# PLAYBOY

For the names and/or nature of the authors, good times, love trials, Charles Cora, or even Cicero and associate writers who backlit the best work and life and life they are, A true correspondence which is included in behalf of a few, a, and the some, and beloved of them.

ALSO BY JOE THOMAS

THE SÃO PAULO QUARTET

*Paradise City*

*Gringa*

*Playboy*

*Bent*

**Joe Thomas** is the author of the critically acclaimed São Paulo Quartet – *Paradise City*, *Gringa*, *Playboy*, and *Brazilian Psycho*, which was longlisted for the CWA Gold Dagger – and *Bent*, which was a *Guardian* Best Book of 2020 and an *Irish Times* pick of the best crime fiction of 2020.

# PLAYBOY

JOE THOMAS

First published in Great Britain by Arcadia Books 2019
This paperback edition published in 2022 by

Arcadia Books
An imprint of Quercus Editions Limited
Carmelite House
50 Victoria Embankment
London EC4Y 0DZ

An Hachette UK company

A CIP catalogue record for this book is available from the British Library.

ISBN (MMP) 978 1 52942 659 5
ISBN (Ebook) 978 1 911350 74 3

10 9 8 7 6 5 4 3 2 1

Typeset in Minion by MacGuru Ltd
Printed and bound in Great Britain by Clays Ltd, Elcograf S.p.A.

MIX
Paper from
responsible sources
FSC® C104740

Papers used by Quercus Books are from well-managed
forests and other responsible sources.

For Martha Lecauchois

# Author's note

Although based on actual events, this is a work of fiction. Certain names, dates, organisations, etc., have been changed for this purpose. A postscript and a glossary of Brazilian Portuguese follow the text.

Brasil is the only country where – in addition to whores cumming, pimps being jealous and drug dealers being addicted – poor people vote for the right wing

Tim Maia

A plague a' both your houses

William Shakespeare, *Romeo and Juliet*

*Playboy, n., Brazilian Portuguese, slang: rich young man*

# Brasil, who pays for us to end up this way?

*São Paulo, 2015 –*
    *Year of the Goat.*
    *Nem fodendo, cara. No fucking way. Year of the Snake.*
    *The snake? President Dilma Rousseff. The boss. The head honcho. The Marxist with the mostest. The* **Presidenta**, *she calls herself. It* burns.
    *Rumour has it she's been skimming off the Petrobras oil kickback scheme like a proper Russian oligarch. All power corrupts after all.*
    *Cash-heavy bitch.*
    *Yeah, Year of the Snake –*
    *The snake? President Dilma Rousseff. Lula's prodigy. Leader of the Workers' Party. The balancer of one tricky-as-fuck left-centre coalition. A balance that has, for years, been achieved through very questionable means.*
    *They don't like her in São Paulo.*
    *Well, some do…*

# Article by Eleanor Boe

## OLHA! Online magazine, 16 March 2016

**What is Operação Lava Jato, Operation Car Wash?**
**(And why does this particular corruption scandal threaten to topple the government?)**

It began in March 2014 as a routine federal investigation into money laundering through a car wash and garage complex in Brasilia, the country's capital. Two years later, and half a million people flooded the streets of São Paulo to call for President Dilma's impeachment. How did this happen? And where will it lead?

What started it all was the discovery of a Land Rover bought illegally by Alberto Youssef – a convicted money launderer of some distinction and considerable reach – for Paulo Roberto Costa, an executive at Petrobras, one of the biggest oil companies in the world, a company that accounts for an eighth of all investments in Brazil, and provides hundreds of thousands of jobs in construction, shipyards and refineries across the country.

And what this purchase led investigators to uncover was a far-reaching mechanism of corruption in which Petrobras overpaid on contracts to a cartel of construction companies, and, with the guaranteed business, this cartel channelled a percentage of each deal into offshore slush funds. Bribes, leaked documents have shown, were built into the contracts themselves, which made their illegality harder to spot.

So far, so your-basic-traditional-corruption model.

However, things might be about to change. Last week, on 8 March, Marcelo Odebrecht, CEO of the international Odebrecht construction conglomerate, was sentenced to nineteen years in jail for corruption, money laundering and criminal association. And it doesn't look like he wants to go quietly. To reduce his sentence, he's allegedly been outlining the epic scale of this kickback scheme. And exactly which politicians – and their parties – have benefited directly.

Last week, we saw the results of all of this: calls for Dilma's impeachment. On Sunday, we'll see the other side of the coin, as hundreds of thousands plan to march in solidarity, in her defence.

If nothing else, it appears that this unfolding scandal runs deep. And the question many people are asking is what's really more important: political ideology and policy-making, or being free of any association at all with corruption in a country in which it is considered systemic.

Brazil, quite clearly, is divided.

**São Paulo, 20 March 2016**

*The thing about wealthy, or comfortable, Paulistanos when they first get a job – and this is something you English do better for once – is that they're not used to authority, don't know how to respond to a boss, how to behave professionally. In São Paulo, your first job is your career. You very rarely get the middle classes working through college, in a bar or restaurant, or doing something menial in the holidays to make a bit of pocket money. So when they turn up for work in their mid-twenties, in their first position, they don't know how to behave. They think they've made it. I'd make every upper- and middle-class Paulistano do a month in McDonald's. That'd be a start.*

Camilla, 34, teacher

Leme sat at the counter, chopsticks poised. He was in the cop-friendly Chinaman's dumpling joint, deep down in Japa-town. Off duty and happy about it.

He angled his empty bottle of Chinese lager at the waitress and she brought him another. The TV was on with the sound down. Military Police in riot gear were hosing down troublemakers on Avenida Paulista, not a fifteen-minute walk away.

'An elegant business, Mario,' the Chinaman said, his hand on Leme's shoulder.

Leme had been coming to the Chinaman's for donkeys. He had spent time just across Avenida Vinte e Três de Maio in Bela Vista. Bixiga, as the neighbourhood was known by locals: the bladder of São Paulo. Leme's old man had a hard-on for crispy duck and took him on Sundays to feast. Everyone else was in the eye-talian canteens end of a weekend, but Leme was picking a fattened roast bird out of a line and watching the Chinaman tear into it with a machete. Habits, ne?

Leme nodded at the TV. 'Which side is this lot on?' he asked.

'Well, the nature of the affair seems to be more about the conflict than the ideology.'

Leme smiled. He thought of Renata, his late wife. It was her kind of an appraisal.

The Chinaman went on: 'But, shortly, we'll be engaged by the pro-Dilma rally and our chubby, gyppo fuckwit Lula will be pronouncing some political untruths.' He paused, took a pull at his own lager. 'So those young men getting their heads serviced by the Militars will be anti-Dilma, I'd wager, and God bless them for it.'

Leme laughed. He'd forgotten. The rally would cause him problems getting home. Since his run-ins a few years back, he no longer drank and drove for fear of angering the wrong Militar. He'd planned to walk across Paulista and down through Jardins until he got tired, then jump in a cab. This changed things.

'You not a fan then?' Leme asked, only half-serious.

'Dilma? Fuck no,' the Chinaman said. 'The puta don't got a noble bone. Sour-faced lefty cunt that's richer than God? On our dollar? No, Senhor. I form my political allegiances elsewhere.'

Leme grimaced. Nodded, slowly. 'It's your right as a citizen, my friend.'

'Yes, I know my rights,' the Chinaman said. 'Don't forget, young man, I was made by this town in the seventies. With your father.' He smiled. 'So, as you can imagine, I do know my rights.'

Leme raised his lager and they knocked bottles. 'So was Dilma,' he said.

The Chinaman chewed this over. 'Yes, I suppose so. It was a dishonourable time that affected many fine young minds. Though she seems reluctant to desist harping on about it. You know they tortured her when she *started* talking.' He paused, cracked a grin. Winked. 'It was the only way to shut her up!'

The Chinaman roared.

Leme winced. He smiled. Faz o que, ne? he thought. *What are you going to do?* Old-school Paulistanos have their reasons for being suspicious of the rise of the left.

He wondered what Renata would make of all this. He knew where she would be spending her afternoon. Which is what made up his mind.

He popped a prawn dumpling. He nailed the rest of his lager. He threw some notes on the counter.

'Ciao,' he said. 'I'm going to see what the gyppo and the slag have to say for themselves.'

He upped and left the restaurant. The bell rang as the door shut behind him. He turned left. Across the road, a man wheeled right and studied a window display in a Japanese supermarket. His arm was bent at the elbow. He flashed a look behind him as he spoke on his phone. The look seemed aimed at Leme. Was it? Leme slowed, eyed the man, couldn't place him – at least not from the back of his head.

It's not the paranoia that kills you, Leme thought.

He kept a slow pace. He didn't make the guy on his phone.

Leme hit Avenida Paulista twenty minutes later. There was a sea of red T-shirts. Cheap red baseball caps. Red balloons. A shit-tonne of them. And the odd, menacing black flag. Meaning: trouble ain't *too* far away.

Leme rubbernecked the crowd. The usual student rabble, the air around them hash-thick. A good number of workers: tough-skinned and gnarly men; grinning, dancing women. Lots of condo-dwellers eating out tonight, Leme thought, then felt a flash of repugnance that he had thought that. Some middle-class do-gooders, Renata's old mob, he expected. Gaggles of slouching anarchists in heavy metal slogans, bandana-ready. Standard. A textbook lefty bash, attendee-wise.

He bought a can of lager from a gawker with a cool box and worked his way slowly against the flow, aiming at the MASP building. Its outsized, red spider's legs fit right in. Even the museums were on Dilma's side today.

There were placards – everywhere.

*Brave heart: there will be no coup*

The Chinaman would have loved that one, Leme thought. There were placards with photos of a gurning Lula, '2018' emblazoned across his chest.

*All Support*

Leme studied the placards. All of them were stamped with #. His girlfriend Antonia had tried to explain to him what # meant only the other day.

'There's nothing more boring than a middle-aged man shrugging at the idiocy of the modern world,' she'd said. She'd gestured at their living room. 'An analogue throwback in a digital world. How original.'

He'd laughed at that.

The revolution is a click away, he thought. It's just a click away, click away. He smiled. Jagger-Richards it up a bit, entendeu?

He came up with his own little slogan: *vai tomar no coup*. Bilingual magic, that pun. Go take it up the… coup. He'd work on it.

He wormed through the crowds, south side of the avenue. It was a pertinent fucking contrast, the corporation towers flanking a marching band of anti-capitalists. Or pro-democrats. These days it was all so black and white it was hard to tell the difference.

Antonia let it wash over her: no nuance, no séance.

Or as the Chinaman was fond of saying: no barley, no parlay. Meaning: you wanna chat, we gonna drink.

There was a surge. Leme was pushed back against the Conjunto Nacional mall. The grill was down. A janitor peered through. Sensible positioning, son, Leme thought.

Then another man caught his eye, also just the other side of the grill. Leme, brow-furrowed, tensed. It was the guy from outside the Chinaman's – no doubt. Coincidence?

It's not the coincidence that kills you.

He gave the guy the sidelong fisheye. Definitely him. He was unshaven, hair unwashed, filthy little tache, corpse-pale, stick-thin, jittery.

Leme turned away so the guy wouldn't see his face, and tried to place him.

He acted crowd-curious.

He turned back to study the guy again. And he was right there, next to him, the grill separating them. Leme could feel the guy's heavy breath.

Bingo. Leme half-knew him. His detective partner in the Polícia Civil, Lisboa, knew him. His journo friend Silva *knew* him.

'Remember me?' the guy asked. 'Don't run now. Be cool, ne?'

Leme smiled, didn't look at him. He tiptoed and craned. Ah, Lula's on the stage. He couldn't see much beyond a bloated red shirt.

The sweat stains were *ominous*.

'I remember you. Fat João. Helluva joke that. You're even skinnier than I remember. Why are you following me?'

'Something for you.'

'What?'

'A tip. Something you want to see.'

Leme nodded. The guy was textbook-rat, informant-type working for chump change. He'd seen him once, twice, three times over the years, maybe. Never directly and never one to one. This was new.

OK.

'And what, I have to make it worth your while?' Leme asked.

'Not necessary – taken care of. I've just got a message for you.'

'Who from?'

'Not part of the deal.'

Leme weighed it. Lisboa, Silva – they can vouch for him. That's good enough.

'OK, shoot.'

'Know the dodgy little park in Praça Alexandre de Gusmão?'

Leme nodded.

'You might want to take a look. Like, *now*.'

Leme raised eyebrows. 'That the message?'

'Don't shoot the messenger, chief.'

Leme turned. The rat had skedaddled.

Leme let it marinate a moment.

It's not the curiosity that kills you.

He made up his mind. He could scoot over; pick up a cab nearby either way.

Leme edged further away, just catching a key line crackling through the inadequate PA: *Democracy is the only way to allow people to participate in the government's decisions.*

Leme wondered what that had to do with accusations of pilfering state funds and harvesting kickback money.

He tossed his beer can and got off the main drag.

Leme edged through Jardins towards the park. There was a taxi rank there he was sure would be freed up despite the rally. Old-school hardheads, no fans of The Snake.

It was Sunday-quiet. No real overspill from Paulista. Side-street dirty. Fast-food wrappers and empty cans blew about. Mangy dogs dug in. A group of drunk students let fly at them, laughing. Boot-heavy thumps turned to rib-cracking. The dogs yelped and whimpered. The students kicked cans and scarpered, singing.

Leme followed at a distance down Alameda Santos. They passed the Intercontinental Hotel and arrowed towards the square and Parque Tenente Siqueira Campos behind. Leme figured he'd pass by and boost a taxi down Peixoto or Azevedo if the rank was empty. At night, the park was a hotspot for hopheads and noias – paranoid crackheads – homeless bums and sex pests. It was getting dark. Leme wondered what exactly this tip was. Some Vice shit, he'd guess.

It's not the assumptions that kill you.

The students crossed the road in a drunk-spread, arms-wide traffic-taunt.

Though there were no cars.

It seemed the city was giving the Boss Bitch the swerve today, Leme thought.

Aside from the swarm of lefties just up the road.

He scoped the cab options. There were none. The students were gathered by the park railings. He watched them. They laughed and kicked jokes to and fro.

They sat on a moped that was propped against the gate.

Leme eyed them.

Something not quite right.

Ah, leave it, he thought. I'm off duty. Not my problem, no Senhor, not today.

Wide-berth it.

Kids, joshing.

Then a shout: 'Caralho, bicho!' Mate, look out!

And another: 'Puta, que isso?' What the fuck's going on?

A different, deeper voice. An instruction: 'Get the fuck off. Embora pentelho! Drive. Let's go. Vamos, vamos!'

The students jumped back.

The students fanned out.

The students turned and scrammed, five-ways.

Leme watched.

Two men in black T-shirts and black balaclavas jumped on the moped and gassed it the wrong way down the square. Then burned off up Jaú.

Leme looked – hard.

Number plate blacked out.

Leme waited.

Nothing.

He scanned the street both ways.

Nothing.

He cocked an ear.

Rally-traffic. Cracked voices and cheers.

He studied the buildings above street level and the shuttered shops.

Nothing. No obvious lights.

He crossed the road.

And he saw why the students had left in such a hurry.

At the bottom of the railings, poking out from beneath a bush – A body.

Leme pulled his phone and began to spear in the emergency number.

He examined the body as he did.

A kid. A bloodied pink shirt. Sleeves rolled up. Smart pair of jeans. Slip-on black leather shoes. No socks.

Leme stopped dialling.

He got down on one knee. Looked more closely.

Chest wounds. Face untouched.

Good-looking lad. How old? About twenty-something. Hard to tell *exactly* these days.

Pink shirt.

No socks.

*Aha*.

The lad was rich. A playboy type.

*Not* the usual corpse to wash up on these shores.

Leme needed the cavalry and double-quick time.

He stood, turned, phone to his ear.

A blue-red flash.

Fuck.

'Good afternoon,' said an especially ferocious-looking member of the São Paulo Military Police.

These boys did not like Leme's mob, the Polícia Civil side of things, the *detectives*. Didn't like to get their hands dirty was one complaint. Cerebral and fresh with it. Bunch of fucking pussies was the general feeling.

The Militar had a sadistic look in his eye. 'And what the fuck do we have here then, old man?' he said.

'Less of the old, eh,' Leme said.

Leme hit the hang-up button and raised his hands.

# Article by Eleanor Boe

## OLHA! Online magazine, 20 March 2016

**ONE HUNDRED THOUSAND ATTEND PRO-DILMA MARCH**

Avenida Paulista turned red as a hundred thousand people took to the streets to show their support for President Dilma, who is battling calls for her impeachment.

Earlier in the day, Military Police dispersed crowds of anti-Dilma protestors. They used limited force, including tear gas and water cannons, justified, a statement issued late last night reads, to prevent the possibility of 'serious violence' between rival political factions.

As this took place, a Supreme Court Judge took the step of suspending former President Lula's ministerial nomination. Dilma's critics claim that by attempting to make her mentor part of the government, she is effectively shielding him from money laundering charges, charges he vigorously denies.

Many of the crowd waved red flags, defending the Workers' Party. Banners depicting Lula as a bodybuilder were among many creative displays of support, in stark contrast to only a few days before, when an anti-Dilma protest featured two huge inflatable dolls of Dilma and Lula – dressed as prisoners.

Lula, wearing a red shirt, addressed the crown to rapturous applause. 'There will not be a coup against Ms Rousseff,' he said, to cheers and raised fists. After he left the stage, the rally became a street party, with singing, dancing and pro-PT (Workers' Party) chanting.

The recent nationwide protests against corruption called for Dilma's removal due to 'economic mismanagement' and her alleged part in the far-reaching corruption scandal based around state-sponsored oil company Petrobras.

Dilma denies all wrongdoing.

*More to follow*

# PART ONE: **FUCKHEADS**

**Same day, same place:**
**São Paulo, 20 March 2016**

*My family is a political institution. I saw relatives arrested only to later host a former President of Brazil seeking support. People who didn't know me believed they had the right to judge me when they did not. My family wanted me to be someone I was not. São Paulo is a part of my family; my family is a part of São Paulo. We helped make it what it is. We helped build this city, build its infrastructure. Sometimes, I look at São Paulo with ambivalence; there are things you have to do to make a difference, politically, which are not always pretty. They say you can't choose your family; I wouldn't change mine.*

Marina, 19, student

# Junior

*Less of the old?*

Jesus, the fucking front on this guy. The *face* on the lad. Serious bolas. The cunt's caught leaning over a corpse by two Militars and he's got the garra and nouse to crack wise.

May not be the smartest move, however, thought the younger of the two, Junior. Old Assis had a temper on him, and there was no one around and they could easily make this an in flagrante-type scenario.

Bang, bang, medals and honour and all that jazz: just got to make sure the bullets are in the right place.

Junior scoped the street. Assis cuffed the guy.

Assis said, 'You going to tell us what the fuck you were doing, son?'

The guy smiled. Shook his head.

Assis nodded at Junior. Flicked his chin at the body. 'Have a look,' he said.

Junior did as he was told. He gloved up and examined the John. He could see he was a kid, about the same age as Junior, maybe a few years older. Who knew when a corpse flattened things out a touch. Different type of kid, though. Caucasian glint to him, for starters. Dressed rich.

The body wasn't too well hidden. A few leaves, a couple of branches, almost discarded, it seemed. It was the bottom end of the park and the slope down was steep enough the stiff wouldn't be seen too easily though. Like maybe he'd been rolled down the hill in the trees – good cover – and then pushed through the railings. There was a stillness to the air. Junior could hear the rally, but the distance pulled that stillness closer to him.

The park was deserted. Not a surprise. Normally was at that time of the day: the cusp of night. Any respectables well away by then, before the hopheads and noias, perverts and paedos turned up. Snide little line of underage rent-boy cocksuckers available to those who sought it. Drop-out schoolgirl pussy for hire for your less than discerning nonce, too, Junior had heard.

Takes all sorts.

Fuck knows what this lad was up to, but Junior guessed it wasn't pretty. He looked like he could afford a lot better.

'ID?' Assis called out.

Junior frisked the stiff. Not his first time and harder, in fact, than rifling the pockets of a real live human. Not called stiffs without reason. He was no medic, but Junior didn't think the kid had snuffed it too long ago.

In the pockets, he found:

Cigarettes – Marlboro Red

Lighter – a gold Zippo

Keys – house and car

A wallet – Louis Vuitton, brown

In the wallet, he found:

NADA.

Not a sausage. But it was old, well-thumbed, and recently emptied, Junior reckoned.

'Então?' Assis called out.

'Nothing, Senhor,' Junior replied.

'Cash?'

'Nope.'

'Shame.'

Junior raised an eyebrow. Assis continued, 'Rich kid gets robbed, gets merced. Textbook.' He pulled his radio.

Junior held tight.

'That how it usually works?' the guy asked.

Assis glared at him. 'Ask your opinion, did I?'

The guy smiled. 'Only it's an odd decision to take the poor cunt's ID and bank cards, as well as his cash, *and* button his coat while they're at it. Tad risky, entendeu? Somewhat incriminating, perhaps?'

Assis said nothing. Junior flanked the guy, wondering if the old temper might just kick in and kick off. Junior fingered his revolver, spread his legs a touch.

Assis got back on the radio. Assis barked some instructions.

Junior held tight. The air thinned, cooled, as the fat sun, once raw, hostile, sloped off.

Moments later, a Militar SUV pulled up. A colleague, Edu, hopped out. Assis bundled the guy into the back.

'You two stay with the stiff. There's people on their way.'

The SUV gunned, then squealed, then roared.

'Nasty business,' said Edu, nodding at the stiff.

Junior sighed. 'Pois é,' he said.

'What happened?'

'No idea, mate,' Junior said. 'We found that guy standing over him.' Junior gestured to where the SUV had been. 'It ain't even obvious how the kid was ironed out. He doesn't look that bad, to be fair.'

Edu smirked. 'That guy? Didn't you recognise him?'

Junior shook his head. 'Sure didn't. Nem fodendo, cara.' No fucking way.

'Ride-along in Paraisópolis couple of years ago. You were green as, proper rookie. Driving, I think you were. *That* guy was a mate of Big Carlos. Polícia Civil cunt, though I forget his name.'

Junior ran the ride-along in his mind. He remembered it well enough. He'd barely looked at the guy. Sensed something was messed up there, something best not to engage with. Alarm bells, it was personal, a fucked-up type of scene.

'Assis know, you think?' Junior asked.

'Meu, I don't doubt it.' Edu snorted. 'Good old Carlão. He's going to have to untangle a total clusterfuck.'

Junior shook his head. Laughed – rueful.

The blue-red flash of the Militar SUV lit the gloaming as it pulled away.

Junior worked his jaw hard – three fresh pieces of gum, tension thin.

They stood either side of the body. Motorbikes with their sirens flashing silently either side of them.

Junior narrowed his eyes as the sky darkened. He sniffed the air. He nodded up the hill towards Paulista.

'Fuckers had better turn up before the rally is over,' he said.

Edu turned to look at him. 'Ah, don't sweat it. Any minute now, no doubt.'

Junior nodded. Fact is he was nervous. Two Military Police standing over a dead body at a left-wing rally? There were better places to be stationed, sunshine, no fucking doubt about that, he thought. Their mob weren't exactly popular with the hundred or so thousand wankers just up the road. Automatic weapons or not, this was by no means a desirable stand-off.

'Know what?' Junior said.

Edu pulled a face – mock dumb. 'No. What?'

'Ha ha, yeah, very good. You're a hoot to work with. Know *that*?'

Edu laughed. 'Ah, don't be such a pussy. Please. Continue. Tell me what I should know.'

Junior shook his head, took a breath. 'OK,' he said. 'Something weird. About the body.' He angled his back towards it. 'Assis told me to search it, right? So I checked his wallet – no money, no ID, nada, entendeu?'

'Yeah,' Edu said. 'I'm following, mate. Complicated stuff.'

'OK, but I didn't think of this at the time. There was no phone on him.'

Edu sighed. 'Son, he was mugged. Pronto. Or looking for some dodgy action and misbehaved. Or his fucking boyfriend had enough of his whiny little backside and snuffed him himself.' Edu shook his head. 'Phone? Course there was no fucking phone.'

Junior – chastened. 'Alright, settle down, it was just a thought.'

'Piece of advice,' Edu said. 'When our boys turn up, you keep your thoughts to yourself. You've been with us, what, about four years?'

Junior nodded.

'So you don't know the different ways these things can go.'

'What does that mean?'

'It means, amigo, that you watch and fucking learn, entendeu?'

Junior shifted from foot to foot. He heard a siren.

'Anyway,' Edu said, 'they're here in moments, if you can hear that. So stand up straight and look sharp. I'll do the talking.'

The response vehicle pulled over and two uniforms jumped out the back with a stretcher.

The passenger door opened and a senior officer swung a leg out. He *glared* at the scene, like he was appalled and disgusted by it, like it was a personal affront to him, like it was nothing more than a monumental waste of his time, and anyone connected with it an equally monumental waste of his – and anyone else's – time.

Junior knew the sort.

He swung the other leg out and John Wayned it towards them, dead slow, legs wide, both hands resting on his belt buckle, just beneath his well-earned belly, residing there, firm, defiant, as if to say, 'Yep, my cock is exactly as big as my swagger suggests – you got a problem with that?'

Yeah, Junior knew the sort: classy guy. Proper swashbuckler.

The Swashbuckler took a deep breath and hoisted his trousers up. 'Right, cunthooks,' he said. 'What the fuck, eh? Talk.'

He looked away from them. The last of the sunlight flashed in his mirrored aviators.

Edu started. 'Junior here, and Assis, spotted a character acting suspiciously. They engaged and discovered the body. Assis apprehended the suspect, called for a tactical response unit and took the suspect into custody. My orders were to wait with Junior until the second unit arrived.'

'And here we are,' said the Swashbuckler.

He clicked his fingers and hissed something at the two uniforms. They rolled the body onto the stretcher, secured it, covered it and bundled it into the back of the vehicle. They checked the area, and, satisfied there was nothing else there, nodded at the Big Man and climbed into the car.

'Right, you two, jog on then.'

'But – ' Junior started.

The Swashbuckler grinned. 'But what, young man?'

'I – '

'I do hope you're not querying my methods, son.'

'No, I – '

'Insubordination is a serious charge, young man, ta entendendo?'

'Yes, I – '

The Swashbuckler hawked and spat. He looked at the two of them. Junior looked down.

'Now, you two are going to fucking jog on, and, while you're doing it, you're both going to think long and hard about where you got the fucking front to question a commanding officer, when said *commanding* officer is taking charge of and diffusing a potentially delicate, even, yes, even *dangerous* situation. You got that, sweethearts?'

They both nodded.

'So what are you going to do?'

'Jog on, sir,' Edu said.

The Swashbuckler smiled. 'Good lad.'

He turned and walked to the car, even slower, Junior thought, than when he'd ambled over towards them.

It seemed to take about five minutes.

'Nice one, dickhead,' Edu said.

Junior said nothing. What he was thinking: *isn't this a crime scene?*

'Come on,' Edu said. 'Let's fuck off, eh? Before something else goes wrong.'

And Junior could think of no reasonable argument against that idea.

Junior sat on his bed. Home.

He could hear his sisters and his mum in the kitchen down the corridor, arguing over something while they cooked. He could smell the onions and the thick drift of beans stewing with pork. He was hungry. He played with his rosary beads.

He heard the roar of his dad coming home. Laughter. He pictured his father lifting first his mother and then his two sisters off the floor in a bear hug, smothering them in dirty-lipped kisses, his helmet dropped where he stood, his orange, state-maintenance overalls tied at his waist, his vest oily, his breath sour with beer and cheap cachaça.

Don't judge, Junior, he told himself. Most people should be so lucky.

A shout – his mother. 'Junior! Vamos jantar, filho!'

'Coming, Mum,' he shouted. 'One second, eh?' he said to himself.

He studied the two text messages one last time before dinner. One from Assis and one from Edu. He didn't know what to make of them, mainly as it seemed there was nothing to make of them.

He read Edu's first:

**cara, foi legal hoje, ne? really was cool. nice one. you did ok**

This did not sound much like Edu at the best of times, let alone after Junior's misplaced comments to the Swashbuckler.

He swiped to Assis's message.

**Today wasn't straightforward and you handled yourself and the situation very well. You did a good job. Your part is done. Get some rest. Tomorrow's another day.**

He switched his phone off. His dad couldn't abide it at dinner.

# Roberta

Idiota, Roberta thought. *Idiota*! It was typical of him, *typical*. It was typical of *her* too, and that made her angrier even than he did. *Why could she never control herself*?

She'd heard a phrase once: she's got a lot of buttons and he's got a lot of fingers. It was spot on.

Like every bloody argument they'd ever had. All she'd said was that there was no debate anymore, that this talk of impeachment *claimed* to be a debate, but that it was, in fact, the opposite, it was *closing down* the debate by polarising the country, dividing families, friends, colleagues. It was us and them now, and that is not democracy, not what politics is, should be, we no longer deserve the democracy we'd earned, and Dilma had been a part of achieving it, but now, who knows, ne? And she's either a snake in the grass or a terribly wronged woman in a society that is more misogynistic, conservative, backward-looking than ever.

'Settle down,' was all he'd said, but with that snide little smirk, and that had set her right off. Her last words to him: you can go and join your playboy, fuckhead friends and leave me well alone, you machista filho da puta, and then she'd stormed off, and there was no way she was going to find him, but she'd made the mistake of giving him her phone as she hadn't wanted to take a bag for fear of thieves, and the dress she was wearing was dead-on ripe for some ladrão, pickpocket.

So what now? Wait for Lula to get on the stage and speak? Listen to his pronouncement of support for Dilma on her own? Or go and find her old uni gang – they'd be there, for sure, and she'd likely spot the flags? Or go home and sulk. Pride, Roberta, pride. Don't let the man-child get you down. *He* should be looking for *her*.

Stay.

Yes, she thought. She'd see him later, yes, the fucker would likely turn up at her apartment with a swagger and a look of faux-contrition that would annoy the fuck out of her, but also likely make her laugh and he'd get back into her good books – the *fucker*.

Yes, *stay*. She decided to stay.

She needed to get a view of the march from above, or, at least, a little higher up, to see if any of the flags and banners were recognisable and she could find her friends. She snaked across Paulista in front of the Conjunto Nacional shopping mall, threading through the mass of bodies, which swayed to the music, and edged forwards and backwards in time to the whistles and horns. On the other side she climbed the steps of the Santander building and sat down at the top. If she looked too hard, she thought, she'd never see them. She rolled a cigarette. She lifted her sunglasses onto the top of her head. She closed her eyes as she drew hungrily, and the cigarette scratched, dry, harsh, at her throat, and the sun throbbed, pulsing, spreading its warmth in increments across her face, warmth which intensified as she breathed in and relaxed and let the sounds and excitement of the day settle into the background, acknowledging they were there, but allowing her feelings and calmness to be present too.

Fucking Antonio, she thought, after a moment or two of serenity, serenity that was short-lived precisely because she was aware she was having a moment or two of serenity. She'd been using a meditation app but she didn't want to pay the subscription after her ten trial 'lessons', and so she tried to remember them and do it herself from time to time. Perhaps, on reflection, she thought, the biggest political rally in years might not be the most conducive spot for achieving mindfulness.

The app was just the kind of thing Antonio mocked her for, the prick. His entitlement knew no bounds: a clear conscience, a clear head, an innate mindfulness, really, she supposed, were his for the taking. When you're brought up to believe everything you do is right, then you never understand when you're doing something wrong. Not quite a lack of empathy, but not far off.

'Guilt is for Catholics and the poor,' he'd once joked, adding: 'Actually that might be tautology.'

'You might want to try a literary elective, mate,' she said. 'But the sentiment is still deeply offensive.'

She sometimes wondered if they were right for each other.

'What does that even *mean*?' he'd asked. '*Right* for each other?'

He'd had a point. She couldn't answer that.

'Are *we right* for each other?' he'd mused. 'Right? *Right*. Funny word, when you examine it, ne?' He'd smiled, put his hand on her cheek. 'I think we're *good* for each other.'

He had these moments when he'd completely disarm her, see right through her, to the best version of herself, and she'd see the best version of him, and she'd believe that his playboy shtick was exactly that, bluster, nurture not nature, and that she could handle the rare-enough moments when it annoyed her.

She scanned the crowd, looking for the red-and-green flags her uni mob would be waving. There'd be the usual gang, all Masters and PhD students in political science and its various offshoots, most of them, like Roberta, interning at NGOs.

'All very Universidade de São Paulo, querida,' Antonio had said on first meeting some of them at a conference, spinning out the full name to add an extra layer of patronising, as nobody called it anything other than USP.

'Yeah,' she'd nodded across the courtyard where they were holding the drinks reception, 'and your pastel Polo-shirted, playboy crowd are very TAAP, entendeu?'

'Stereotypes everywhere.' He'd given her a wolfish grin. 'Who'd have thought it?' He'd leaned closer, his arm against a tree above her.

She'd kissed him then; that'd sealed it.

He was really good at kissing.

She spotted them.

The flags were huge, emblazoned with 'USP pra Dilma', and there was a fierceness to the chanting group beneath that marked them out.

That and a cloud of marijuana smoke thick enough to knock over even your most dedicated Bahia stoner. Roberta smiled and skipped down the steps and aimed herself at the biggest of the flags, and after a few minutes of tussling and being spun through gaps too small for her, squeezing her shoulder blades and pressing her arms together, trying to avoid touching anyone or being touched, she was with them.

'E aí, menina!' Roberta's friend Lis squealed as she grabbed her shoulder. 'How are you? Where have you been? Hanging with Antonio's boys, ne?'

Roberta laughed. 'Just him, but the malandro pissed me off so I'm all yours now, querida.'

'Ta, ta ótimo. That's great. Monica's here somewhere. Malô as well. Manu, over there, ta vendo, you see her? Ellie, you know, the gringa journalist? She's heading over too.'

Roberta saw Manu and nodded. 'And the speeches?' She pointed at Lis's hand. 'Give me that.' She'd had a smoke earlier with Antonio, something he rarely did, something she felt he did for *her*, and she needed a fucking top-up.

Lis passed the joint. 'Ah, I think soon, ne? But they're not really the point, right? It's about a show, não é? Main thing is we're *here*. *All* of us, entendeu?'

'Ta certo, cara.'

The noise level increased and Roberta craned to see why. There were cheers and arms raised in fists, or up and across one another in imitation of the sickle and hammer, solidarity. That was what this was all about, Lis was right.

'I mean,' she was saying, 'these attacks on Dilma cannot stand, sabe? Corrupt, old, right-wing white men accusing her of, like, what, ne? *Corruption*? Fuck off, know what I mean?'

'E isso ai,' Roberta said. That's exactly it. She agreed, of course she did, but they'd all had these discussions a million times and she was feeling a little looser after the hit, and her mind, if she was honest, was drifting away from politics and back to Antonio, and she was *here*, wasn't she, and so was he, *somewhere*, and isn't that the whole point?

She was aware of Lis and her friends shouting something, though she wasn't sure exactly what and suddenly it didn't really matter, and it was all a little bit too similar to the protests about the World Cup a few years before, and really what was the difference between shouting 'Fuck FIFA' or 'Fuck Temer'? Essentially, it was the same thing, 'Fuck the elite', and yet at least a dozen of the people standing closest to her were part of this elite, at least their families were, at least their paternal grandfather or whatever, and, yes, Antonio too, but *he was here*.

He was here.

And that meant something. She grabbed Lis's arm. She should go. She should.

'Oi, Lis, I think I'm going to head off.'

'You're going? Ah, vai. Why?'

'I'm not feeling great.' She pointed at the joint. 'Knocked me a little sideways, entendeu?'

Lis smiled. 'Fair enough, dude, you fuck off.' She gestured around her. 'There's plenty of us here.'

They embraced and Roberta wriggled through the tight space beside them, pushed past a group of students from a private university, forced her way through a group of manual labourers dressed in their orange overalls and white helmets, nailing their lagers with a certain grim efficiency, past a group of cleaners who were laughing, heads back, hips moving, and then she was on the other side of the road, and Lula was speaking, and she wasn't sure what to do next.

She headed up towards Paraíso, where she lived. It suddenly seemed important that she get home. She knew she could be a pain in the arse, and Antonio knew he could be too. They had been together two years. They made each other laugh.

'Laughter and orgasms,' he'd said, one weekend morning. 'It's a potent combination.'

It really was. It was around that time she began to understand properly the word *intoxicating*.

'It's high-low culture, querido,' she'd said. 'Philosophy and blow jobs, entendeu?'

He'd laughed. 'All the major food groups.'

'Nourishing, ne?'

'What's that joke? The brain: it's my second favourite organ.'

She smiled as she remembered the exchange. His friends were his friends and you can't escape your past and really his loyalty to them was admirable, and it *was* a trait he seemed to possess in spades. He wasn't your average rich-kid pussy-hound, that was for sure. And anyway, his friends *could* be fun, and they'd certainly had some good…

'Oi, Roberta! Roberta!'

She looked up. And there were his friends, about a dozen yards away. She smiled, shook her head, tried to refocus her dope-smudged brain, smiled again and fixed her grin in preparation. She would be nice.

'E aí,' she said. 'How are you lot getting on, eh?'

The guy who had called her name, Alexandre, narrowed his eyes. 'You're not with Tônico?'

'No, I thought he was with you.'

The noise of the crowd rose as someone shouted slogans through the tinny PA.

'Ah,' Alexandre said. 'I'll ring him.'

'Please. Idiot's walked off with my phone.'

Alexandre put his phone to his ear and lifted his finger to quiet her. Roberta seethed.

He took his phone from his ear and looked at the screen quizzically.

'Então?' Roberta said.

'Nada. Didn't even ring.' Alexandre raised his eyebrows. 'Huh,' he said.

'Ah, well, signal's likely jammed with all these people, ne?'

'Yeah, I guess.'

Alexandre fiddled with his phone and neither said anything for a moment. Roberta stood patiently, waited for him to finish.

She said, 'When you get hold of him, tell him I'm at home, certo?'

'Sure, of course,' Alexandre grinned. 'Getting the dinner on, right? Good girl.'

Roberta shook her head but found she was smiling, despite herself.

'Exactly,' she said. 'And tell him if he stays out too late with his good-for-nothing, layabout, playboy friends, he'll be *wearing* his fucking dinner.'

And with that, Alexandre laughing, she ducked down a road that led off Paulista and set off home, looking forward to, excited, even, about the evening ahead.

Roberta's apartment seemed even emptier than it normally did. Standing in a crowd of thousands will do that to your sparsely furnished, though sizeable, studio flat, with its bed, its piles of books and its wicker rocking chair that you 'borrowed' from your grandparents' farm years before. She put water to boil on the hob and jumped into the shower, immediately relieved to scrub off the dirt of the street, wash the smoke from her hair, feel the heat from the day rinse away from her. She was in the shower for what felt like a long time, and when she came out wearing only a towel, hair fresh and damp on her shoulders, the kettle was boiling ferociously, and clearly had been for some time. She'd burned through three of these kettles in exactly this way over the years. Amor fati, she thought, smiling at her pretentiousness, the love of one's fate, Nietzsche's eternal return. Meaning: we never fucking learn, querida.

She made a cup of mint tea, put on a sweatshirt, sweat pants, her slippers and a thick hair band, and thought about what she should do next. It was a little after seven, the light fading, the heat dissipating and the excitement of the day, which, at its beginning, had felt contained and trembling, like the coiled spring of the hick fazenda rifles her grandparents' farm workers used to carry to scare off intruders, had now settled, and she heard only the odd shout, the occasional firework and empty cans and rubbish blowing down the road below.

She sat in the wicker chair, her legs folded underneath her, feet crossed, and she sipped at her drink, both hands around the mug. She blew gently on the tea, closed her eyes and let its aroma and heat waft up her nose and into her eyes, a little like, she realised, her mother's ritual sinus cleanse with her bowl steaming a heavy menthol vapour. It felt calming, meditative, and she focused on her breathing – as the app had taught her – and tried to let go of any thoughts that interfered with this moment, with her sensual *awareness*, sensual appreciation of what she could smell and hear both in the immediate vicinity, and a little further away, where, she hoped, Antonio would be, laughing with his friends and preparing to set off to see her. The idea occurred to her that, as he had her phone, he had an excuse to stay out later, and she acknowledged it, understood where it had come from and why, refused to judge herself for having the thought, and then dismissed it, consigned it to the ether.

Minutes passed.

Her breathing settled as she focused on it again, counting to ten each time she exhaled, then starting again. She sipped at her tea. It was cheating, she knew that, to drink tea while trying to achieve mindfulness, but she'd always figured even Buddhists have to multi-task every now and then. All that infinite space had to be useful for something.

She stopped the counting and let her mind drift.

She saw his face, smiling, turning to look at her, tanned, hair salty and wet, his shoulders dusky, sitting next to each other on the beach at Camburi, watching the last of the surfers at the end of the afternoon, sharing a cold beer and a joint, talking about what happened next. This was eighteen months ago.

'I never thought I'd say the words "so where is this going then?"' he laughed. 'But there you are, I'm saying them, can't take it back.'

She was smiling then and she was smiling now. 'Ah, it's natural, Tônico. Don't sweat it. *Own* that shit, querido.'

'Natural why?'

'Six months, ne?' she said. 'Six months we've been seeing each other. We've had our wobble and we're through it, sabe? It's "shit or get out of the woods" time now, meu amor.'

He laughed. 'Que romantic, ne?'

She took the beer from his hand, placed it in the sand and kissed him.

Yeah, they'd had their wobble, their whole Gaugin moment, as she'd later called it: *Where do we come from? What are we? Where are we going?*

'Hiding behind your learning again, sweetheart, but I see your point,' he'd said.

They'd decided that the key was that wherever they were going, they'd be going there together, for the foreseeable.

Roberta let the memory settle, slowly opened her eyes and took a final deep breath.

And another.

A wave of panic, of guilt, seized her, stabbed her and she shuddered and stood up. He wasn't here. Why wasn't he here? Perhaps this time she really had fucked things up? Perhaps he was more patient with her than she had realised, and now was like, chega, querida, enough, entendeu? She might not blame him, she thought. Perhaps she had driven him away; that was her deepest fear – that her behaviour, prompted by her love for him and fuelled by her own inescapable nature, would mean he couldn't love her anymore, that he could no longer live with *her.*

'You knew what I was like when we got together,' he'd say when they disagreed on something, when they argued, or discussed anything that might provoke discord.

It was a supremely confident assertion –

*I'm me and I will not be a different person just for you.*

She respected, envied and resented him for that – and the truth that she knew was contained within the statement.

Oh yes, she had a lot of buttons and he had a lot of fingers and he knew just what to say – or not say – and do – or not do – to push those buttons and engineer a scenario where she was apologising, where she was chasing him to reconcile, to make things right, which meant, of course, to make him tell her she was forgiven and that he loved her.

And he did tell her –

Often. He told her he loved her every day.

She smiled, let go of her anxiety.

What was she supposed to do *now*?

She turned on her TV and got into bed, and hoped she'd find something inane enough to fall asleep to, so that when he arrived and woke her up, the fight would be nothing more than a distant memory, perhaps even funny, considering the context, where it took place, and they could get on with the getting on with.

She yawned and sighed, and she settled.

# Mario

Leme leaned back. Shifted to give his wrists a little space. The seat was hard, blood-soaked to its core, no doubt. No point crying over spilt PCC, the unofficial Militar slogan. AC roaring. Leme's sweat cooled. Toxic shivers. All that. And fear. The Chinaman's beer dripping out of him – fast.

'Mate,' Leme said, 'take the cuffs off and I'll show you my fucking badge and we might be able to speed all this up a little, entendeu?'

The Militar snorted. 'I know who you are, son,' he said. 'And those cuffs are going nowhere.'

Interesting, Leme thought. That'll be the old Carlão connection. Which is either a relief, or very fucking worrying indeed.

Leme hadn't seen Carlos in donkeys. Not since they had agreed to go their separate ways after the incident with Ellie and all that Cracolândia land deal beef. Carlos got a decent wedge of dinheiro. Leme got –

Peace of mind.

No one'd find out he'd been part of the Militar gang that stomped the gold-toothed kid dealer to death, way up high in Paraisópolis. The gold-toothed kid dealer old Carlos had made as a dead cert for the triggerman in Renata's murder. She was killed by a stray bullet, a bala perdida, in a firefight between the Military Police and the PCC drug gang in the favela Paraisópolis where she ran a legal aid office. The community mourned her. The community was quite happy for the police to do whatever was necessary to bring about justice. Most of them, that is, the village elders, though they kept it quiet, of course, didn't let on to the big men with guns who ran the place. And what did Leme care, in the end? It'd troubled him – at first. He'd done the thing he'd said he'd never do and blah blah blah.

But, you know, menos um, as they say with a shrug, one less villain, entendeu?

Some kid dealer gets merced, no one gives a fuck.

But –

But this was a my-word your-word type of situation and Leme didn't trust old Carlos anymore. Not as far as he could wrestle him. And he certainly wasn't called Big Carlos for nothing.

'What's your name then, pal?' Leme asked. 'You know, let's even the scores here a little.'

The Militar laughed. 'You've trod on the ball here, son. My name ain't gonna make an ounce, entendeu?'

Leme decided to keep his counsel.

Leme hoped they were going somewhere official.

He didn't have a cat's chance if they weren't.

He playbooked it:

Fat João, the skinny rat copper's beak, tails him from the Chinaman's to the rally and tips him off –

Militars witness Leme poking about the corpse –

Leme causes a stir, uses his copper nouse and whatnot –

Leme's ironed out in a classic he-tried-to-do-one scenario.

Bullet in the back. Textbook Militar.

Leme had *better* hope they were going somewhere official. And if they were, he'd have to call Antonia. She wasn't the worrying kind, but he wasn't the stay-out-all-night-on-his-day-off kind either.

And after the Cracolândia land deal and her involvement –

Minor, of course, and forgivable, but it meant she had an insight into the workings of the mind of someone like Carlão, and she could handle him, yes, she *had* handled him, she had handled him better than Leme ever had, but she *knew* him now, and types like him, and she did *not* want anything to threaten, well, to threaten *them* –

Point is, it all worked in the end: they really did live happily ever after.

'I need to ring my bird,' Leme said. 'You going to let me?'

The Militar laughed again. 'Patience, lover boy. All in good tick-tock, entendeu?'

Leme noted where they were headed: Lapa-bound.

Could go either way: plenty of official buildings in Lapa. But only a stone's throw beyond and you're in bandit country.

'Hold tight, son,' the Militar said, laughing.

Leme thought he probably didn't have much choice.

Leme gave up wondering where the fuck they were going.

And guess what? Moments later they arrived.

They ghosted into the garage of a medium-sized condominium building in Lapa, a little way off the main drag, not far from the Polícia Federal building, not that that meant anything at all. Only bureaucracy boys in there.

Leme didn't like the idea of a private residence. But the condo was modern, slick, and they had lowered all the windows for the seguranças, the usual phalanx of condo security guards behind bulletproof glass, so there was no doubt they knew he was there. These seguranças didn't seem too bothered by the Militar SUV –

Cash-happy, no doubt.

The old aspirational-Militar-assist. The money's good and the hours are minimal. Zero contract: you're paid *not* to do anything.

So this felt like a could-go-either-way type of scene.

Leme thought he'd have taken that, an hour ago.

The cunt with no name bundled Leme out. A younger one flanked him.

They were elevator-whisked to the eighth floor.

Usual swank condo set-up.

Narrow corridor, one apartment either side of the lift.

No Name knocked once on the door to the right. He waited a beat and opened the door. Leme clocked the number: 8B.

The sala stretched out in front of them. Dark wood floors, a dining table and four chairs to the left, a black sofa to the right and two brown leather armchairs either side of a fireplace. A fucking fireplace, Leme thought. Antonia had friends who used theirs once a year. Get their polo-necked jumpers out and their wedding-present fondue set and play at being your sophisticate Alpine swingers for an evening. Leme quite enjoyed it. Never stayed late enough to drop his keys into the empty fondue pot, mind.

There were three men out on the balcony. All in uniform. All with guns in their belts. All huge men, wide around the middle, shoulders pinned back, straining to keep themselves upright.

Leme could see two faces. He recognised neither.

One of these two noticed Leme and his guard dogs and he nodded at the room. The third man turned. The third man shook his head, smiling.

Carlos.

Carlão. Big Carlos.

Not a surprise. Leme grinned back. Winked.

Why the fuck not? Not a great deal to lose at this point. Might as well go down swinging, entendeu?

Carlos stepped into the room. He examined the two Militars with Leme.

'Cuffs off, and fuck off, certo?' he said.

The younger one uncuffed Leme and the pair of them nodded at Carlão and skedaddled. Leme stretched his hands out.

Carlos nodded at Leme and smirked. 'You'd think they'd be used to a bit of work, your wrists,' he said. 'Kitchen.' He turned and pushed through a door at the end of the room.

Leme decided not to comment on this stain on his impeccable, and followed.

Carlos had his head in the fridge. He pulled a beer and tossed it to Leme. He pulled one for himself and they both cracked their cans.

'Saúde,' Carlos said, raising his can.

Leme nodded.

'Long time,' Carlos said.

'You miss me?'

Carlos smiled. 'Yes, mate. I brought you here to mata saudades, entendeu?'

Mata saudades. To kill the longing. Leme always liked the phrase.

But the word 'kill' escaping old Carlão's meaty chops wasn't too sweet.

'That's what I figured. A drink and a catch-up, ne? We've earned it.'

Carlos's expression shifted. He muttered, 'Cheeky cunt.'

'What was that?'

'You heard.'

They nailed their lagers. Carlos belched and popped the fridge. 'Another?'

'I got much choice?'

'Good point.'

He tossed Leme another can. They drank deeply and said nothing for a minute or two. The lager gave Leme a nice post-work glaze: a two-cans-by-the-fridge sort of deal, even before you've said hello to your missus. He felt good, but suddenly hungry.

'Any nibbles, Carlão?'

Carlos snorted. 'Turn it in, son. This is a safe house, not a fucking padaria.'

'So it *is* safe, then?'

'Vamos ver, ne, cara?' Let's see.

Leme was reassured – just. Safe house meant negotiation, deal, protection. It didn't mean an on-the-sly whack job. Might as well figure the next steps then.

'So what's the play, Carlão? I'm fairly sure I ain't here to help with the investigation, sabe?'

'The grand detective,' Carlos said. He tapped his right temple. 'Not just a hat rack, ne?'

Leme laughed. 'Então?'

'Então,' Carlos said, 'I brought you here as a reminder – and to give you a little info that you won't have worked out yourself, certo?'

'A reminder of what exactly?'

'You know very well, amigo.'

Leme did know very well.

It had been three years. And two since the Cracolândia land deal beef. It was a score draw at this point: 2–2.

They both had the death of Gold Teeth over each other.

Leme had Carlão over a barrel in terms of the dodgy Cracolândia resident benefits and the suitcase of cash and what all that meant.

Carlos had been running a protection and drug racket in Cracolândia, Crackland. It was a desperate place, a lawless area in downtown São Paulo where crack cocaine was openly sold and taken.

But Cracolândia was a part of the old, colonial centre. Leme remembered how his friend Ellie, the young English journalist had described the place, her foreigner's eye. You approached from Praça Julio Prestes. It smelled of urine baked in the heat. Palm trees swayed drunk in the breeze. Small groups of dark, defeated faces scurried about, occasionally words escaping their toothless mouths, either an offer or a request. Smashed windows and black, gaping doorways, toothless and dust-rinsed women and men. Groups of swollen-bellied women sat on the road, cackling. Dead-eyed, rail-thin men wrapped in dirty blankets, passed out on each other on sofas underneath streetlights. Couples in rags shuffled back and across the road, arm in arm, muttering. Carlos was clearing the nastier elements of the place, disappearing them, Leme heard, making the downtown neighbourhood palatable again for visitors in time for the World Cup.

And Carlos had, by association, implicated Antonia – her law firm was connected to the relocation aspects of it, so he had that over Leme.

So score draw, and extra time and pens if they weren't careful.

Complicated scene.

Or not, really. You scratch mine and I'll scratch yours seemed to be the order of the day. Until today, that is.

Aha –

Leme thought maybe he'd got it.

'So this,' he said, gesturing around them, 'is what, some sort of further insurance?'

Carlos smiled. 'Cookie-sharp, my son,' he said. 'What happens next is up to you.'

'Seems unlikely.'

'Well, you're in the frame, mate. At this point, there's a stiff and a man – *you* – poking around next to it.' He paused. 'We Military Police are always very grateful when a member of our Civil counterpart assists in an investigation. A real relief it was, when we found that Detective Leme was already on the scene, doing his job, asking the right kind of investigative questions.' He looked at Leme. 'That's one way this could go.'

'And the other?'

'Don't make me laugh.'

Leme nodded. 'You know who the kid was?'

'I told you not to make me laugh. Sleep on it. We'll be in touch. Assis downstairs will give you a lift home.'

'He's a real heartbreaker,' Leme said. Assis. He noted the name.

Carlos laughed. 'Total charmer. Now fuck off, eh?'

Leme did what he was told. He had about forty-five minutes in the car to decide what he was going to tell Antonia when he got home.

She'd be fucking delighted old Carlão was back in touch.

# Article by Eleanor Boe

## TIME OUT SÃO PAULO, 21 March 2016

### OPINION: SEX AND THE MARCH IN MARCH

The colours of Brasil used to be yellow and green. Not anymore. These days they're black and white. Politically speaking, there isn't a single shade of grey; erotic fiction has never been less relevant in a country where nothing used to get in the way of the old horizontal samba. Not anymore.

It's us and them in every sphere now, *queridos*. Flirting has become a partisan activity; Dilma divides. You say the wrong thing on a first date, and you are *not* going to score, no *Senhor*. Oh, we'll lie about being in a relationship, about our jobs, about where we live, about who we know. But politics? Not anymore.

No right-thinking, left-leaning Dilma fan is going to put out for any member of the conservative elite calling for her impeachment, no matter how enticing they look. The whole swipe left / swipe right conundrum has got an edge to it now; alignment is everywhere!

And the march in March proved this beyond reasonable doubt. Yes, there was a fair amount of booze flying around, and the air was, ahem, pretty pungent, but I'd wager that a good number of the hook-ups that took place – both at the rally and in the evening that followed – were driven by solidarity, a we're-all-in-this-together, like-minded sexiness. A quick trawl of social media and you'll see it – good place to pull, a political event in this day and age.

The age of Black and White / Us and Them. Families and friends divided, the country *triste*, saddened by the lack of political discourse, debate, nuance, the abundance of hostility and anger.

There's got to be an upside, *ne*? Or as one of the placards I saw put it:

**Progressive liberals are better lovers**

And speaking as one myself, there's really no need to put that policy to a vote.

**São Paulo, 21 March 2016**

*I'm very privileged. I've always had a very good life. But everything I've got out of life was obtained through dedication and a tremendous desire to achieve my goals… a great desire for victory, meaning victory in life, not as a driver. To all of you who have experienced this or are searching now, let me say that whoever you may be in your life, whether you're at the highest or most modest level, you must show great strength and determination and do everything with love and a deep belief in God. One day, you'll achieve your aim and you'll be successful.*

Ayrton, deceased, driver

# Junior

They used to do blow before work in the locker room, back in the day.

So Junior had heard. Get them good and jacked up for all the law-enforcing and strong-arming and head-banging they'd have to do. Level playing field, then, you see:

The villains were all up to their eyeballs in the stuff, after all.

Bit of Colombian courage, know what I mean? It was sanctioned from the top down, apparently. The headquarters of the *2°BPChq Anchieta*, the second battalion of shock troops in the São Paulo Military Police, was in Lapa, and Junior had arrived early.

He always did –

He'd grown up in the neighbourhood; it was fifteen minutes from home. He remembered the hopped-up Militars, blitzed and on the prowl. Quite a ruckus on some days when he was a kid. Muito heavy.

This morning, troubled by the day before, he sat in the locker room and reflected on his role, his job. He listed his responsibilities, his missions: control of civil commotions, policing in sports areas, policing during artistic and cultural events and ROCAM (ostensible patrol with motorcycles).

As he sat and waited for the day's tasks to come in, it occurred to him that dealing with a dead body was absolutely not something he was professionally supposed to be involved in.

He had been there in a different capacity. Civil commotion, he supposed –

Or would have been, had the anarchist Black Blocs turned up. There were a few in the battalion who had been well up for giving them a kicking, turning them over in a straightener for a change, instead of that snide form of terrorism they usually practised when no one was looking.

'It's going to be old school today, son,' an older Militar, Araken, had told him. 'Rocks and fists, shields and truncheons. About time we had a proper tear-up. Too much firepower with the old PCC. I fancy getting my hands dirty, know what I mean?'

Junior had said nothing. He didn't like the fact that the week before they'd been out for the anti-Dilma protest, and this week it was *her* supporters. What did that *mean*? If he was an instrument of the state, then what exactly was he protecting? And who?

And now, why could he not get that playboy kid's face out of his mind?

Fuck it.

*Not your problem, Junior, seu filho da puta,* he thought, forget about it.

The door swung open and smacked against the wall. A slight, damp echo. Boot heels clicked across the floor, slowly. Junior was alone; someone had come to see him. He readied himself –

The locker room was not well known as a venue for negotiating a promotion, after all.

Look sharp.

'Junior, isn't it?' Carlos said. 'Remember me?' He smiled and held out his hand. 'It's been a while, ne?'

'Sim, Senhor,' Junior said, standing up, feeling the firm clasp of Carlos's handshake.

'Quite a night that, wasn't it?' Carlos said. 'Please, sit down.'

Junior nodded and sat back on the bench. His first ride-along, a good four years ago. A gold-toothed dealer interrogated. A Civil police detective. He and Carlos had shared a burger when it was all done. Something of an initiation.

Carlos smiled again. He stood over Junior, put his left foot up on the bench next to him, leant his left elbow on his knee. 'Interesting few weeks we've been having,' he said. 'Civil unrest means we're busy as fuck. Difficult to get any perspective, though, you know, politically speaking.'

'Sim, Senhor,' Junior said. He tried to keep Carlos's eye. Failed.

'At this point, the key thing is to remember what it is we do here, entendeu?'

Junior nodded.

'Our role is to keep the peace, that's all. To make sure things don't get out of hand. We don't judge, we don't take sides, certo? It's simple enough when you think of it like that. Make sense?'

Junior nodded. 'Sim, Senhor,' he said. 'Makes total sense.'

Carlos levered his leg off the bench and turned away slightly, rolled his bulky shoulders, clicked his bulldog neck first left, then right. He was a *biiiiig* unit, old Carlos –

Heavy man. His team were known inside as the Heavy Mob. Junior twitched, waited.

Carlos went on. 'You might have recognised the lad we boosted yesterday evening. Mario Leme, a detective in the Polícia Civil. Did you?'

Junior nodded.

Carlos pursed his meaty lips, grimaced, smiled again. 'Thought you might. He's an old friend. Helping us out, entendeu?'

Junior nodded. 'Sim, Senhor.'

'The John Doe is a young man, not much older than you. Wrong-place wrong-time type of scene. It's taken care of.' Carlos smiled again. 'It's done, ta ligado? No follow-up required. We're on it with the Civil lot now. Ta entendendo?'

Junior did know what he meant. Carlos meant –

*Nothing to see here.*

Junior nodded. 'Senhor, I understand,' he said.

'Good lad,' Carlos said, cracking another big smile, nodding his swollen head. 'You know what you're doing today?'

'Not yet, Senhor,' Junior said. 'Waiting orders.'

'Good lad. Fact is,' Carlos went on, 'things are a bit topsy-turvy right now, what with the corruption investigation, you know, this Lava Jato nonsense. And let's not forget this Dilma impeachment business.' He smiled. 'No official opinions on the slag, of course. Everything else is a bit on hold for now. We've just got to focus on doing what we're told, entendeu?'

Junior nodded.

'But hold tight. Play it straight, son, and there might be a place on my team in not too long.' He smiled again, his eyes danced. 'Benefits of a good set of peepers and a tight gob, know what I mean? I'll see to it that you come out with my lot today, certo?'

'Sim, Senhor.'

Carlos turned, walked a few paces towards the door. 'You're alright, son,' he said. 'Important that.' He laughed. 'Enjoy your moment's respite, young man. We'll call for you shortly.'

Junior said nothing. The door swung shut. He exhaled –

Yep, he thought, he knew his responsibilities, his missions.

And he knew not to think too much beyond that.

He'd have to try and forget this dead playboy, whoever he was –

And this Polícia Civil detective named Leme.

Though after that night in Paraisópolis, that night high up in the favela, and whatever the connection was with yesterday's palaver, he was pretty sure forgetting anything might be a fairly tough fucking assignment.

Half an hour later: Militar SUV, Carlos quarterbacking. 'Então, young man,' he said to Junior, 'we're going to be putting the wind up a few rich cunts today. That suit you alright?'

Carlos wolfed a mixto quente. He guzzled at a jug of foaming coffee. Grease dripped from the cheese and ham sandwich. He back-handed milk from his top lip. He levered his bulk around in the passenger seat of the Militar SUV and winked at Junior, who sat in the back, squashed between two of Carlos's boys. The Heavy Mob.

'Learning on the job, son,' Carlos barked between mouthfuls. 'Never fails.' He sprayed liquid, breadcrumbs.

'Sim, Senhor,' Junior said – with purpose. Sunglass-set expression, dead ahead.

Carlos laughed. 'That's enough lip from you, querido.'

They were, ostensibly, on a follow-up to the previous day's rally, wheedling out provocateur types. Junior wasn't sure what this meant exactly, but he had his suspicions. The phrase 'rich cunts' rang in his head like the long note of a bell. A warning bell, perhaps, he thought.

The SUV moved through the traffic like a shark. The Heavy Mob either side of Junior held their automatic weapons from their windows, showing their teeth.

They feathered through the posh part of the city, arrowed through the traffic: floored it.

A rush of images, of colour, as foreign to Junior, in the lives they represented, as Europe or Africa or, in fact, anywhere outside Brazil, outside São Paulo, outside *his* São Paulo –

Low-rise, light-brown, red-brick housing; green spaces; pedestrians in smart navy clothes, suits and shirts, well-cut jeans, shining black shoes, shining black Lycra sports kit, well-groomed dogs obediently trotting alongside; *dogs* in smart clothes; glass security booths with painted green doors; cars neatly parked, in lines of black and silver and white; black maids and nannies dressed in white, holding children's hands, while their white mothers and white fathers chatted to other white mothers and white fathers, laughing, making dinner plans outside expensive schools; black maids dressed in white carrying shopping bags from smart supermarkets, while white men and white women walk behind; white men and white women in suits and sunglasses, sitting at pavement tables, served at these tables by black waitresses and white waitresses in smart black and white clothes, drinking black coffee and sparkling water, talking on black mobile phones, tap-tapping on white mobile phones, stepping into chauffeur-driven black cars, cars that look like they were bought from the foreign concessions that line the roads with their foreign, sophisticated goods, concessions that scream their message in their simplicity, lines of expensive, foreign, sophisticated goods, concessions that a man like Junior has no place in, no more place in them than he does in –

No more place in them than he does anywhere else, he thought – anywhere else but home.

And driving through these wealthy neighbourhoods in a Militar

SUV with automatic weapons and an obvious show of force, of authority, Junior was still invisible. The men and the women chatting by the side of the road didn't notice them, and if they did, it was out of a sort of expectancy, an ownership: *oh good*, their expressions seemed to say, *here go the people that get their hands dirty to protect us*.

'Cinco minutinhos,' the driver said to Carlos. About five minutes.

The Heavy Mob grinned at each other. They grinned and nodded at Junior.

But five minutes until what?

'Young Junior here is technically on watch, that's all,' Carlos said. 'I mean, *technically*, sabe? It's not up to us to police his *every* move, entendeu?'

The driver laughed. The Heavy Mob laughed. Carlos winked, raised his eyebrows. Junior looked dead ahead, eyes on the road.

They stopped outside a bar in Itaim. The name: Vaca Veia. Clientele: young, good-looking, professional. Cash flow: heavy. Tables dotted inside and out. A lunchtime buzz. Some drinking. Plates of food picked at. Not much on them, Junior thought. Memorabilia on the walls, hanging from the ceiling.

'Vamos,' said Carlos.

The five of them bounced. They lined up in front of the bar in formation: Carlão at the head, a Heavy Mob flank, driver and Junior fanned out behind.

Heads turned. Heads looked up from tables. Eyes shot other eyes glances. Conversations stopped. Nerves: jangled. Junior could feel the equivocation – it throbbed. This sense of power, this ability to *impact*: he liked it. He was, for a moment, *seduced*.

They stood and waited for the bar's attention. It was quite a scene. It was quite a performance. *São Paulo is Shakespeare*. Junior had heard some smarmy fuck at the academy once say that. He understood, suddenly, the power of a show of strength, the power of a *show*.

Carlos grandstanded. He paraded. He *prowled*. He rested his fat hands on his fat hips, hoisted his fat belly up, scowled and swaggered. Another fucking John Wayne in the cavalry, Junior thought.

Another swashbuckler type. Except Carlos was far more dangerous. This was *not* just for show. The tension crackled. The air stank of it.

Carlos grinned. He prepared to speak. Silence.

Carlos scanned the bar. His eyes ran over the tables, they ran over a couple holding hands, over a group of men and women in smart work clothes, over another couple, but these two were not holding hands, they were sitting more stiffly than the first, backs straight, expressions strained. His eyes ran over a second group of colleagues, dressed the same, laughing. They ran, Carlos's eyes, over all these people before they landed on a table of three young men, three good-looking, healthy-looking, tanned, confident young men, three privileged young men dressed in expensive polo shirts and tailored shorts, wearing boat shoes, shoes with tassels and no socks, three young men who could absolutely be described as classic Paulistano playboys, three young men who –

'Mind if I join you?' Carlos said. He gestured at the empty chair at their table. 'This taken?'

The bar, it felt to Junior, held its breath.

'Not at all, it's yours,' one of the young men replied. 'Please, join us.'

The bar, with great relief, exhaled –

Except for the table of three young men where Carlos now towered.

Each of these three young men reacted in quite different ways to the situation, to the intrusion, to Carlos.

The young man who had spoken wore a look of pure nonchalance, casually, loosely, he wore this look, like a sweater tossed and knotted, casually, loosely around his neck.

Carlos raised his arm, clicked his fingers and whistled. A waiter appeared. 'Another round for my friends here,' Carlos said. 'And the same for me.'

Carlos sat, heavily, down. He sat opposite the young man who had spoken. The young man Carlos sat next to did not have the same breezy, casual disposition as the first.

In fact, Junior thought, the lad appeared to be shitting bricks.

Carlos spoke to this nervous-looking young man. 'I suspect you're wondering what this is all about,' he said. 'To what, exactly, you might owe this honour and whatnot.'

The young man nodded and looked down at the table. His hands fidgeted with each other, and the way that he examined his hands made Junior feel as if this nervous young man were looking down at some distinct object, something separate from himself, his volition, some entirely *foreign* object.

The waiter appeared and dumped four glasses of beer on the table. Not hanging around to see if they wanted to order anything else, he scuttled off sharpish.

A hubbub returned to the bar. The other customers, very self-consciously, were ignoring the drama being played out in front of them.

Junior looked them over –

They did not want to be there –

But nobody was going to be the first to leave.

The Heavy Mob jawed their gum. They scowled. They glowered. They did their best to keep the bar guessing. Driver slouched, leant against a lamp post, his hand by his side, close to his holster, but not too close, giving the impression of some quick-draw kid, like he should be chewing on a match and flirting, stone-faced, with a woman. How often, Junior thought, had they done this sort of thing before? Could *he* do this sort of thing, again and again, he thought, could he, *willingly*, really do this sort of thing?

Carlos nailed his beer in one long, thirsty gulp. 'Puta que pariu,' he said, 'that hit the spot.' He grinned at each of the three young men in turn.

They did not grin back –

They sipped at their beers. They tried not to look at each other.

Junior was, by now, sweating profusely. Even in the relatively leafy neighbourhood of Itaim, there were few trees, there was little cover, the concrete baked from all sides.

The heavy flak jacket, the boots, the weight of the weapons, the *accessories* –

It was quite a workout in this weather.

Carlos was speaking more quietly now. Junior tried, but failed, to follow the conversation. The confident young man remained confident. He drank his beer. His body language said: I'm doing *you* a favour, and it's fine, not a problem, entendeu? The nervous young man twitched and fidgeted. The third young man, Junior couldn't get a read on. But he sat, broadly speaking, involved –

Then things happened very fast.

Carlos placed his hand on the nervous-looking young man's shoulder – and it was definitely not a friendly gesture.

The Heavy Mob bristled.

Driver turned back to the vehicle.

The third young man pushed back his chair and bolted.

Carlos barked an order.

The Heavy Mob hotfooted it.

The lad managed about half a dozen yards before doing what he was told –

Arms up legs spread hands behind the head, son.

Carlos signalled for the other two to relaxa the fuck out and sit the fuck down, entendeu –

He signalled to Junior to keep an eye, and he walked, slowly, purposefully, down the road to where the Heavy Mob waited.

The bar gasped, then hushed.

The two other lads kept their hands where Junior could see them –

This was not common, boosting playboys like they were on a favela roust –

Carlos better know what he's doing, Junior thought. You can't fuck with these boys too much, you don't know who their old man went to school with.

Carlos instructed the Heavy Mob; they patted the lad down. They pulled his wallet. Carlos opened it up, rifled through it, flicking cards – credit and business, gym and loyalty – onto the pavement. He, quite obviously, quite deliberately, lifted the cash, held it in the air and pocketed it.

Then –

'Bingo,' Carlos sang. He held up, between thumb and forefinger, a small bag of something most definitely not sold at the bar.

The young man, resigned, nodded. He offered his wrists. Carlos laughed.

The Heavy Mob led him to the SUV. They ducked his head, pushed him in. They jammed themselves either side. Doors slammed, driver popped the siren and the car squealed off, screeched away in a blue-red flash.

Carlos, grinning again, pulled his phone and turned a circle, jabbering –

Junior held tight.

Carlos finished the call, waved at Junior, gestured for him to sit down at the table with the two other lads.

'Another round,' Carlos called out to the waiter. 'Rapido, ne?' He looked at the two young men. 'You two best fuck off then. If I need anything from either of you, your mate will tell me how to find you, certo?'

They nodded. The waiter returned. Carlos looked up. 'Second thoughts,' he said, 'it's just the two of us now.'

The waiter nodded and placed a beer in front of Carlos and one in front of Junior. The two young men scraped their chairs loudly, so eager were they to be up and away.

The bar watched them leave. There was audible relief, tangible fear that this wasn't quite over.

'Cheers.' Carlos raised his glass, knocked it against Junior's. 'Drink up,' he said. 'Car's on its way, we don't have long.' He grinned. His eyes sparkled. 'We'll go back and have a quiet word with young Scar-face, entendeu?'

Junior took a sip of his beer. Christ, he thought.

Here we go then.

The interrogation room buzzed. The stuffy, cramped interrogation room really fizzed. It *popped*. Carlos drove his hand into the wall with a smack, hard, flat palm, no more than an inch or so to the right of the young man's head.

The young man's name, it transpired, was Gabriel.

Junior watched. Gabriel's old man, Junior now knew, was *somebody*. And that was all they needed. Somebody, in fact, who was not going to appreciate his son on a little drug-possession beef. Best for everyone if young Gabriel here does what it is we want him to do, was the gist of Carlão's little opening speech, his opening *salvo*.

Junior learned.

'Now you listen to me, son,' Carlos spat, his right hand still pressed against the wall, his left now threatening to tighten up around young Gabriel's neck. 'We are not going to fuck around. I have you, in front of a bar-load of witnesses, not to mention four of our finest Militar officers, such as young Junior here, running away from a perfectly civilised meeting, *resisting arrest* even, you could call it, then apprehended, searched and discovered with a decent-sized bag's worth of high quality bugle, not the yellowing, sulphurous shit you'd find in a boca in Paraisópolis!'

He leant back off the wall. Indicated that Gabriel should sit back down at the interview table.

'Favela, you got it in the favela.' Carlos shook his head. 'You're having a fucking laugh, son.'

Gabriel said nothing. Carlos sat down in front of him and leaned across the table. Junior imagined his sour breath, his rancid tongue, his pores *alive* with rankness.

'Fact is, Gabriel, I don't give two fucks where you got this from.'

Gabriel looked confused.

'And by that I mean to say that if you *don't* do what I tell you, we'll be pursuing a particular line of enquiry that means the person you got this sample of expensive and exquisitely proficient cocaine from, is in fact, you!'

Carlos smiled. 'Do you know what I mean?'

'You're saying that the deal is I do something for you, all this disappears?'

Carlos winked. 'Clever boy.'

Gabriel processed this.

'Course,' Carlos added, 'you don't, and all this gets a hell of a lot worse.'

Junior watched as Gabriel fingered his jewellery, a silver bracelet on his left wrist, a gold signet ring on his right hand. Gabriel's expression was one Junior had seen before in these sorts of situations. It was one of *understanding*: there is no choice to be made; it is out of your control. So.

Gabriel nodded. 'What is it you want me to do exactly?'

'Good boy,' Carlos said. He stood. 'We know that you lot, you posh lot, you boys who went to the private international schools and the private universities and now work as lawyers and in finance and whatnot, you all know each other, certo?'

Gabriel nodded. 'Mais ou menos, sim, ne?' he said. More or less, that's true.

'OK, good, look like you want to help.'

'Sim, I do, yeah.'

Junior thought of the way that he himself agreed to Carlos's demands, the way he cowered – at least on the inside – always aware of who he was, where he came from, always a little favela fuck with a bit of luck, none of the bargaining or entitlement of this Gabriel, even with the violence in Carlos –

It was something.

'So, look,' Carlos said. 'We think at least one, if not two, of your sort of people might well be AWOL. Certo?'

Gabriel nodded.

'We don't know who or why or where, but we think this is the case.'

Junior clocked Carlos's shift in tone, shift in manner –

He was feigning ignorance to get the lad on side. Carlos was letting Gabriel feel like *he*, Gabriel, would be doing them all a very big favour indeed, and that in some way Gabriel was, in fact, the boss man here.

'OK,' Gabriel said.

'Here's my card.' Carlos placed one on the table and pushed it across with his finger. 'You're going to call me every three hours, from now, with any news you get, anything you find out. Entendeu?'

Gabriel nodded.

'Just ask around, that's all. No mention of anything else. We just want to know if anyone isn't where they should be, ta ligado?'

'Crystal.'

'But you call me, right? Through the night, too. One word: nada, if there's nothing. We'll talk if you find something.'

The air in the room thinned. Their limbs relaxed.

'One thing,' Gabriel asked. 'What's the timescale here, roughly?'

'You mean when are you free from this binding contract and no longer in danger of being made as a dope-hound and a pusher?'

Gabriel smiled. 'Yeah, I guess I mean that.'

Junior admired the balls on this kid, the *front*. Serious front. It comes with the knowledge that this whole thing is based on a bluff; he walks out the door, nothing will ever happen – legally. So essentially they've become partners. They're working together now.

Carlos stood up. 'Mate, we don't find out by tomorrow night tops, it'll be too late for everyone.' He moved to the door. 'See him out, Junior, will you?' he said.

Junior nodded. 'Sim, Senhor.' He moved from the back of the room closer to the table.

Gabriel keyed Carlos's number into his phone. When he was done, he holstered his mobile, smirking. He pushed the card towards Junior.

Junior pulled a pen. He pushed the card back towards Gabriel.

'Write your number on this, cara,' Junior said. 'Quick.'

Gabriel read Junior's expression, understood it, nodded:

He scribbled digits.

Junior pocketed the card.

'Vamos, ne?' he said, and they left the room, Junior's hand on Gabriel's arm, his tight, firm grip on Gabriel's now limp, exhausted arm, and Gabriel breathed a helluva sigh of relief, an enormous, deep breath of relief as the door banged behind them and they were on their way down the corridor and back towards the sunlight of the front entrance.

'You probably don't want to pick up a cab right outside the building,' Junior said.

# Roberta

Roberta woke.

A whiff of him – just in the moment before her eyes opened, his hair product faint on the pillow next to her and she smiled and clutched it to her, and then her eyes did open and it was gone and she was alone.

She shook her head, shook herself awake, half-crawled, half-fell out of bed. She put water on to boil and took a shower, the same ritual she acknowledged each day.

In the shower, she'd decided what to do. For a start, she needed her fucking phone, Christ knows what she might have missed, and she needed to go into college and retrieve her laptop, and there were at least three or four people there who might know something, might know where the hell he was. Or, at least, she'd be able to try his or her phone; not for the first time she lamented how her generation never wrote anything down, never knew anyone's number or email address without checking their contacts, fucking millennials, she thought, laughing, generation sext. That was one of Antonio's jokes. He was funny, old Antonio. Good old Antonio. She felt happy, suddenly, knowing she'd see him soon.

She drove to the university. It felt, distinctly, a Monday.

Her head soupy with the draw she'd smoked the night before, traffic buzzing, an irritant to be swatted but just out of reach, streets lined with rubbish, the odd placard, socialist newspapers strewn about. Post-rally city-slump.

She weaved down through Jardins. Mid-morning quiet, which meant it only took about twenty minutes longer than it should. She feathered through the quieter side streets, coming out at Rebouças and the shopping centre, crossed the bridge and headed right, out towards Butanta and USP and she wound down her windows as the air thinned, felt immediately fresher, just a few kilometres out from the centre.

She negotiated the roundabout at Praça Vincente Rodrigues. It was unusually quiet. More often than not, Roberta found herself riding the horn; her car, and its staccato, jarring movements, would course through her, jerked this way then that by the awkward, selfish flow of the traffic, shunting forwards, jamming the brakes, gesturing with middle finger...

...not today. She glided around and along Avenida Afrânio Peixoto, circled the second of the three roundabouts before campus, then accelerated, her left arm hanging from the window feeling the sun and the breeze along Avenida Universidade.

She parked in front of the Economics department. There were hardly any cars about. She looked up at the clock tower in the central plaza, the Praça do Relogio, as she always did. Habits, even on a day like this, an uncertain day, held fast. The tower had always fascinated her. Its vast, concrete flat front and back, its jutting rectangle rising skyscraper-high from a circular pool of green brackish water, its modernist, yet indigenous etchings, and the clock itself, high up at the top, like an afterthought, so you had to squint to see the time.

It made a stark contrast with the functional, low-level brick-and-glass boxes that made up the departments and teaching and research areas. When Roberta was an undergraduate, her professor had showed her class – political economy – photos of New York projects and London council estates, to interrogate the distinction of the first world favela from their own; but many students were impressed at how their university didn't look so different.

She sat back for a moment, the engine off, the AC off, the driver's window wound down, and she closed her eyes and let herself listen to the noises around her. In the distance, faint but constant, the low hum of Marginal traffic by the river, coming into the city, leaving the city, *stretching* the city, it sometimes seemed; more immediately, the buzz and snap from the electricity cables that fed the medical and science facilities in the next buildings; and next to her, in the space she claimed as hers, nothing really at all.

She was calm, she acknowledged this, but there was something more, something persistent, which she couldn't identify, something that made her stomach shrink and her eyes narrow, something about powerlessness, she thought. She was proud of the way she'd handled it yesterday, practical and realistic given that she had no phone, no computer, no way of contacting anyone save going round to their house, and pleased too that she'd had the self-possession to manage all this without panic, without fear, without too much anxiety from the uncertainty, from, yes, she thought, the *powerlessness*.

She nodded to herself three times and, in three quick motions, wound up the window, grabbed her bag from the passenger seat and jumped out of the car, locking it remotely with a beep as she walked towards the Economics block and her on-campus locker.

She couldn't help but notice something: there didn't appear to be a single person around. Had she missed some sort of holiday, or strike? The building, too, looked empty, all the lights out, almost derelict in the muggy heat of the morning.

And yet, despite the heat, despite the clammy space between her shoulder blades, the tight wetness where her thighs had melted on the car's leather seats, she shivered as she keyed in the six-digit entry code.

Half an hour later: Roberta stood, confused, in front of the reception desk at Antonio's office. 'So what you're telling me is that I can't ask questions about employees unless I have a prior appointment?'

The receptionist gave her a thin smile. Actually, Roberta thought, thin was being generous. This woman's smile was a slit, knife-sharp; it was barely even an acknowledgement of Roberta, of her existence, let alone her presence.

'That's right. I believe I told you this over the phone.'

This was true, she had. Back at university, Roberta had picked up her laptop from her locker, gave it a quick charge, then set about getting some numbers, firstly hers and Antonio's, sitting easily as they were in her contacts folder. She scribbled them down. She then got online and found his work number; it made sense to call him there if the mobile phones were out of battery, even though she never had before, had never even possessed the number, nor, in fact, the desire to do so. She also noted the address; it would likely be her next destination.

'You did, of course,' Roberta said, smiling, though reluctantly, herself. 'But I really need to talk to him. He's my boyfriend. Can't we imagine I'm making an appointment with you now?'

The phone conversation had gone about as well. After jotting down what she needed, she'd headed to the Economics department admin office. There was no one there. She hadn't seen a soul since she'd arrived. But it was unlocked and there were telephones. She tried the two mobile numbers, and both went straight to voicemail. She didn't leave messages. No one did anymore, only parents. She was yet to decide what she felt about it. It used to be a pleasure to receive a message from a friend she wanted to hear from. Now it was a faff, pressing this number or that – or was it a faff, really? Had everyone simply become even *more* impatient? When friends didn't answer when she called and then sent her a text to see what she wanted, it made her furious.

Right now though she wanted to speak to Antonio. That was all that mattered.

'I'm not sure you've totally understood what it means to make an appointment?' the receptionist said. And that smile again, though a touch more joy in it this time, perhaps pleased with the joke, or retort, or witticism.

Roberta swore under her breath. 'Do you think you could at least tell me if he's here?' she said, and as she said it – as she was saying it – she realised quite how desperate or vulnerable or sad the question made her look, and she felt all at once miniscule and hot and morti-fied and enraged by the whole thing.

The receptionist arched an eyebrow, made a tight, ironic face.

'Please.'

Her expression softened. 'OK.'

'Thank you,' Roberta said.

She'd driven over from the university fast – and twitchy with nerves or confusion or uncertainty, she wasn't sure which, or, in fact, if she really thought that for her there was any difference between the three things. She had expected to see friends – or possibly even friends of his – and had hoped she would get some company, some support, if that wasn't too dramatic, and some good practical advice. Instead, it seemed that everyone had disappeared and she had no way of tracking them down bar actually going looking for them, which was sort of unthinkable, not something any of her generation ever really did.

She smiled in genuine relief as the receptionist fiddled first with her computer then with her headset earpiece. She turned away from Roberta and spoke in a whisper, nodded, spoke a little more. She looked up at Roberta and flashed another tight smile, but this one wasn't hostile, no, it was something else, something…

Roberta didn't know much about Antonio's work. This was not a reflection on their relationship, though, thinking about it, if it were, it was a positive one, she thought. There were several reasons why she didn't. The principal reason, it seemed to her, was that Antonio was basically ashamed of what he did, realised that it was an easy route from expensive school to private university to finance sector, that he had taken, knew that, yes, he was after money and status, and knew this to be a superficial approach to life, knew that he was in fact better than this, and so only spoke of it to her in ironic and dismissive tones. And she, realising all of this, *understanding* it, and not wanting to be judgemental or be seen to be pushing him, wanting him to improve, to *be a better man*, never really asked him any questions or asked him for any details beyond the very broad generic sketches he gave her of the world in which he moved.

Yes, she thought now – this was a good reflection of their relationship; they didn't *need* to know that much about each other's work.

She was a PhD student and an intern at an NGO; he worked in a small, but prestigious, private finance company, a hedge fund, she thought. These were not incompatible things. Not at all.

'So?' Roberta asked, sweating now that her body heat had cooled.

The receptionist kept her eyes on her screen. 'Antonio Neves, you said, ne?'

'Yes.'

She nodded. 'He's not here. He's not due in until Thursday. In his calendar it's marked off. I've spoken to his manager, I – ' She shook her head, gave Roberta a sympathetic, pleading look.

'You're sure?'

'Yes.'

Roberta nodded. 'Holiday... makes sense, of course,' she said. 'Absolutely. Thank you. You've been really kind.' She smiled again, but she felt the panic in her smile.

She drifted from the desk, tripping slightly as she gathered her things.

'I can call someone if you – '

Roberta moved away, shook her head, stumbled, called out, 'No, don't worry at all, thank you!'

She staggered through the revolving doors and out into the blistering midday sun, light-headed and alone.

Roberta swore to herself. She shook as she drank the herbal tea she'd just about managed to order in the café across the road from Antonio's office, order without quite bursting into tears, without embarrassing the poor girl who served her with a curious glance, a curious, not unsympathetic glance, a look, really, and it had taken all of her willpower not to burst into tears, to cry, freely, to *weep* –

And then she had an idea.

Well, she thought, not really an idea, as such, more of a realisation. And a pretty fucking simple one at that, but one that about twenty minutes before she was incapable of having.

She didn't have her phone, but she did have her laptop, which meant she had email. And she was in a café that had Wi-Fi. What a millennial genius.

*You've gone on fucking holiday!? Without telling me!? You fucking prick! I can't believe you'd even* think *about doing that. And you've got my phone, caralho. I need it. You'd better reply to this – soon.*

Sending that message had felt good. But where did it leave her? No closer to any sort of resolution, or closure, or, fuck, I don't know, she thought, *serenity.*

She read it again. She read it three times. And then she realised something else.

She looked at the words she had written: *I can't believe you'd even* think *about doing that.*

Interesting words to have chosen, she thought. Yes, she can close read it and see the indignation, the anger, the disbelief that he could ever be so insensitive –

*I can't believe you'd even* think *about doing that.*

But of course a close reading can be a psychological one too, and she slowly, on her fourth or fifth reading, realised that she'd used the words *I can't believe you'd even* think *about doing that* precisely because she couldn't believe he'd even *think* about doing that, she couldn't believe, she *didn't* believe he had done that, didn't believe he'd gone on holiday without her, let alone without telling her –

Which means what exactly? she thought.

And then she *did* start to cry.

# Mario

Leme was smiling before he'd even opened his eyes.

Positively beaming, he was –

What a sop. This was getting to be something of a regular occurrence. What was it, contentment, is that what they call it? Quite the headline: man enjoys living with his girlfriend.

Two noises: the shower and the kitchen TV –

Morning routines. Antonia's pre-work rinse, then catching up on the latest skulduggery that Globo offered up as news over a pingado – a sweet milky coffee – and a little pão na chapa, bread fried in a hefty wallop of butter. Old-school Brazilian breakfast.

Leme breathed a rattle, cleared his throat, snorted like a horse. Lips buzzed. He swung his legs out of the bed and lumbered into the en suite. Antonia was hum-singing something that sounded like 'I'm in my little rowboat', which made his heart zoom and his grin widen. Naked, he pissed, heavily, straight into the bowl, no hands, back arched, scratching at his chest hair and clawing at the sleep in his eyes; it was a *proper* piss, a real *man's* piss, and he took great pleasure in doing it while Antonia showered.

'Mario, really, caralho,' she'd said the first time she'd seen him do it. Well, *yelped* the first time she'd seen him do it. 'Don't we have any mystery left?'

He'd laughed. 'Intimacy is what this is, querida. We don't share this with anyone else, after all.'

She'd shaken her head, smiling, and kissed at him through the glass of the shower, smudging the impression of her lips and mouth.

'At least put the seat up,' she said.

Antonia sang; Leme mooned. Leme swooned. He stood and watched her a moment then wrapped himself in his dressing gown and went through to the kitchen to make breakfast. He wanted to ask about her period. But he didn't want to ask about her period. He didn't want to be that guy. They were being consciously less careful. This was an agreed and agreeable position. He wanted to ask and he didn't want to ask. Most of all, he wanted her to want whatever it was that the answer was.

Leme flicked through the channels. TV news:

All pro-Dilma rally. Numbers of attendees smudged depending on the network. Connections to Lava Jato implicit or outright. Criticism, or congratulation, of the rabble. No one seemed to know much, though.

Nothing on the kid. *Nada* –

Thank fuck for that.

Not exactly a surprise though. He'd shelve it, for now – stick it in a box.

This was the thing about living with Antonia:

*When he's with her, nothing else matters.*

Leme cranked the coffee machine. It gurgled. He filled the milk frother and pressed play. It swirled. He whacked a heavy cast-iron frying pan onto the electric hob. It beeped heat immediately. He forked a wedge of butter into the pan. It slid and softened. He cut hard bread like wood, in a sawing motion. He tossed two slices into the pan from across the room.

Back of the net.

He mixed the coffee and milk, flipped the bread and pushed it down hard into the butter, the heat, then plated up on the breakfast bar.

Morning routines.

There was a time when he mixed a different kind of drink first thing. Or chased his pingado e pão com manteiga with a cachaça shot and a cigarette –

Old-school labourers' and night-shift breakfast, that one.

Two and a half years they'd lived together now. He was giddy with domesticity. It was a sharp contrast to the dope-fiends and gash-hounds and freaks and shooters and knife-men and balaclaved hoodlums he scouted and collared each day at work –

He was still stuck in that petty criminal rut:

Not exactly a surprise though. No senhor, no surprise *at all*, not given his last couple of run-ins with the big men and the Heavy Mob.

Suited him though. His partner Lisboa, too.

Quiet life, that's the goal, no drama.

*Church.*

Antonia breezed in. Perfume and lines. No real make-up. She kissed him. She smiled. 'Thanks, love,' she said.

They ate and the TV jabbered.

Antonia nodded at it. 'Anything?'

Leme shook his head. 'Same old, same old, entendeu?'

He'd arrived the night before and it wasn't too late. She was out with a friend and home not long after. They were both jazzed on a little too much booze. It was easy to shelve what had happened, to stick it all in a box. *When he's with her, nothing else matters.* To put Carlos and the playboy corpse in a box. *When he's with her, nothing else matters.* To put the consequences, for now, in a box. *When he's with her, nothing else matters.* They shared some leftovers and watched the news and then half of a film that Leme wouldn't have been able to pick out of a line this morning, if asked about it.

Antonia ate slowly. She drank slowly. She looked at her coffee. She nodded. She gestured with her chin at the TV, mouth half full of bread. 'Know what all this is?' she said. 'I've been thinking about it all night.' Leme raised his eyebrows. 'Well, you know,' she said. '*Some* of the night. It's the old cafézinho, but on an epic scale.'

Cafézinho. The old Brazilian bribe. A little coffee, a quick coffee, bought to grease the wheels. The whole public official service lived on it. To *expedite*, in any other language. You can't even get an ID card without wetting someone's palm. Cafézinho. An outlandish euphemism for systemic corruption. That diminutive ending: cute. They'd both done it, Leme thought. And not long ago. To sort out documents and other admin when they'd moved in together.

Everyone does it. *Everyone.*

Leme grunted.

'Point is, querido,' Antonia went on, 'it happens – and *this hap-pened* – because of the general belief that everything – *everything* – is corrupt. And therefore everything *is* corrupt. Even if you don't have to buy a cafézinho, you still do. Why not? It might speed things up. Even though everyone else has done too, so the queue is just as it would be. Too risky not to, though, ne? Lava Jato is simply an understanding of scale.'

On the TV: a vast oil refinery construction project. A name: Odebrecht.

Antonia chewed. She nodded again at the TV. 'Scale, see? Can you imagine the size of that project? Of course not. They thought they'd get away with it purely because how on earth can anyone really get their heads around the scale? The difference between zero and 60 million dollars is vast and fucking easy to see. The difference between 120 and 160 is fuck all. *That's* what these fuckers understood.'

'They might not get away with it.'

'Well, yeah, and that's because we don't know what it is yet that they're getting away with.'

Leme nodded.

He poured them both more coffee. He spritzered the coffees with milk.

*When he's with her, nothing else matters.*

'Course it's not the companies or the politicos who are suffering, you know, on the ground.'

'Only the poor get arrested,' Leme said.

'Not quite what I mean.'

'No?'

'No. I mean the economy's in the tank, unemployment's up, massive construction projects are frozen, precisely because of this. Petrobras is told to suspend work with its chosen contractors, that fucking cartel, then the country suffers, right or wrong, end of story. Well, at least this exacerbates it all. The recession is more than just that, but you know what I mean.'

'Uh-huh.'

'Hence the backlash. Last week and yesterday.'

*When he's with her, nothing else matters.*

She smiled. 'Might be the first time the economy has become political, you know, big picture-wise. I mean, the question that your average Joe wants answered is quite simple, really: *where the fuck is all our money?*'

Leme laughed. 'Fair point.'

'What was it Tim Maia used to say?'

Tim Maia. Leme's all-time favourite Brazilian singer. Renata had introduced Leme to his music. That series of four eponymous albums in the early seventies *shone*. He was a hero to a lot of people, old Tim Maia.

Leme said, 'Oh, you know, that his doctor told him to give up drinking, drugs and fast food for two weeks and all he lost was a fortnight.'

Antonia laughed. 'No, not that. About the poor, and the right wing.'

'Huh,' Leme said. He thought about it. He smiled. 'He was bang on. What he said was Brasil is the only country where you have whores cumming, jealous pimps, addicts for drug dealers and poor people voting for the right wing. Something like that.'

Antonia nodded. 'Good old Tim Maia. One day it's going to happen, I'm sure of it. This whole thing will not end well.' She shrugged on her coat. 'Anyway, querido. I'll see you tonight?'

'You will.'

Antonia smiled. Leme smiled. And she was gone and then he was alone.

*When he's with her, nothing else matters.*

Last night hit him with a sucker gut-punch. He shook his head, took a breath, nodded, game-faced it.

He ran it:

A tip-off from a low life, dedo-duro, a textbook rat, Fat João –

Leme becomes a suspect or at least an accessory –

Old Carlão reminds him of their somewhat chequered past, who owes who, who did what and blah blah blah –

Old Carlão threatens to put him in the frame –

*Why?*

And who was the kid?

If he is in the frame, be nice to know who he's supposed to have ironed out, Leme thought.

He playbooked it:

One thing at a time: first talk to Lisboa –

Then find Fat João.

Leme was not a happy rabbit.

And he was confused. 'So you're telling me,' he said to Lisboa, 'what you're *telling* me, is that there's no report or record of anything from yesterday other than a few arrests for agitation, a couple of weed pulls, and, what, one or two *traffic* casualties?'

Lisboa made a face. 'I'm telling you what they're telling me. End of.'

They were sitting in a padaria round the corner from the Polícia Civil building that they worked out of at the bottom of the Jardins hill. It was mid-morning, second breakfast-time –

Half a lager and a plate of cheese pastel, smothered in hot sauce.

Lisboa called it the happy ulcer. He said, 'Look, this is coming from our boys only. If you're saying the Military lot carted off a dead body...'

Leme nodded.

'...well if you're saying that, then I'm not sure our boys would necessarily know. *That's* what I'm saying.'

'And there's been no reports of any missing persons?'

'Nope. Nada. Not a sausage.' Lisboa laughed at that. 'Sorry. But, you know, it's likely a little early for that.'

Leme raised an eyebrow. Thought: true.

'I mean,' Lisboa went on, 'you said the kid is, what, early twenties? A playboy? Ah, it's not even twenty-four hours. Who's going to report that just yet? Any cunt with any sense would assume the poor little fuck's off the grid for a little fun, sabe?'

Leme thought this was about right.

Missing persons cases were rife, and reported promptly, on the whole, a hysterical mother weeping at a police block in the favela –

Fear of the old bala perdida. Or an unjust stop and search that ended in resisting arrest and a self-defence shooting in the back –

But not with this demographic, not with a playboy.

There was less worry of a random event. If one of these boys disappeared, you could bet that the kid's rich grandfather would be getting a call sharpish, an empty-a-considerable-part-of-your-bank-account call and tell no one.

But there was a body. Leme had seen it and it existed, so where the fuck was it?

They'd met in the padaria as a lay-low move. Leme had phoned Lisboa, told him to meet there. He gave him the lowdown and Lisboa had skedaddled, made some calls, asked a few questions –

Leme sat tight and made a few calls of his own. He was trying to find a way to get hold of Fat João. The only contact he had beyond Lisboa was his old journo friend Silva. But he wasn't answering. Leme sent him a text in no uncertain terms.

'Strikes me the Militar lot are holding the kid somewhere,' Lisboa said. 'Question is why. And it strikes me there are three basic scenarios here, given your little bate papo with Carlos post-corpse bait and switch.' He laughed.

'Not very reassuring, mate,' Leme said.

As Lisboa was making his enquiries, Leme had let his mind drift, let his mind hear her voice, Renata's voice. *That* was reassuring, the sense that no problem could not be overcome. That's what she was telling him: you overcame grief, you can do anything after that. He'd never got over *her* – he never would; he didn't have to – but he'd got over grief.

He knew what she'd be saying about this whole business, about the fortnight of protests, about what it meant –

*A plague on both your houses.*

That sort of thing: anger at the lack of debate. Fear at the lack of nuance. One thing she'd often talked about was the inherent weakness of a political system that requires citizens to vote. She believed, and believed that she was – that *they* were – lucky enough not to have experienced it in their lifetime, which was, what, five, six years ago now. Christ, how quickly things have normalised.

Her point: you have to vote, you have to vote for some*one*. And in a system that preyed on fear and division, relied on corruption and sleight of hand to maintain a political majority, that some*one* will one day sooner or later be the populist demagogue type; will, in fact, very closely resemble the promises and government of the military dictatorship. And it's hard not to vote that way when you have nothing, when you're invisible and erased, disenfranchised and under-represented –

And there are an awful lot of people like that in Brazil.

A lot more of them than us, Leme thought now. Difficult to know quite what *us* is anymore. He knew that Renata would be worried about the way things were going right now.

Let alone if she knew what had happened to him only the day before.

'OK, so, three options, if you ask me,' Lisboa said. Leme opened his mouth to speak. Lisboa raised his palm. 'Settle down, Mario, I'm telling you what I think whether you've asked me to or not.'

Leme smiled. 'Então vai,' he said. 'Pode falar.' Go ahead, be my guest: tell me.

'Number one. The body is in the Militar deep freeze up in Lapa or somewhere, and they're doing an autopsy, etc. They haven't ID'd the poor sod and they're not sure what's going on exactly, but they don't like the look of it.'

'Crime scene,' Leme said. 'There isn't one.'

'Maybe not, but they had to get the lad out of there before the rally turned. Short cut, but maybe, *just about* like, doable.'

Leme grunted.

77

'Number two. The body isn't in the fridge, they had something to do with it, for whatever fucking reason, it's not like they need one, really, and our dead rich boy is wrapped up in a hula hoop of burning tyres in a favela.'

Leme nodded. 'And the only other cunt to know about it is me.'

'Hence,' Lisboa said, 'Carlos's little reminder of your history, and his threat: stay out of it. That's all.'

'It makes sense. If I don't know who it is, then why push it? But then why did our friend Fat João tip me off?'

'Which leads me to scenario number three,' Lisboa said. 'Which is a combination of one and two, stiff-wise: either the lad's in the deep freeze or a well. Point is someone wanted you to find it. Right?'

Leme nodded. 'It seems that way.'

'And this someone knew that the Militars were very close behind.'

Leme said nothing.

'Which puts you in the frame. They iron out the playboy and you swing for it. Or you don't, and they have one in the bank in case things get complicated.'

'So, what, I'm an insurance scheme?'

Lisboa grinned. 'It might be the most practical use you've ever been.'

'You know,' Leme said, 'your three scenarios are kind of all the same scenario.'

Lisboa laughed.

'It's really a question of how soon I'm fucked.'

'*That's* the scenario, son,' Lisboa said. 'And Carlos is either straight up with his threat or it's a bluff and they'll be coming for you when you're not expecting it.'

'Great,' Leme said. 'What a fucking start to the week, eh?'

Lisboa laughed. He signalled for another round of beers. 'They can't do anything while they're keeping the information – and the fucking evidence, let's not forget – of the dead young man to themselves. While the kid isn't even missing, *officially*, you've got nothing to worry about.'

'So the answer is?'

'Find out who's the fucking kid. And don't hang about doing it.'

Leme smiled. His phone beeped. Silva. A text with an address and a time.

They nailed their beers. They slapped hands, embraced.

'You keep your ears pinned and your eyes skinned,' Leme said. 'I'm off to meet Silva.'

Lisboa roared. 'Batman and fucking Robin.'

Leme watched him leave. His heart swelled. Lisboa would protect him – always had. Family.

And Silva might just know what lay behind all this.

After all, if Leme was sure of one thing, it's that *something* did.

The address in the text from Silva:

A bar. Of course it was.

And when Leme arrived:

Silva tucking into bife a cavalo com fritas. Of course he was. *Cowboy Beef.* Huge plate, two steaks, smack bang in the middle, topped by fried eggs, a cholesterol island surrounded by a sea of chips. Proper lunch. Silva slurping at a bucket of red. Lips purple and swollen. Suit: shoddy. Tie: egg-stained, though who's to know when this happened. It was probably clean a few years ago. But there's been a lot of bife a cavalo since then.

Leme smiled. It'd been a while. He *liked* Silva.

Silva looked up as Leme approached his table, quickly looked back down at his plate. Between mouthfuls he said, 'E aí, seu gayzão. Beleza?'

Leme shook his head, a sort of half-reluctant, half-smile.

*Alright, you big homo? How's tricks?*

Charming.

Leme sat. The waiter approached. Leme waved him away.

'That's rude, mate,' Silva said. 'You're not going to leave me to chow down all alone, surely?'

Leme laughed. 'Good to see you, Francisco.'

Silva raised his eyebrows. 'I doubt that. You only ever seem to want to see me when you're in trouble.'

'Ah, don't be like that, querido,' Leme said. 'I didn't think social calls were really your thing.'

Silva grunted. He applied himself to his rapidly diminishing plate of food. He waved at the waitress and ordered another red wine, one for Leme too.

'Shape up, man,' he said. 'Think of it as a cafézinho. Paying for my time.'

Very apt, Leme thought. He said, 'This one's on me, mate.'

'Don't be cheeky.'

They knocked glasses and drank. It was a typical Silva haunt: an old-school joint on Rua dos Pinheiros, up towards the turnoff to Vila Madalena. At that end it was all still pretty basic: you had your corner bars and their grumpy regulars, their plastic awnings and rickety tables and chairs, doing burgers and shoe-leather steak, cheap cachaça and beers in frozen bottles, the odd, starkly lit buffet restaurant with its piles of day-old feijoada and gleaming veg. Further down: trendy taco chains and concept micro-breweries, a high-end French restaurant, a couple of live music venues where São Paulo hipsters covered Pink Floyd and moneyed men and women drank R$20 glasses of Guinness. The street as symbol: it roughly divided posh Jardins and hippie Vila Madalena. In between, there was something of a mash-up. You were making a point drinking there. Or, you used to be. Leme was well out of touch, on that score –

And thank fuck for that, he thought.

'You well?' Leme asked.

'Let's talk about why you're here, shall we?'

Leme allowed himself a smile. 'OK,' he said.

Silva finished his meal. He coughed and lit a cigarette. He plucked a toothpick from the dispenser on the table and forked at his mouth. It looked painful.

'I'm all ears, mate,' he said.

'I'll get straight to the point,' Leme said. He decided not to fuck about. He and Silva went *waaay* back, a lot of history, a lot of incriminating work they'd done together, and they trusted each other, so it seemed a waste of both of theirs to not get *straight* to the point. Question was how to frame it.

'The rally yesterday,' Leme said. 'I've heard that the body of a wealthy young man was found not far away. But it's not been made official. So I've got two questions for you.'

Silva nodded. 'Vamos lá,' he said. Go on then, let's hear it.

His interest was piqued. Leme could tell by his body language: he didn't look like he was about to fall asleep.

'OK, so,' Leme said, 'firstly, is there anything at all you know that might connect a playboy type with this political clusterfuck? And by that I mean, obviously, anything that might not be strictly legal. Make sense?' Silva nodded. 'Two… actually, you know what,' Leme said, 'let's just stick to the first question for now.'

'OK,' Silva said. 'First up, I'm guessing you're asking me as you reckon there's a fair chance that I might be balls deep into something like this myself?'

Leme smiled. 'Ah, vai, come on. I figured you know more than I do, that's all.'

'Flattery will get you everywhere, my son,' Silva said. 'And yes, of course I know more than you do.'

'So let's hear it, então.'

Silva nodded, sat up. 'Key thing, obviously, is Lava Jato and the way it's going. I'm sure you know it's got political. I'm sure you know what's happened this year has led to this state of affairs. And I'm sure you know that at first it was a straightforward corruption and money-laundering deal.'

'More or less, sabe? I read the papers.'

'Good for you. It's a lost art.' Silva lit another cigarette. 'Point is that it started like all serious criminal enterprises start: money. Illegal, dirty money. And the need to shift it, right? You ever heard the phrase follow the fucking money?'

'Yeah, matter of fact your young colleague introduced me to it.'

'Ellie?'

'Ellie.'

Ellie. Eleanor Boe. Leme's gringa friend. She'd started out as a messy bird with a job writing arts listings in a local bilingual rag. She was now full on with the investigative journalism scene, a part of Silva's mob. Quite handy, by all accounts. He hadn't seen her in a little while. He'd saved her life, not long ago, she'd tell anyone that'd listen.

More or less, *sabe*, was the truth of it.

'We'll come back to her,' Silva said. 'So look, if you're going to shift and clean dirty money, you need some dirty fuckers to do it for you, villains, right? At least at first. That's how it starts. The *doleiros* – the bagmen – doing the pick-ups and drop-offs are all at the criminal end of the social spectrum. But then things changed.'

'OK.'

'Yeah, suddenly there was more money than anyone knew what to do with. A fucking car wash and a few mules with shrink-wrapped packages of cash strapped to them just ain't going to cut it, *entendeu?*'

'So.'

'So. They need lawyer types and finance types to set up offshore businesses and companies to get the money out and about in order to get it back in.'

'Which means –'

'Which means that whereas a year or so ago, we – well, your mob – were dealing with low-lifes, now you're having to have a pop at the establishment. My guess is that your dead playboy was one of these. How old you say he was?'

'I didn't.'

'Any idea?'

'Early twenties, apparently.'

Silva weighed this. 'Fair enough. Most likely a fairly low-level middle-management type at a private finance company or law firm.'

'And he's doing what, exactly?'

'Well, fuck knows, I've no idea who the kid is, *was*, but my guess is, if he's carked it and no one's saying anything, he was one of these new doleiros, these new bagmen.'

'Sort of virtual bagman?'

'Yeah, why not? Some online, some wire, some cash. So I've heard.'

'Oh yeah?'

'You mentioned Ellie. She's just got back from London, couple of days ago, following something up.'

'London? That's quite an investment for a pão duro like you.' Pão duro: hard bread, a skinflint.

Silva glared – ironic. 'Holiday, fucksticks. And she funded it. As you say, I'm not swinging for a shot in the fucking dark. And it's just a hunch. A hedge fund, that's all, with some São Paulo connection. Could be anything. She's back now. You can fucking ask her yourself.'

Leme smiled. 'Bagman and Robin,' he said.

'You what?'

'Nothing.'

'So what's the second question? I ain't got all day.'

Leme grinned. 'How do I find Fat João?'

Silva laughed – loud. 'Urgent, is it?'

Leme nodded.

'I'll give him a tinkle right now,' Silva said, keying in a number on his phone.

'Good lad,' Leme said. 'Let me buy you lunch.'

Silva winked and waved for another drink. 'Hello mate,' he said into the phone. He stood up and moved away from the table. 'I need a little word with you.'

Leme smiled. Good old Silva.

# Article by Eleanor Boe

OLHA! Online magazine, 21 March 2016

**São Paulo: the capital of the world? A tale of two cities…**

I'm afraid not, readers. That title goes to London. São Paulo is the capital of South America, *Latin* America, I'll give it that, but I've just come back from a visit to the Motherland, and, well, London takes the cake. Forgive my shameless click-baiting.

São Paulo makes London look like a village. I've said that before. I've *written* that before. The two cities have a surprising amount in common. There is gentrification and social cleansing; there is a political elite deaf to the plight of the disenfranchised; there is the recent, tragic collapse of a social housing project; there are acid attacks; there is the dichotomy of a thriving construction industry, and yet a deepening housing crisis, luxury buildings inhabited by ghosts. And like São Paulo you feel energised, politicised, important.

Back in my old home, I realised a few things about my new home. One thing about living in São Paulo is how quickly you get used to the normalisation of crime, the threat of crime. Everyone knows someone who has suffered some terrible experience. Driving in the city illustrates this: the winding up of your car windows when you stop; the jumping of red lights after a certain time of night; the constant checking that your doors are locked. It became clear to me that preparing for crime, or its prevention, is the same thing as living with its threat; one way or another, it very quickly becomes a mundane part of your daily life.

São Paulo exists in a state of heightened paranoia that lends itself to massive gun ownership, distrust of the police and armies of private security. Drive around any relatively wealthy area and you'll find high walls ringed with barbed wire, doormen, security teams and CCTV everywhere. That this is normal terrifies me. And it's now completely normal.

In London, I listened to a lot of Brazilian music, especially the Cazuza song, *O Tempo Não Para* – time doesn't stop. Cazuza died young due to complications with AIDS. He remains the poet of the disaffected. His work is discursive and profane, preaching inclusivity and tolerance. It is a staunch representative of a growing alternative movement that rejects the nepotism and vulgar capitalism of the country's elite. The political protests of the last two weeks recalled one of his songs, 'Brasil', and a specific line:

*Brasil, mostra tua cara, quero ver quem paga para a gente fiche assim.*

Brazil, show your face, I want to know who pays for us to end up like this.

His lyrics were prescient in the early years of democracy in the post-dictatorship period, and now they reflect a deepening dissatisfaction with the political system. Many Brazilians have had enough of the endemic corruption, the widening inequality: the general passivity in the face of societal injustice. There's a recurring slogan: *O gigante acordou.* The giant awoke. In Portuguese the verb 'acordar' means to wake up, and, as in English, there is the connotation of stirring yourself to action. One couplet was a refrain on my visit home:

*Transformam o país inteiro num puteiro*
*Pois assim se ganha mais dinheiro*

They turn a whole country into a whorehouse
Because that way it makes more money

**Later that day, same place:**
**São Paulo, 21 March 2016**

*In São Paulo we thrive in the mess, enjoy the confusion – it's alive!*

Marcos, 44, restaurateur

**Brasil: love it or leave it.** *This was the nationalist slogan of the Brazilian military dictatorship. The regime was repressive and there was media censorship and torture, but it was popular, too! Don't forget we saw the Brazilian Miracle, a period of considerable economic growth. You forgive an awful lot when you're making money. Brazil feels like a young democracy. The legal obligation to vote is… I don't know. Let's just say the legacy of the dictatorship is felt keenly. But for the young people like me, in the sixties and seventies, we saw those Tropicália guys in exile – Gilberto Gil, Caetano Veloso, Chico Buarque – and it gave us hope. They seemed to be thriving, and we thought we could too.*

Clayton, 66, retired

# Junior

Junior stood outside the door of the flat where Gabriel had told him to meet, not half an hour after he'd received the text. An address, a time and an instruction:

**don't knock**

He'd watched Gabriel leave the building and turn left. Junior had waited a moment, turned right, then scampered around the block, doubled back, in effect, knowing exactly where Gabriel would end up. Junior knew the neighbourhood, he'd grown up there, and he knew there was only one place nearby where Gabriel might find a taxi:

A small, informal cab rank on a quiet street outside a stand-up corner bar that catered to manual labourers and anyone else who dared chance their arm at getting served –

Which weren't many.

Junior was quicker than Gabriel. He could see him dawdling on his phone, heels clicking, moving with a confident economy that surprised Junior, given that this area wasn't exactly his comfort zone.

Junior went straight for him. Gabriel, startled, dropped his phone, scrambled for it, kicked it forwards, tripped –

Junior grabbed him by the lapel.

'Vamos, cara,' he said. Let's go.

Junior dragged Gabriel down the tiny alley that led off to the side of the bar. No one paid them any heed. Or chose not to. Either way. The alley ran between the backs of two rows of improvised houses and was a common place to have a quiet word, or make a drop, or simply take a short cut between the two main roads that flanked this residential pocket.

'OK, let's make this quick,' Junior said. 'What exactly do you know?'

Gabriel was hyperventilating, no longer a privileged young man and now just another bleat in trouble. Junior examined him. He was fairly pathetic, Gabriel, at this exact moment, fairly desperate, pretty wretched; he was well out of his depth. And it was then, watching this rich prick blub, that Junior understood why he, Junior, was doing this: he didn't want the fucker to get away with it, simple as that. Junior wanted to *know* that he wouldn't. This power Junior had, for a moment – and he recognised that it *was* power – this power, over a young man whose whole being was based on power, on being *in* power, this power was intoxicating.

'Relax, man, breathe,' Junior said. 'I'm not going to hurt you.'

Gabriel nodded. He swallowed, took a breath, exhaled, settled –

'OK, come on, we haven't got all fucking day, entendeu?'

'I don't know anything,' Gabriel said. 'I've no idea why your boss chose me. I've no idea what he wants. I'm just going to do what he said. I swear, that's it.'

Junior pulled Gabriel's face close to his own. He could smell his beer-soured tongue. He could hear the phlegm-rattle of a smoker, the nasal-dust of a gak-hound.

'Tell me the truth.'

Gabriel tried to pull back, squirm free, raised a hand –

Junior gripped his wrist and pushed him back against the fence that ran behind.

'I'm telling you the truth, please, you have to believe me.'

Junior pressed his forehead against Gabriel's. 'I don't have time to fuck about,' he spat. 'You want me to turn you over and let you rot? You playboy fuckhead prick. You ain't going to last long here, son, believe me. Talk.'

Gabriel breathed. 'I'm serious, there's nothing I can tell you. What was I supposed to do? I'm being blackmailed and I don't know why. You saw yourself! Come on, please.'

Junior took a step back. He studied the lad's face –

He didn't look a liar. He looked like a dozy cunt in well over his pretty little head, like a scared little boy.

'OK,' Junior said, letting him go. 'Go straight down this alley. In about a hundred metres you'll come out onto a main road. I'll watch you. Get a taxi there and go wherever it is you're going. And you call me when you call my boss, certo? You've got my number.'

Gabriel nodded.

'Good, now jog on.'

Gabriel didn't need a second invitation: he was down and out of the alley like a cockroach across a kitchen floor.

Junior took stock.

All he could think at this point was that he needed to know the ID of the dead kid. And this was the only jeitinho, the only way that he could think of to maybe get a jumpstart, maybe get a sense of what the fuck was going on and why Big Carlos was keeping him sweet. This was the only thing he had to hold on to.

So here he was, a few hours later, and Gabriel had news –

He waited for the door to open.

And when it did, right on time, right on the fucking nose it was, he got a helluva shock, a serious jolt –

*Jesus fucking Christ*

He should have known –

Idiot.

Junior clocked the plastic sheet on the floor.

He clocked the chair in the middle of it.

He clocked the figure slumped in the chair –

This was a relief. The chair was not meant for him.

There were dark stains, puddles, pooling at the feet of the figure slumped in the chair. There was a slow, steady drip, like ink spilled from a school desk, Junior thought. There was no one else in the room, that he could see –

The door closed behind him and he turned –

A sharp explosion at the front of his head, a crack-crunch in his nose, pain spreading behind his eyes, an instant light, a flash of incomprehensible pain, he felt his features form an expression of shock and confusion –

Then blackness. He felt himself fall, quickly, into nothingness.

Then:

A wet rush of cold, a light slap, and he opened his eyes.

'Glad you could join us, young man,' Carlos said. 'And right on time. Good lad.' Carlos nodded at the Heavy Mob, gestured at Junior with his chin. 'Get him up.'

They pulled Junior to his feet and gave him a cloth to wipe his face.

'Sorry about that,' one of the Heavy Mob said. 'Needs must and whatnot.'

Carlos laughed. 'That was just a little warning, lad. You had to take one for the team. The bruising will come in *very* useful in our report, entendeu?'

Junior widened his eyes. He wiped his face. Carlos handed him a beer. Junior looked at it without understanding quite what it was, why he was being given a *beer*, what, the chair, the figure, Gabriel's text, who, what, I don't –

Junior's head rolled. Junior's head *lolled*. Junior's head flopped –

Junior, at this moment, was thinking *very slowly*. Time, he realised was passing, but passing in a way that it hadn't ever really passed before. It flowed, slowly, time did, flowed like a river weighed down with sludge.

Junior shook his head, loosened, and then tightened, his neck.

Time wasn't there, but it wasn't *not* there either.

Junior's eyes were glazed, empty –

For that moment, he was all in his head, Junior.

There was movement from the chair. Junior saw it, in a blur, as if underwater. Carlos noticed Junior's eyes drift to the slumping figure.

'Don't worry about him.'

The room slid into focus.

A wooden floor covered in a plastic sheet.

A fireplace.

A long, curved balcony to the right, beyond a closed glass door behind which Driver smoked –

Nothing else. Whitewashed walls. Furniture cleared, if there ever was any. Junior made out dark shapes in a doorway at the end of the room that led to a corridor, so perhaps piled up there, he thought, making space for, for this –

Whatever *this* was.

Junior coughed, caught thick coppery blood at the back of his throat –

'Who is it?' he asked.

'You what?'

Junior rasped, hawked phlegm. He looked down at the plastic sheet, then back up at Carlos, enquiringly.

'Knock yourself out,' Carlos said.

Junior spat. 'Who is it?' he said again, louder, clearer this time.

'I told you not to worry about him. Come.'

Carlos gestured for him to come closer to the chair. He nodded at the slumping, groaning figure, the murmuring, bleeding figure. Through dazed eyes, Junior had a gander. The poor cunt had been knocked about a fair bit, taken a hell of a leathering, it seemed to Junior through his tired, anxious eyes.

'Recognise him?' Carlos asked.

Junior shook his head, his groggy head. 'I don't know him.'

'For the best,' said Carlos. 'I tell you what though, son, you're not going to forget him, so have a good look at that face.'

Junior did as he was told. The face, the bloodied swollen face, swam into focus. Its mouth was taped shut. Its left eye was closed. In its right eye, Junior saw fear and anguish, and, as he looked deeper into this bloodshot and blackened eye, Junior saw resignation, Junior saw *tiredness* –

Junior saw relief.

'Like I say, you're going to remember this one.'

Carlos nodded at one of the Heavy Mob. He approached Junior and handed him a weighty object wrapped in an old cloth, still oily from use on some shitheap car or other.

Revolver. Junior opened the cloth. An old-looking street weapon: *not* standard Militar issue. Junior turned it over in his hands.

'Who's is this?'

Carlos grinned. 'Don't worry, lad, we'll find out, we'll find him. Sharpish, too, I'd say, entendeu?'

The scene, quickly and definitively, sharpened, shunted into focus.

Carlos handed Junior a pillow. 'Through this, we don't want to frighten the neighbours. Three, got it? This is going to look like a PCC interrogation and execution, so don't be too precise.' Carlos nodded at the Heavy Mob. 'These two will carpetbag him and take him home, leave him in bed.'

Junior did nothing. PCC, First Capital Command, a gangland interrogation and execution. Huh. There had been little happening with the gang and the Militars for a while, everyone knew that. Since 2012, and the snide eye-for-an-eye that had been going on, there'd been an uneasy sort of peace. Fact is, ROTA, the Military Police top boys, crossed a line a few years before when they undertook the in-custody snuff job of a lad who was resolutely not on the turn. And the parking lot incident, too. Six villains offed with automatics, self-defence the claim, but there were no bullet marks on any Militar SUVs, let alone any injuries. Rumour was the lads they picked were low-level workers, sorting out a delivery. It was, Junior had heard, very much a show killing, a disruption, a power-grab, a your-boys'-families-will-suffer type of move, no strategic value. So what was this? There were whispers the PCC were planning to end their twenty-year truce with the Rio mob, Comando Vermelho, Red Command. That would be a bloody move. Prison bloodshed, first off, most likely –

Riot, riot.

This was something like a calling card then, perhaps, a pre-empt, get the game up and running, blow the whistle and kick the fuck off.

'You didn't think we wouldn't find out, Junior?' Carlos said. He paced the room. 'I'm going to put it down to a well-intentioned, but misguided, act of diligence, certo?'

Junior said nothing. He weighed the revolver, weighed the pillow. He watched as the slumping, bleeding, murmuring figure, breathed heavily, wheezed, as he slumped, his blood trickling, dripping in time with these heavy breaths, these final, heavy breaths –

'People don't forget, Junior,' Carlos continued, a new steel in his voice. 'Your first outing with us, back in spring, what, four years ago now, you remember that?'

Junior nodded.

'Well, then. This is the same thing. Work, sabe? This is work and it's an order.'

Carlos turned to the Heavy Mob. They both unclipped their holsters, rested their hands on their guns. Driver came in from the balcony. He closed the door. He shuttered the blinds.

Carlos slapped Junior on the back. 'I'll be in the car park downstairs. We'll go for a bite. On me. You'll have earned a top-notch steak dinner, son. And a chat about your future.'

Carlos turned and took two steps to the door. He turned back. 'You're a very lucky young man, Junior.'

Junior nodded.

He heard the door close behind Carlão.

He gripped the gun, felt its warmth, slid off the safety catch.

The figure on the chair roused himself at this, squirmed, tried to talk through the brown tape over his mouth, then tried to shout, then tried to scream, then tried to squeal –

Junior took a step towards him, this poor, squirming man, a man he didn't know, a man who was a pawn in some miserable game, a man who had committed crimes, perhaps killed, who had contributed to chaos and misery in this miserable game, a squirming, cowardly snake, a nasty fucker, a man who Junior now saw as work, OK, work, it doesn't matter, it doesn't matter, this is a consequence, a consequence of a bad choice, a well-intentioned but fundamentally bad choice, a real stinker, and so this, and if not him then anyone and this way, now, this way, it's over and you're in, and steady, but not too steady –

And Junior smothered the muffled squealing, smothered the bleeding face, smothered it, *it*, as that's what it was, it –

Three shots, not too precise.

# Roberta

Roberta didn't cry for long.

Not her style. She'd taken a deep breath, thought about the person she'd like to be, how she'd *like* to behave in this moment, in this uncertainty, in this not-quite crisis.

So she'd done what she often did in moments of confusion:

Made a list.

Well, she made several lists, lists that detailed what she knew and what she didn't know, what she could do and what she couldn't do, what was verifiable and what was not, and who she might contact – and why. And *how*, of course.

And it all felt so dramatic.

And she didn't like that one bit, she wasn't that person – she was unflappable! She hated any feeling of helplessness or powerlessness or confusion, and so she always assumed control, she eliminated confusion on her terms, assumed that others – her friends, her family, her lovers – were all as independent-minded as she, all as far from that sickening, cloying, clinging dependency in their relationships with her as she with them, all as –

But, when it came down to it, he wasn't at work, had taken *holiday*, for crying out loud, and she didn't know where the fuck he was. He had told *other people* he wasn't around on this day, people he barely knew, he had told other people and not her.

*Other people and not her.*

That was the gist of the email she sent to Lis, who she'd seen at the rally, and who knew she'd argued with him, and knew she'd stormed off, knew the context of the day, or some of it. That was the *gist* of the email, though it was couched in rather more relaxed terms, rather more the *can you believe it, amiga! What a cheek!* sort of terms –

Within half an hour of sending the email, Lis was sitting across from her. And this made Roberta think.

First thing Lis said when she arrived:

'Let's go and get a proper fucking drink.'

They went to Bar do Juarez on Juscelino Kubitschek in Itaim, a local haunt of some of Antonio's friends. They sat on the upper balcony and ordered draught beers, glasses of choppe. Mid-afternoon and the traffic was chock-a-block on the main road. It was basically stationary on the side street they looked down on, the lights were on the blink, the taxistas and the motoboys swore at each other and the world in general. Roberta took all this in despite how she was feeling –

*Funny how the world never stops.*

'Right,' Lis said. 'You drink and calm yourself, menina. I'm going to make some calls.'

'Just keep it casual, please,' Roberta said.

Lis gave her a look. 'Querida, I know you, I got this. This was me, though, I'd out the fucker on social, entendeu, then we'd know what was going on.'

Roberta made a face. She did as she was told.

Lis called anyone she knew who knew him or who was connected to him, on the premise that she had a surprise lined up for Roberta and needed to get hold of *him* to help her set this little surprise up –

But, então, couldn't ask *her* for his number, sabe? Don't want to ruin nothing, you understand? Could you get him to give her a call or something?

Clever girl.

It got the response they wanted –

But not the response they wanted.

*Funny how the world never stops.*

Nobody could get hold of him, anyone who had his number got voicemail, he wasn't at work, he wasn't at home, he wasn't at his parents' place, he wasn't at his parents' place out of town –

After about an hour of this and five beers –

'There's something fucked up going on here, querida,' Lis said.

'Remember my English friend Ellie, journalist? You've met a bunch of times. I used to work with her at the magazine?'

'Sim, of course, I remember her, she's cool. Why?'

Lis made a face. 'She might have some ideas. You know what she's been doing last few years, ne?'

Roberta nodded. The booze suddenly took a hold. She shook.

'It doesn't mean anything, menina,' Lis said. 'Just not a bad idea, get another head on this, sabe?'

Roberta took a deep breath and saw the sense in mapping this out to, and with, someone else. 'Call her,' she said.

'It makes sense.' She picked up her phone and dialled, put it to her ear. 'Either this is your boyfriend dicking you about or it's not. And if it's not, well – ' She raised her palm. 'Sweetheart! How is my English princess?'

And half an hour after that, Ellie was with them.

They told Ellie everything that had happened.

Ellie took it all in. Roberta noted her expression, which was serious, sympathetic, concerned, but not panicked, and with just the hint of something in her eyes, something Roberta thought looked a little like excitement –

Bit snide.

'So,' Ellie said, eventually, 'if you can't contact him, he's not at work, you've heard nothing from anyone else, it's pretty likely, it seems to me, that you're not going to, sabe? He'll either turn up and explain, or he won't. I reckon it's down to us to figure out where he is and why, ne?'

She paused. Roberta felt a heat creeping up her neck, felt her stomach tighten and contract, felt the hunger she'd been obliterating with beer and cigarettes come back, sharply, she felt, suddenly, lightheaded, weak.

'I think,' Ellie said, 'I know just the person we can talk to.'

Lis smiled. Roberta felt her take her hand, felt her own, damp and clammy in her friend's grip.

'I was hoping you'd say that, querida,' Lis said.

# Mario

Leme watched Silva leave. He had a few hours before he was set to meet Fat João.

His phone beeped:

**hello stranger**

He laughed –

She was right on cue.

Leme returned Ellie's message quickly.

They arranged to meet the following day. He was looking forward to it. He hadn't seen her for almost a year, he thought. They'd kept in touch; he'd kept himself apprised of what she was getting up to, work-wise. The Olha Online stuff was entertaining; he liked her mix of serious and silly, a bit high-low. She was good at it, and for a gringa she had a real feel for the pulse of São Paulo, seemed to know instinctively what mattered to Paulistanos –

And how the different city tribes would react.

She'd matured, he thought, too. It felt patronising to voice that thought, but it was true. She was only a kid when he first met her, a kid who was a long, long way from home. When he met her, investigating the disappearance of her best friend, her only real friend, she was just a careless gringa, just that, a gringa –

So yeah, she'd matured. She'd *lived*.

And she'd handled the situations she'd found herself in extremely well, given the circs. And her presence had been helpful, effective; she was a worker, she got her head down and got on with it, and Leme understood why Silva had taken her under his wing.

So yeah, he was looking forward to seeing her. He'd tell Antonia in the evening. She wasn't Ellie's biggest fan, but that was really only because Ellie knew what she'd got up to in the Cracolândia land beef a couple of years back. Ellie knew and didn't do anything, didn't write anything, didn't suggest any follow-up at all. So Antonia felt like she had one over on her, which, he supposed, was exactly the case.

And Antonia's way of dealing with people who had one over on her:

Not to like them –

And make that fact very clear.

This was not something that they had in common –

Leme was scared of anyone who had one over on him. Largely as anyone who did was usually pretty fucking scary.

While it was not his style, he did respect and even envied a little Antonia's approach, her philosophy, if you could call it that, if that wasn't too *grand*.

The ability to not worry about what others thought of you.

Leme reckoned that was a quality he had never quite mastered. Renata had encouraged it in him, and Antonia too. He wasn't convinced it was a bad thing that he hadn't got the hang of it.

But it did mean he had to watch his nature, his instincts, around the likes of old Carlão.

They might well have something over each other, but Big Carlos was a lot scarier than Leme –

Old Carlos, Leme's former friend, had a lot more nasty surprises at his disposal.

Finding Fat João's place of residence was a fair bit harder than Leme expected.

The address Silva gave him was *waaay* out past Lapa, textbook bandit country –

It was, Silva had said, one of a stretch of semi-shacks in a grid almost slap bang on the Marginal. But, Leme was finding out, you couldn't simply make a right off the main road: you had to go beyond and then double back and the grid was fluid and the houses packed tight and the roads single-track and in bits and there were deposits where mudslides had hardened so it wasn't even possible to negotiate some of the corners –

And there was hardly anyone about. This was not reassuring. This was a place it would be very easy to get lost in –

And very easy to *stay* lost in.

Leme was not in the best of spirits. He was tense. He was sweating in the heat. He was aware that the longer he took, the more likely he'd be stuck in an almighty traffic jam on his way home.

A woman, dressed in little more than rags, pushed a shopping trolley slowly past his car. In it: piles of moody Adidas tracksuits.

Classy. Leme wound down his window.

'E aí,' he said. 'You know a little fucker called Fat João?'

The woman grinned. She revealed a dark expanse for a mouth. The few teeth she had were brown-yellow and mismatched, oddly shaped. When she smiled, her face looked like the beginnings of a construction project, all soil and rock and brick strewn about all over the shop, no evidence at all of any rhythm or planning. She rolled her dark, fat tongue. She spat. She licked her cracked, muddy lips with her blackened tongue. She was still smiling.

'Então?' Leme said.

'Over there.' She pointed down the road. 'The horrible-looking one, see it? Filthy yellow door, the real shithole of a house,' she said, laughing. 'Lucky you!'

Leme thanked her. He watched her wheel her trolley down the road in the other direction. He smiled to himself. She was a character.

He swung out of the car and crossed the road. He stopped by the filthy yellow door, which was in fact filthy, and had once, long ago, been yellow.

He looked up and down the tiny cramped street –

Dogs slept.

Cars rusted.

Rubbish bags heaved and sweated.

Washing dried.

A heavy odour sat just above the row of tiny cramped houses –

An odour of decay, of stale food, of rank water –

The river, you could almost feel it, slopped and sludged, throbbed and pulsed its way past, just beyond the wall of traffic, the constant lines of belching cars and trucks.

This was proper no-man's-land. The very fringe of the city –

And exactly where a dirty little grass like Fat João would end up.

Leme knocked.

Nothing.

Leme knocked harder.

The door gave slightly, creaked and opened.

Leme, again, checked the road, up and down.

Nothing.

He pushed into the tiny, cramped shithole of a house –

The smell was intense. A very different smell.

The living room was empty.

A wooden crate was covered in dirty plates and dirty cutlery.

A smaller, wooden box for a chair.

No carpet over the concrete floor.

No windows.

Like a cell, Leme thought. But without the facilities.

Leme edged to the bedroom. The smell thickened.

It was then, he realised, that he knew –

Fat João in his bed, dead, lying in his bed but wrapped in a carpet, wrapped like that so that his cremation would be straight-forward, but left like that as there would be no cremation. The body, his body, had been left to be found by someone, an old PCC calling card –

His face: a pulp. A real mess. A battered, beaten, oozing piece of rotten fruit. Somebody had gone to town alright. Old Fat João had never stood a chance. Leme doubted he'd been given one at all.

Something didn't add up though. The place, while undoubtedly a shithole, was not disturbed. There were no signs of a struggle, no signs of a break-in.

Leme weighed it:

The execution – the torture and execution – and he was sure it was both these things – had taken place somewhere else.

*They'd brought Fat João home*

First thought:

*Who the fuck is trying to stitch me up this time?*

Here we fucking go again, old son.

# Article by Eleanor Boe

## OLHA! Online magazine, 21 March 2016

### What is the PCC and why should we even care?

Here's a story that answers these questions.

The PCC gang runs São Paulo crime. The men that run the PCC run it from prison. These men want to watch the 2006 World Cup on large, flat, wide-screen TV sets. The PCC is like a corporation – none of the flip-flop / assault-rifle shtick of the Rio gangs. They are *very* organised. And they generally get what they want.

So the PCC leaders ask for large, flat, wide-screen TV sets. They pitch for more frequent conjugal visits. These requests are nixed. In response, the PCC leaders tell the authorities that they will 'cause some chaos'.

For three days, São Paulo experiences some righteous, PCC-brand chaos. Gangbangers attack the police. They hijack buses. They evacuate them. They set them on fire and leave them burning on major highways. There are rumours of raids on public buildings, that schools and hospitals are next. Over a hundred and fifty people are killed – police, gangsters and the inevitable unfortunate bystanders. The stray bullets: the *bala perdidas*. The city goes into lockdown. The authorities throw in the towel. The PCC get their TVs and, I believe, their conjugal visits.

I have friends at the British school who were there when this kicked off. I speak to the headmaster. The chief of police's son studied there, he told me, and his father dropped him off the morning after the weekend's violence. The officers who had been shot were receiving danger money. Trauma and whatnot, apparently, so the chief of police is supposed to have said. Thing is, hearing this, a number of officers have shot at their own police stations. The bullet holes can be used as proof they've been attacked. They too, the chief of police said, are claiming danger money.

São Paulo is a city of great contrasts. That weekend in 2006, according to those I've spoken to, the gap between the have-nots and the elite seemed to close a little. The peculiarity of the crime, the brazenness of the requests and response, and the behaviour of the police seem distinctly Brazilian to me.

**PART TWO: AWAYDAYS**

# The week before

*We flirt, but we don't flirt. There's a difference between São Paulo and London. People say I'm flirting when I'm not. I'm quite reserved, but they say that's the point. Something about the look in my eyes, poking fun. I'm just chatting, laughing, enjoying myself with the playful banter. It's normal. When I flirt, I think I make it fairly obvious! English colleagues don't get it. When you came in to talk to me, they were sure we were flirting. It's the Brazilian way of chatting, which we have, that physical to and fro, the gestures and eye contact, the smiling. Affectionate and always keen to make the other person laugh, to communicate that warmth we feel for our friends. That's all it is. And I love it. And that's something São Paulo is the best at in the world. Not that I've ever dated a Brazilian. Too jealous, too insistent on doing everything together, too much cheating. In São Paulo there are more beautiful women than in London; but in London there are more handsome men.*

Gabriela, 28, receptionist

London: *we will be arriving at London Heathrow in one hour.*

Back to Blighty! Ellie thought, half-dreaming, half-laughing. She yawned. She massaged her neck. She ran her dry tongue round her cracked, dry mouth. She shifted in her seat, bending her knees and rubbing at her lower back. She lifted her eye mask and looked around –

Premium Economy. What style. The Prodigal Daughter. The returning hero –

Ghengis Khan across the fucking Alps she was.

Shame there was no one to see it, really. It didn't matter which bit of the plane you were in when you came through Arrivals to a barrage of Ealing's finest mini-cab drivers, dressed like chauffeurs. No one *there*, no one in *Arrivals*, knew about your extra legroom, your ample buttock space, enough for *both* to really settle in, your early dinner service, your tiny, basically non-existent queue for the British Airways snacking tray, the fact – the key, incontrovertible fact! – that there were only two of you in your row, *even though you had a window seat.* You only ever had to disturb *one person* if you fancied a piss. This was, many would agree, the height of civilisation, pure *class.*

Pure Premium Economy Class.

She thought that maybe she'd had about an hour's sleep, had drifted off – well, nodded off, with a jolt, *finally* – at the same time as she'd given up on a predictable romantic comedy, turned off the entertainment system and realised that she'd run out of peanuts from the British Airways snacking tray. She liked to fly long haul. Who wouldn't? Free booze, free food, free films. The British Airways snacking tray behind the stewards' curtain was a thing of beauty to an Englishwoman coming home after a few years living abroad without any of her cultural reference points, her *staples*. The brackish clarity of a Walkers Salt 'n' Vinegar crisp. The elevenses snap and crunch of a KitKat. The reassuring heft of a Mars bar. The punch in the teeth of your European can of Coke, somehow more unpleasant – and all the better for it – than the Brazilian equivalent. The warm miniature of London Pride ale.

She looked out the window and down towards where she assumed the city must be. The stewards were delivering breakfast. The plane was waking up, shafts of yellow through partially opened blinds. Stiff-backed men and women shuffled in queues for the toilets. (But not in Premium Economy. The queue in Premium Economy was basically non-existent.) Children whimpered, confused. Teenagers slept on. There were others, like Ellie, who had barely slept at all, and they gulped at water, trying to create some distance from the last half-bottle of red wine they'd drunk not an hour before.

The light was sharp, otherworldly in its brightness. The horizon stretched out, piercing blue, translucent, lazy in the effortless way it rolled on beyond the clouds, beyond the light, beyond. Ellie thought she could make out a faint green, but she didn't think they could be over England yet. There was still a good hour or more until they landed. There'd likely be all that holding-pattern palaver. London: the gateway to Europe. Was that a phrase?

'Tea or coffee?' the steward asked.

'Oh, tea,' Ellie said.

'Breakfast?'

Ellie nodded. 'Cooked, thanks.'

The woman sitting next to Ellie turned to her.

'You're English,' she said.

'Very.'

'Ha.' The woman smiled. 'Well, your Portuguese is impressive then.'

'Merci,' Ellie said.

'You're funny.'

'Only first thing in the morning.'

'Or last thing at night, ne?'

Ellie smiled. They sat in silence for a few moments. Ellie sensed that now was the time to duck out of this conversation, if she wanted to.

'*Your* Portuguese however – ' she said.

'You *are* funny.' The woman offered her hand to shake. 'I'm Giovanna.'

Ellie smiled. 'I'm Ellie.'

They shook hands.

'What are you doing in London, Giovanna?' Ellie asked.

Giovanna smiled. 'Visiting family. Work. You know. A holiday, I suppose.'

'Here for long?'

'Couple of weeks.' She smiled again. She took a sip of her coffee. 'And you?'

'Same thing, basically.' Ellie laughed.

'What do you do in São Paulo?'

'I'm a writer. Well, a journalist.'

'There's a difference.'

'There is.'

'What's the difference?'

'It's a bit like the difference between Economy and Premium Economy.'

Giovanna smiled. 'Financially?'

'Not at all.'

'What do you write about? Sorry, *journal* about.'

'Very good.' Ellie laughed. She turned slightly towards Giovanna, in her ample seat, her vast writerly seat. 'I do a few bits and bobs, you know, online, sometimes print stuff.'

'Anything I might know?'

'Ah, the question any writer – sorry, any journalist – loves to hear.'

Giovanna made a face.

'Sorry,' Ellie smiled. 'I, oh thanks – '

The steward handed them their meals. They considered them and they set to work. They peeled back their plastic covers at almost exactly the same time, and, in this moment of triumph, steam rose, ominously, *wafted* from their meals, briefly filling the space between them, like in a sauna.

It felt, to Ellie, quite intimate.

She inspected the goods. Volcanic scrambled egg, a sort of blood-yellow tinge to it, rubbery, it would surely bounce if you dropped it; a piece of thick bacon that curled in on itself in disgust, its slimy fat dripping grease, its meat somehow dry from over cooking; a tomato, oozing; a solitary, firm potato –

A sausage.

'You know,' she mused, 'there is a certain type of English person who, no matter how they feel or where they are, will always, always, without fail, order the cooked breakfast if it is an option.'

Giovanna laughed. 'I think there's the exact same type of tourist.'

They worked diligently and uncomplainingly at manoeuvring their food around in the plastic tray with their sets of plastic cutlery.

'This is the main difference between Premium and Business,' Giovanna said.

'The food?'

'The cutlery. You get a proper knife and fork, an actual glass of wine.'

'With breakfast?'

'Ha. I'm sure you can ask.'

They laboured on. The sausage work, Ellie noted, was especially Sisyphean.

I *am* funny, she thought.

'You were about to tell me what it is you write?' Giovanna said.

Ellie smiled through yet another mouthful of sausage. The hum-rattle of the aircraft was a constant once more. Her ears cleared, popped.

'I suppose you could call it political journalism, now,' she said. 'I write a sort of column for Olha Online. Reflections on politics, that sort of thing, but not very serious, or at least not always.'

'Interesting.'

'And it's written in English,' she added, quickly. 'I think the idea was to try and reach a quote unquote *international audience*.' Ellie made the quote signs, then immediately hated herself for doing so. 'Or, you know, more likely,' she said, 'reach a few expats who have yet to learn any Portuguese.'

'And that's why you came to São Paulo?'

'Not exactly.'

Giovanna raised her eyebrows in that dry, amused, mock-shocked Paulistana manner that was not so much an invitation to continue as an instruction.

'I was working for *Time Out* São Paulo at first.'

'I know it.'

Ellie smiled. 'But I wanted to do investigative stuff, you know?' She paused, made a face. 'I had *ambition*, entendeu?'

'And you've achieved your goals. Muito bem. Brava, querida.'

'Mais ou menos, ne?' More or less.

Of course she wasn't going to tell this stranger what brought her into contact with the kinds of people who could help shape a career in this kind of journalism. Even if this stranger was making her feel remarkably relaxed, forthcoming. No, she wasn't going to tell her about what had happened with her best friend Ana, with the politician Jorge Mendes, with snide Alex, and sweet Fernando, with the redevelopment of Cracolândia, Leandro, and her first forays into politics, into corruption, into storytelling as whistle-blowing, she wasn't going to tell this stranger about how this had all come about through her friendship – and professional relationship too, come on, Ellie, don't do yourself down *that* much, with Leme, and, oh yeah, fuck, *that's* who this stranger reminds you of –

Antonia: Leme's missus. Identikit type:

Muito droll, drolly bird –

Ha. Clever girl, Ellie.

They continued to work on their breakfasts.

'What is it that you do?' Ellie asked.

'I'm a lawyer.'

Bingo. *Very* Antonia.

'And that's why you're over?'

'Partly.' Giovanna gave a thin smile. 'And my daughter studies in London, at King's. Work, family, holiday, all that. At my age,' she said, 'you have to combine these things, sabe?'

Ellie wasn't exactly sure what she meant by *at my age*. Resigned – or lapsed – feminist and whatnot, she thought.

'You said you were doing some work here too. A story?'

Ellie nodded. 'More of a hunch.'

That arched eyebrow thing again.

'Lava Jato, you know,' said Ellie, knowing that it was something of a catch-all now, the phrase, what with everything it entailed.

'Uh-huh. Like the international angle? Follow the money, that kind of thing?'

Ellie laughed. 'I've written that phrase before. But yeah, something like that.'

'The world's financial playground now, London, so they say.'

'And I've heard that phrase before too.'

'It's the Wild West, totally unregulated, much of it, apparently. Only thing that matters is cash. What a city.'

'Europe, eh?'

'The old world.' Giovanna smiled.

Their breakfasts were, by now, basically done with, the debris drowning in congealing grease. The steward collected their trays, refilled their tea.

'Well, good luck with it,' Giovanna said. 'I'm going to use the heavy fuel we've just consumed to help me commit to a quick nap before we land.'

'I like your style.'

Giovanna slipped on her eye mask.

Ellie looked out the window. The light refracted, dispersed, through cloud. The air looked thin, fragile, out there.

Not long now. *Home*, quite soon.

She'd be with her mum in not too long. She hadn't seen her for almost four years. She'd done exactly what her mum had said she would – *stay away*.

And this hunch –

Gawd knows what the week would bring.

São Paulo: the toilets of a mercilessly swank bar in Itaim –

Business time.

'Mate, trust me, it's a piece of piss and it's – hang on. Here.'

Antonio took the silver coke straw his friend and slightly older, *slightly* senior colleague Rafael handed him.

'Classy,' he said.

He hoovered his line. It tasted good. The back of his throat was briefly numbed. The whiskey fire was doused. The coke snapped into his brain. He felt his eyes widen, for a moment, in agreement with what he'd done, applauding him with a smile, then narrow again, more focused.

He grinned.

'That's some decent chop,' he said.

'Ah, you get what you pay for, entendeu?'

Rafael flicked the lock of the toilet cubicle and shouldered the door. He nodded at the attendant, who fingered the fifty Rafael had palmed him when they went in.

'Textbook,' Rafael said.

Antonio looked at his phone. A little after nine on Monday. Pretty late – or early – to be getting on the bugle, but fuck it, why not? No messages or calls from Roberta. Likely for the best, for now. He would see her tomorrow. Last thing she needs to know is he's out and about on a Monday. She's never been one for the drunken late-night cuddle, he thought. Though fair play, really, not a great deal of romance in being pawed and slobbered over by a half-continent, ethanol-breathing, coke-chattering dragon. Antonio used to tell her that he'd love it if she came round to his, drunk and horny, clamber-ing all over him.

It had been a lie; he knew that now, after the one time she'd tried it –

Turns out when you go to bed early, when you want an early night, you go to bed early because you want an early night.

They sat back down at their table. It overlooked the dance floor. A waitress hovered. Rafael made a circle with his finger around the drinks on the table indicating another round. The waitress smiled. Rafael smiled. 'Get one for yourself, too,' he said.

'Maybe later?' she said. 'If you'll both join me?'

She left.

'Christ,' Antonio said. 'It's like walking into a cliché in here.'

Rafael grinned. 'Ah, you get what you pay for.'

'She's too expensive for you, mate.'

They looked around. The music was loud. They peered over the edge of the VIP area, watched as young women danced self-consciously in groups, their eyes over their shoulders, their purses held casually in one hand, like ping pong bats, protection, Antonio thought, as young men circled, talking only to each other –

It wasn't exactly a sociable scene.

Rafael worked his jaw. Antonio suspected that it wasn't his first line. It rarely ever was Rafael's first line. The lights flashed low, the music changed gear, there were cheers from the boys near the dance floor, demonstrably recognising the new tune, half-hearted enthusiasm from the girls.

At least, Antonio thought, doing drugs in here felt like you were doing drugs for *something* and not simply doing drugs to do drugs, sitting in a friend's apartment until the sun rose and calculating to the minute the sleep you might get in if you left in a cab *right now* before showering and heading to work. And then instead getting a patchy half-hour on a sofa, hopeful the shower made up for the lack of sleep. The elusive pursuit of drug-taking, and especially the mirthless, relentless, joyless pursuit of taking cocaine –

They had a mate, Octavio, who would sit at the kitchen table, plate in front of him, hammering out, then distributing, line after line, endlessly *working* his way through the diminishing pile, really putting in a shift, like, well, like a production line, Antonio supposed.

Ha.

It wasn't always like that, of course, he reflected.

Though, to be fair, he was always delighted on the nights when he *hadn't* taken it. It was such a relief! That next morning, fresh, productive, applying himself in new and interesting ways.

Fear of *not* missing out, Roberta had joked.

But he was enjoying it now, and the waitress was back with their whiskeys and he felt that little tug he sometimes did to misbehave –

'So, it's a piece of piss, right?' Rafael was saying. 'Honestly there is nothing to it, and if you're in, if you *help*, the dividends are heavy. It's not a percentage cut of the transactions, nothing like that, it's a salary; the weeks you work you're paid. They *employ* you, so that way the activity goes on regardless, there's no risk, no red flag fees or changing amounts, no odd giveaways like divisible movement through multiple accounts, and some weeks you make more even than the money you're moving. Some weeks nothing like it, but, you know, that goes without saying, ne?'

'OK. So what about where we *are* employed, what do they make of it all?'

Rafael made a face. 'Mate.'

'What?'

'It's freelance, they don't give a fuck.'

'But you're using contacts you've made through the firm, it's our clients. That not a bit fucking shady? What's the phrase,' he said, '*conflict of interest?*'

'Nah, it's all good. It's sideline.' He paused, looked around. 'Look, fact is, it's part of the same process – our clients are glad of the din-heiro, glad of the business, and that feeds back into us, sabe?'

'You really think that's true?'

'It's the universal language of love, amigo: cash. And all's fair in love and whatnot.' He smiled, gestured, palms out. 'Mate, trust me, I know what I'm doing.'

Antonio nodded. He was sure of that, at least. Rafael always knew what he was *doing*; he just didn't always realise what he'd done.

'Come on, let's do another line of chang and see when that

waitress gets off.' He laughed. 'Or *how* that waitress gets off, know what I mean?'

Rafael was out of his seat and headed to the gents. Antonio followed. The attendant smiled and shook his head in mock despair.

'You two,' he said.

Rafael shot Antonio a look. Antonio placed a fifty on the tip tray. The attendant doffed an imaginary cap. 'Much obliged, gentleman,' he said, cackling.

'He's making decent bank, that fella,' Rafael muttered, as he closed the cubicle door and locked it. 'It's a fucking *Monday*.'

He opened the silver cigarette case he carried with him, what he called his handbag, or his gak bag, or sometimes, simply, his bag bag. Inside was a vial. He opened it and shook out a fair wallop of powder into the inside of the lid. Using the razor blade he stored in a tiny sheath in his handbag, he chopped and divided the mound into two snaking lines. He took the silver coke straw and offered it to Antonio.

'Much obliged, gentleman.'

Rafael disintegrated into a giggling fit.

'Mate, hold it steady,' Antonio said, laughing.

They both had their lines. They both washed their faces. They both left the toilets grinning, alert. They were both shaping up nicely.

'I guess I just want to know how you got in on it,' Antonio said. 'And how you've got the, I don't know, the authority or whatever, to recruit me, sabe?'

'Fuck me, Tônico, it's not a fucking cult. *Recruit*, Jesus.'

He laughed. They drank deeply at their whiskeys. 'I've got a serious thirst on,' Rafael said. 'Beers, ne?'

Antonio nodded. 'Então?'

'Look, this is not a job interview, entendeu? I just thought you'd be interested.'

'I am.'

'Good.' Rafael glanced this way and that. His eyes darted. He chewed on his cheek, his bottom lip. He was about one bump away from a gurn. 'So, the contact is a client we have, who is a part of Odebrecht, OK?'

Antonio nodded.

'He's got his own portfolio that we manage through the fund, but he wanted to do something different. He spoke to Senhor Matheus, who asked me to set it up.'

'Matheus? So it's sanctioned then.'

'Yeah, mais ou menos.' More or less. OK. Rafael's eyes followed two young women's legs. 'It's sanctioned by him, but off the record. He set me up with a separate account, which is what I'm using. You'll get one too. That's the point, there's more work than I think they realised.'

'OK.'

Antonio turned it over. Senhor Matheus was Rafael's line manager and senior partner of the fund, a board member. It was likely some sort of tax loophole, this off-the-books shit.

'You get an account to handle. Just a number, no names. Trades and payments go through that. And *you* get paid into another account, which is yours, entendeu? Mate, it's fucking golden. I do like two, three trades a week? Takes an hour, tops.'

Antonio was nodding. 'Set it up.'

They slapped hands. Rafael was grinning like a cunt. Antonio felt himself do the same. 'Pocket money, pal, that's all.'

'A fucking paper round.'

'It is almost literally that.'

'Come on, let's go and find someone to talk to.'

They swaggered through the VIP area, two lairy cunts in lairy shirts, drinks in their hands like weapons, a lazy economy to their steps, in time, they were, to the music, in fact they moved almost *around* the rhythm. Their sleeves were rolled up and their arms were muscular and tanned. Their feet: sockless. Their ankles glimpsed from above their expensive shoes, also tanned. They circuited; they turned a slow circle. They jawed their gum for extra swagger, extra nonchalance. They looked away from each other, over heads and shoulders. They spoke without making eye contact, heads nodding in opposite directions. This, they both believed, made their friendship appear greater and more intimate than it actually was, and this, in turn, made them more attractive to women. While they both believed these things to be true, they had never discussed them, never even noted these things in conversation.

It was this that ran through Antonio's head as they plotted their next moves. Plotted without any actual discussion, of course. It all took, Antonio guessed, about two minutes.

'Line?'

'Thought you'd never ask.'

'You're as dry as bone, young man,' Rafael laughed.

They went to the bathroom, and then twice through their little routine. There wasn't a great deal of point, it seemed, to keep turning circuits of the fairly deserted VIP area.

'That waitress,' Rafael said. 'Let's get her and a friend to come back to mine.'

Antonio weighed this. He knew that Roberta would not be pleased if she knew he was even entertaining the idea. But he also knew that he was entertaining the idea only for Rafael's sake. He *knew* that. It didn't hurt, not to misbehave. Fear of not missing out ran deep.

'You're having a laugh, mate,' Antonio said, knowing that this was part of the process, the transaction.

'In what way?'

'She ain't coming with us, and I ain't coming with you, entendeu?'

'Don't be soppy. Roberta's not going to know.'

'That's right, she's not, as there won't be anything *to* know.'

'Selfish. That's what it is, you're being selfish. I'm asking for a favour, entendeu? You're supposed to be a mate.' He paused, smiling. 'Mano, you really do not see anything beyond your own needs, ne?'

*Mano.* Brother. Antonio noted, once again, how often his middle-class friends were so quick to adopt the language and attitudes of gangsters, of the street, of, well, *poor* people. Why is that? Is everyone so uncomfortable in their own skin, or is it just his boys? *His boys.* A case in point, ne? And does this posturing work the other way round, class-wise? Probably not, he reflected. Privilege is the thing you're disabusing, pretending you don't have it.

After all, he thought, I'd rather have hustle than a trust fund; better a pimp than a prince.

Rafael flicked the lock and shouldered the door.

Monday slides into Tuesday.

Monday night *bleeds.*

The next morning –

Antonio sat at his desk. *His head throbbed.* He couldn't really call it the morning after, as the night hadn't really ever finished. *His head pounded.* There was the shower he took at Rafael's. *His head ached.* There was the walk to the office, in the clear light of morning, the clear, promising light of morning, the kind of light that seemed to offer something, seemed to offer at least to clear his throbbing, aching head –

But it didn't last long.

The computer yawned into life and numbers flashed and slid into view. They pounded his eyes, his head, these numbers. Thank fuck, it wasn't a busy morning. Not for the first time, Antonio was grateful for the hours of the finance world, the hedge fund shuffle:

Early start, boozy lunch, slow and easy afternoon, fast and furious night –

It's a lot easier to function at seven or eight in the morning than it is at eleven if you've been hammering at the gak all night. Two espressos and a fried egg sandwich would see him through until ten. Keep your fuzzy, throbbing, pounding head down and don't panic –

Easy to say when the slightest noise sets you off.

Easy to say when you shrink and prepare to take cover or flight whenever a colleague, let alone a stranger, walks towards you.

Antonio had some serious edge on this morning.

And then there were those messages from Roberta, affectionate, playful, but fucking spot on too –

**Hey fuckhead. Late night? ;)**
**I imagine it was Rafael's fault, ne, querido?!**
**Enjoy work! It'll be fun contributing further to a horrendous mechanism of greed and power with your little old self-loathing, baby xx**

*Serious* edge on, he had. It was hounding him, *pulverising* him, it was coursing through him, really giving him a good hiding.

He stared at his screen.

His mind whirred, his mind buzzed, his mind *crunched* –

This hangover was really taking the piss.

His tongue grew fatter, drier, raspier –

He could feel his fat tongue fill like a sponge, then dry out like water evaporating in hot sand whenever he gulped at his bottle of Evian.

His head was piercing.

Bloody espresso.

And then Rafael hove into view, loomed right over him, all teeth and flashing eyes, a right hard-on he's got, really pleased with himself, really *thrilled*, he looked.

*Terrific.*

'Oi, oi,' he said, grinning. 'You alright, mate?'

'No.'

Rafael smirked. 'Settle down. It's only a hangover.'

'Yeah, well.'

'Come on, it was a good night. Ended well, at least.' Rafael looked around. Then leaned in close. 'That thing we talked about. It's on. Meet me downstairs in the bar, nine thirty, we'll sort it, certo?'

'Yeah, sure.'

'Yeah?'

'Certeza, cara.'

'Beleza.' Nice one. 'We'll have a sharpener while we're there. Just a drop, you know, take the edge off.'

'Sounds good.'

'Toast our bright futures and whatnot.'

'If you say so.'

'I fucking do. Now shape up, lad, and I'll see you in about an hour.'

Antonio nodded. What stamina. It's got to catch up with you at some point, hasn't it? Rafael wasn't much older, but he *was* older, he'd been around, been doing this longer. It's *got* to catch up with you.

And *he* can't have got any sleep, Antonio thought.

Antonio would never know if the waitress did have him in mind when she'd decided to stay. But he'd made it pretty clear he wasn't interested, just in case. And the thing was, he *wasn't* interested. He really wasn't. He hadn't been interested in anyone else at all since he'd met Roberta. To the extent that it was kind of a surprise. He kind of almost tested himself once in a while. And the same result: he didn't give a fuck about anyone else.

And it was a relief. Yeah, a fucking relief.

*What a feeling.*

Course, staying up all night at Rafael's with two birds didn't exactly look good.

Neither did calling them birds.

If there was a way he could show that last night was about that urge to stay up, to talk shit, to hang out and feel something, to feel that joy in misbehaving a bit, in chasing *fun*, but also nothing to do with cheating, it'd be fine, it'd be clear and it'd make sense.

But he wasn't sure he could.

Best not to then. Something he was learning in this relationship: What matters and what doesn't.

And sure as eggs are eggs, as sure as fucking mustard, he wouldn't get very far explaining it with this throbbing, piercing, pounding head. His head was a fucking carousel –

He'd sit tight, keep his head down, then meet Rafael and do this thing, do this thing he'd promised he'd do, he wasn't the sort to welch sober on promises made when drunk.

And it *did* seem like a good idea, after all.

Rafael was already in the bar, tucked into a dark quiet corner out of sight of the door when Antonio got down there.

He was nursing a beer and his laptop glowed in the gloom.

Rafael looked up. 'Look what the cat dragged in.' He clicked his fingers. 'Two,' he said to the old geezer that ran the place. The old geezer raised an eyebrow and muttered something about it being alright for some.

Antonio sat.

The old geezer, muttering something about a champion's breakfast, handed them their beers.

Rafael raised his glass. 'To world peace,' he said, cackling. That post- or mid-bender energy crackling away, tangible excitement.

'Yeah, cara. I suspect we can help with that.'

'Mate, you are a right laugh first thing, eh?'

Antonio drank deeply. The beer was restorative, tasted *good*.

Rafael spun the computer round so he could see it.

'Right,' he said. He pointed at the screen. 'Here. That's the account you're dealing with, certo? There, that's the trade.' He flipped the window. 'And here, that's your account, that's where you're paid. Details here.'

He pushed a piece of paper across the table.

'So what's the trade exactly?'

Rafael clicked and pointed. 'This goes here. Simple as that.'

'That doesn't look like a trade. Looks like a transfer, something like that.'

'It's a one-way trade, sabe?'

'You what?'

'You're buying into a fund. *That's* the trade.'

'OK.'

'On behalf of the client. Simple.'

Antonio nodded. He knew the principle. They did it sometimes for their regular clients. A sort of straightforward investment-type situation. Difference was in this trade, in this investment, there were only numbers. Nothing else to identify what he was doing. It wasn't clear at all what the investment was *in*.

What *was* clear was the amount, which was big, real fuck-you money.

'OK?'

Antonio drank more. His head started to clear, just enough to remember what they'd talked about last night, that Senhor Matheus was involved, that Rafael was, essentially, showing him the ropes.

This was a good idea. Pocket money, a paper round, a cakewalk –

'OK,' he said.

'Então, cara, vamos lá.' Let's do it.

Antonio nodded. 'Vamos, sim, cara.'

Rafael pushed the laptop to him. Antonio finished his beer.

Antonio examined the screen.

He clicked –

Job done. You're in, he thought.

'Nice one,' Rafael said. 'You're in like gin, filho. You're not going to regret this, nem fodendo.'

Antonio laughed.

*You're not going to regret this, no fucking way, not even if you're fucking, not even if you are* having sex, *while you're regretting it.*

An apt little phrase, that one, he thought. Nem fodendo.

Good old São Paulo slang, right on the money –

He laughed, raised his glass, smiled –

Right on the fucking money:

Now *that* was an apt little phrase.

*London Calling.* Ellie laughed. Heathrow corridors and the song's already playing.

Except –

Except it was her ringtone. Of course it was. It seemed funny, doing that, a couple of nights ago in São Paulo. Not so funny now, of course. A few giggles, a few eye rolls as she fumbled for her phone.

She should have chosen the other one:

*London calling, Speak the slang now, Boys say –*

Mum.

Of course it was.

'Mum, I –'

'Oh, good you've landed. Excellent. When can you talk, do you think? I expect you've got customs and duty-free and passport and bags and everything else, haven't you? I probably shouldn't have. I probably should just. Oh, yes, please, just the coffee, thank you. No milk. No. You still there, love? Can you? No, no, that's it. No milk. I –'

'Mum. Mum. *Jesus.* Mum.'

'You're still there? Hello? Ellie?'

'Yes, Mum.'

'Oh, you *are* still there. Great, I was going to ring off.'

'Hang up.'

'What?'

'You were going to hang up.'

'Why, you're still there, aren't you?'

'Mum, I –'

'Oh, wait, I need to go, I'll call you back, OK?'

'OK.'

Welcome home.

As uncanny and welcome too, in its way, but infinitely less heartening than the British Airways snacking tray, was the Piccadilly line.

Ellie was on it for *hours*. She was on it for hours, it felt to her, and yet she had only reached Russell Square, where she got off. Zone 1, that was all. Along the Piccadilly line, sitting with her legs wrapped awkwardly around her case to stop it rolling off, trying to read, not trying to read, trying to be entranced by London and its new yet familiar mystery, its *surroundings*, trying to drink it all in, what with the first few hours of the journey on the Piccadilly line actually outside, then trying *not* to drink it in, as, frankly, it's the suburban London nightmare part of London.

She got off the tube and navigated the lifts, schlepped her case past the Brunswick centre, with all its brutal charm really *on show* in the sunlight, and then up Lambs Conduit Street with its extremely pricey clothes shops – Christ, is it actually *allowed* for clothes to cost that much? – and on to Theobalds Road and her digs above a faux-Italian café chain where her friend from school, Lizzie, now lived.

Lizzie. The one friend she'd kept in touch with. Skype calls and texting, so that it seemed faintly ridiculous that they, in fact, hadn't seen each other in years –

'Ellie!'

'Lizzie!'

They hugged. For some time, they hugged.

Lizzie pulled away. 'I have to go to work, like, right now.' She led Ellie down a short, thin corridor. 'This is you. Keys on the bed. I'll be back at sixish if you fancy a drink or something?'

'Nice place.'

'Yeah, thanks. It does me.' She smiled.

'How did you…?'

'Long story.'

'You mean it's your mum's.'

'Something like that. Look I really have to go. You'll be OK?'

'I'll be fine. You crack on. *Definitely* up for a drink later.'

'Great. Make yourself at home. I'm so glad you're here!'

They hugged again, a quicker hug.

'Go, go,' Ellie said.

'What are you going to do today?'

'I said *go*.'

Lizzie made a face.

'I don't know,' Ellie said. 'Take a shower. That's the first thing. Then I'm going to meet that contact, you know, guy I told you about.' Lizzie frowned. '*Work* thing, remember? Then I'm going to spend the evening with you.'

She squeezed Lizzie's hand and winked.

Lizzie smiled. 'See you *very* soon.'

And then Ellie was alone again, and she lay down on the bed in the spare room, which was, for a few days at least, hers. Her mind whizzed with possibilities of what she might do, but the pull of tiredness was overwhelmingly strong, and in moments she sank into sleep.

Ellie dozed, she thought back, she dreamt.

Ellie had always wanted to become a journalist and her degree choice was supposed to set her up for it.

The girls she grew up with were drifting off to colleges of their own, preparing to become lawyers and doctors, though secretly terrified they'd end up as clerks and medical secretaries.

'It's like feminism never happened,' Lizzie said once as they sneaked cigarettes at lunch. 'All those promises that we can have it all. The problem is that if we can *all* have it all, then some of us are not going to have anything, as there won't be anything left. In the current career climate, it makes sense to become a housewife.'

Current career climate. That was a phrase their advisor had used so often and so solemnly that it had taken on political significance, like Global Warming or Teenage Pregnancy. The worst: *Sexually Active*. 'We used to have domestic science and tips on the best forms of contraception,' Lizzie continued. 'Now it's all about marketable personal statements and the right college fit. It feels like if we get this wrong, we'll never recover.'

It didn't stop the frenzied end to their school days, though, with its alco-pop binges and hurried attempts to leave for college without the burden of virginity. And it didn't stop the listless summer in limbo that all school leavers throughout history surely go through, with their promises to keep in touch and resolutions not to change: as if they were fully formed at eighteen and owed it to themselves to be faithful to that adolescent image. Ellie though *was* keen to change, as she didn't want to have to do the same thing again.

She was her friend, her *best* friend. Her *first* friend. Lizzie. Lizzie was the first person to recognise what Ellie could be, who Ellie actually was. That thing she said, 'We've got so much potential, you and I.' That had killed Ellie, lit her up, showed her what it was like to meet a kindred spirit. 'We are muy simpatica,' Lizzie told her just days after they first met. *Muy simpatica!* That was how Ellie wanted to talk.

The days with Lizzie passed in a haze of banter and cigarettes and questionable decisions regarding boys and drugs. And she truly felt she was as clever and funny and vital as Lizzie. Most of the time. On darker days, when she was alone at home struggling over her homework, she felt very different. She realised that what she wanted wasn't to be *with* Lizzie, to be her friend, to be her *best* friend even, but to actually *be* Lizzie. She wanted Lizzie's life. She was clever enough, even then, to give the condition its proper Latin name: invidia.

From *invidere*: to look at something and to want to possess it.

She stirred. She stretched. She smiled. She was glad to be back, glad to see her friend. It was time to get to work.

An hour later and Ellie was in a moderately swank restaurant in the City sitting opposite a well-heeled, well-dressed young man.

'Who are you again?' he asked.

Ellie smiled. 'You know perfectly well. Friend of a friend. A *contact*.'

'Umm.'

Well, he was youngish. Likely late-thirties, she'd guess, but gym-ready with it, a sort of pre-emptive strike. She could imagine him doing something like fencing or equestrianism, no, *polo*. Stomach crunches, that sort of thing. A cruellness to him, there was, a competitiveness that'd suit those activities.

There was something, she'd been thinking that day, about well-dressed men: they're either doing something very right, or they're dressing up to hide the fact that they're doing something quite wrong.

English men were funny creatures, never quite sure how to realise their potential, looks-wise, blindly following fashions with no regard for body shape. Brazilians: they understood body shape. They understood – well, some of them understood, *rich* Brazilians understood – that skin-tight jeans on a round-bellied, wide-hipped, pear-shaped man do not go. And should not go, ever. A surprisingly large number of English men did not, Ellie noted on the walk from Theobalds Road to the City, know how to buy jeans.

'No, of course, I understand *that*,' the man was saying. 'But I don't really know *who* you are, as in, *what* you are. You know?'

Ellie smiled. She was prepared for a bit of evasiveness –

She hadn't been a hundred per cent truthful in terms of why she had arranged this meeting and what she was hoping to get out of it. And that, of course, meant that Christopher, the young, well-dressed man now sitting opposite her in this moderately swank restaurant in the City of London, didn't know what *he* was hoping to get out of it, didn't know, exactly, what he was doing there.

'Christopher –'

Christopher smiled. 'Chris, please,' he said.

'Chris. We have a mutual friend, a mutual colleague, I suppose, as you know.'

Christopher nodded. 'Yeah, of course, Zack, Zack the Yank.' He grinned. 'He told me about you.'

'I'm sure he did,' Ellie said. 'He's quite something, right?'

Christopher examined her. He twirled, delicately, the stem of his wine glass. It was a decent dollop of a red, Ellie thought. She'd give him that.

'How is it that you know him *exactly*?'

'I suppose you could call it the São Paulo expat scene.'

'OK.'

'He works with a friend of a friend of a friend and everyone ends up, well ends up knowing each other, you know what I mean?'

That smile again. 'Yeah, I rather think I do.'

'Barbecues and whatnot. Tennis. There's an English Club where they serve tea, play bowls. I first met him at a thing there. And you worked with him in the States, I think he said.'

The connection, Ellie knew very well, was fairly tenuous between herself, Zack the Yank and this smooth, posh City gentleman. She didn't want to dwell on this aspect; she needed to get him interested in her and sharpish.

'Bowls?' he said. He raised his eyebrows. 'OK.'

'And,' Ellie said, hurriedly, 'he told me I should look you up as a favour to *him* because what I'm doing, in my work, there's a sort of overlap, and he seemed to think there might be some benefit in it for you.'

She grinned.

'So, what is it that you do then?'

'I'm a writer.'

'OK.'

'Political commentator sort of thing.'

'And this is a favour to him *how* exactly?'

Ellie breathed lightly, took a sip of her wine. She leaned forward. 'He thinks it'll help you out, though I've no idea how on earth I might help *you*.' She paused. 'Anyway, that, apparently,' she said, 'is a good thing for him. Doing you a favour, I mean.'

Christopher made a face, a sort of six-of-one-half-a-dozen-of-the-other type of face. A certain amount of male jostling going on in that face, Ellie thought, some calculation in that *expression*.

'OK.'

'So here we are,' Ellie said. 'And just so we're clear on something else, this isn't a set-up, it's not a *date*, yeah?'

That smile again. 'OK.'

'So I suppose you must be wondering how it is I can help you.'

'I'm wondering why I'm here. Not quite the same thing.'

Ellie nodded. 'Fact is,' she said, 'I can't really help you.'

'OK.'

'That is unless you're interested in cleaning dirty money from a political- and construction-based kickback scheme in Brazil?'

Christopher nodded slowly. He raised a finger. 'Do you think we could have another two glasses of the same thing?' he asked the waiter. He looked at Ellie. 'Assume that's OK?'

'Might as well make it a bottle,' she said.

'Sir?' The waiter looked at him.

'Yeah, bottle, thanks.'

Christopher said, 'I *am* interested, yes, but not in cleaning any money, of course. However, I am *interested* in who is or who might be.'

'I'm guessing this is unlikely to be an altruistic interest?'

'It's not. In our game, it's always useful to have something on the competition.'

Ellie nodded.

'So why don't you tell me what you know.'

'OK,' Ellie said.

The waiter brought the bottle. Christopher waved away the offer of a sniff and a taste. 'You can pour,' he said.

It turned out Ellie didn't know very much, after all.

'Look, I'll level with you,' she said. 'I want to know how it is dirty Brazilian money can be dealt with in London. I don't understand how it works, how it's possible. You tell me that – i.e. if it *is* possible – and I'll give you the name of a hedge fund I know for a fact is doing it.'

'Financialisation.'

'You what?'

'Financialisation, it's a term, relatively new. A cultural thing.'

'Cultural?'

Christopher leaned forward. He was purring. 'It's a term that means that finance has become an end in itself,' he said. 'The generation of finance, of more wealth, is what companies are now interested in. Services are no longer important. A company's raison d'être is the generation of wealth, not to provide decent services.'

'OK.'

'I'll give you an example. Let's say you buy something, like a train ticket from a third-party seller. You'll pay a booking fee, right? Something like a quid fifty. Now, you'd think that that charge is a cost in order for this third-party seller to exist as a company to provide a service, wouldn't you?'

'That would make sense, yes.'

'You ever heard that phrase follow the money?'

Ellie laughed. 'I certainly have.'

'Well that little booking fee doesn't simply feed back into the company. Instead it goes on a tortuous journey. It flows up and through a whole host of companies each one owned by the next. It'll take a little detour through somewhere like Jersey, a tax haven, perhaps, off to Luxembourg, then the US, to an investment firm, through all the shareholders, then, eventually more than likely it'll end up in the Cayman Islands, in some anonymous corporate entity, feeding everyone along the way. It's a sort of invisible superstructure, to use a phrase I've read somewhere.'

'So what does that mean for the original company?'

Christopher smiled. 'It means, ultimately, that this company might well be providing a useful and beneficial service, a profitable service, even, but that's not the point, as money is being siphoned off upwards and offshore at every stop on this journey. This is the priority. The services are absolutely *not* a priority.'

'And this is legal.'

Christopher grinned. 'Legal is a funny word.'

'So no?'

'There are various definitions.'

'Bloody hell. And this is sanctioned by the government then?'

'They're the worst of the lot.'

'I suppose that's not a huge surprise,' Ellie said. 'You said it's cultural.'

'Yes, I did. What I mean is that this is how we do business, government included.'

'Example?'

'There's something called the private finance initiative, PFI, OK?'

Ellie nodded.

'In practice, and in simple terms, this means when the government wants to build schools or housing or hospitals or anything else like that, instead of doing so directly, they borrow the money in the City to finance the projects, the construction.'

'And this money follows similar journeys?'

'More or less, yes.'

'And the government pays them back when?'

Christopher sipped at his wine. 'A long, long time later, with interest and incentives.'

'Like?'

'I don't know, tax breaks, things like that.'

'So the taxpayer gets fucked?'

'The taxpayer always gets fucked.'

'Jesus.'

'Quite right.'

They sat in silence for a moment. Ellie let this marinate. 'And what happens to all this new wealth then? Where does it *go*?'

'It lines pockets all over the world. Misallocation costs, it's called. It's worth hundreds of billions of pounds. Privately run, taxpayer-funded public services.'

'That's outrageous.'

'The City is run by cunts.'

'And you work in it.'

'I am, also, something of a cunt.'

Ellie smiled, despite herself. 'So, what's all this got to do with the dirty Brazilian cash I'm talking about?'

Christopher grinned. He was enjoying himself. 'It comes into the system,' he began, 'in an investment, or a trade, and then it goes on a similar journey. The point is, the structure is in place so it is very possible for exactly this: an injection of dodgy money will disappear up and through the chain and end up in an offshore account, or more likely many offshore accounts or offshore corporate entities. The provenance of the investment or trade is no longer especially of interest to anyone. They call it a competitive economy. Means London is in the pink. But as corporation tax is lowered to entice more foreign business, the taxpayer loses out on services, key services. They reckon it's something like a sixteen billion deficit now.'

Christopher sat back. 'I mean that's roughly how it works.'

Ellie chewed this over. 'You know what,' she said, 'it's not so different from Brazil. In fact, in my mind, it's almost exactly the same.'

Christopher raised his eyebrows. 'OK,' he said.

Ellie continued. 'Basically the government hands out construction contracts with kickbacks included, yeah? So it's a bit more blatant than borrowing from the City and everything you've just described, and different people are getting rich off it, different *types*, but it's the same overall effect.'

'The taxpayer's fucked.'

'Exactly.'

'Well we're just as bad as them, I suppose,' Christopher said. 'Now you better give me the name of this fund.'

Ellie opened her purse. She pushed a business card across the table. On it:

**Capital SP**

'Thanks.' Christopher fingered the card. 'And you'll obviously see to it I'm not quoted in the article I assume you're writing? Not that I've really told you anything, of course.'

'I never reveal my sources.'

'Jolly good,' Christopher said.

Some hours later, and Ellie was getting drunk.

On reflection, Ellie was *drunk*.

She and Lizzie were sitting in The Duke, drinking. Ellie had been at it on and off all afternoon, and she'd forgotten about the English and their brutal pace, pounding pints and large glasses, rounds collected before the last is actually finished, the joylessness of those final gulps to make room for the next –

Fun, though, she had to concede.

'So wait, hang about,' Lizzie was saying, 'you've been in mortal danger, *just the once*. Is that what you're saying? Just the bloody once?'

'You know how it is, querida. Brazil's the Wild West.'

'Not funny.'

'No, I mean, there's a lawlessness, totally. I do what I want. I'm an outlaw.'

'*Not* funny.'

Ellie smiled. She took Lizzie's hand. 'It's perfectly safe, sweetheart. But why let, you know, what's the phrase? Why let the truth get in the way of a good story. Know what I mean?'

Lizzie shook her head, smiling. 'You've really developed your London accent out there, haven't you?'

'Totally. I had to. No one's interested in anyone from *Bournemouth*.' She looked around the pub. 'Nice place this. Proper boozer.' She laughed.

'You're drunk.'

'It's the pace,' she said. 'Brutal.'

'Have you eaten *anything* today?'

'Lunch. Those chips.' She pointed at the remains of a bowl of chips and sweet chilli sauce, mayonnaise. 'Proper boozer, bringing over free chips like that. Old-school.'

Lizzie laughed. 'Yeah, well, keeps you drinking, doesn't it?'

'And stops you eating.'

The pub was busy but not rammed. This was rare in central London, so Lizzie told her. And it *was* a cracking boozer. Art deco façade, quiet little dark booths in the back, loads of wood everywhere, dark wood, *proper* wood, not too many cunts, braying –

Ellie liked it very much indeed. She took a hefty swig from her large glass of wine. She examined the glass. She smiled, shook her head.

'Christ, that barely touched the sides,' she said.

'So what about this posh bloke you met today then?' Lizzie asked.

'Friend of a friend of a friend, blah blah blah. Might help with a story, a hunch, anyway. Let's see.'

'Did it work?'

Ellie's eyes twinkled. 'Did it fuck.'

'Your expression, darling, seems to suggest otherwise.'

'Let's just say I know who to talk to when I get back to São Paulo.'

Lizzie's eyes narrowed. 'Lucky them.'

'I'll drink to that.'

They continued to make slow progress on their large glasses.

'What about your mum?'

'What about her?'

'When are you going to see her?'

Ellie thought for a moment. 'Tomorrow,' she said. And then, more firmly: 'Yes, tomorrow. I'll go tomorrow.'

São Paulo, the morning after the morning after –

Or should that simply be the morning after? Fine line, Antonio thought, when all lines are blurred. And snorted. His stomach twisted in some disgust.

He was, he would admit, thrilled that he had managed to put some distance between himself and the shenanigans of Monday evening. Rafael, he had decided, was to be avoided at all costs that early in the week. In a few hours' time he would be at Roberta's flat, where she would cook him dinner. He missed her, simply. He knew he couldn't see her the morning after – the *same* day, effectively – when his spirits were crashing and his comedown toxic and all he really wanted was a hug and a wank. Nope, that would not have been sensible; she did not deserve that.

'Go out as much as you like, porra,' she once told him, 'just steer clear of me until it's well out of your system.'

He wasn't sure if she was being *completely* serious. But, fair play, and the message had got through. The real message:

*Grow the fuck up.*

He wasn't sure it was simply a question of *growing up* exactly. He'd heard older colleagues banging on about this. How they were as game as they had been when they were twenty, just realised that with age, it was simply not possible to sustain it. Their only responsibilities, they seemed to be saying, were to their bodies; the only thing they were respecting was the extra recovery time they had to factor in to a bender.

Or it might have just been mouth: all talk. You couldn't tell with that mob. Bluster was all part of the game, after all. The Hedge Fund shuffle.

Perhaps, then, the message was about *change*, actual change, which might not be the same thing as growing up. And part of the message, implicit in Roberta's words and in her tone, in her expectations, was this: *deserve me.*

Fair play, it was. And he did want to deserve her.

The message didn't matter if he knew what he wanted, of course.

Work was easy and the hours passed quietly, without incident. He ate a simple lunch of rice and beans and salad, prepared by his maid, alone in the sunshine. He let the sun warm his cheeks, and, as he sat on a bench in the courtyard at the centre of the office complex, he looked up into the blue sky, closed his eyes and smiled.

The sun was still hot when he left the office, avoiding the attentions of anyone who might try and entice him for a quick drink, and he decided to walk a little before setting off to Roberta's apartment in Paraíso. Walking was something they had in common, something they both liked to do, which was rare in São Paulo.

'Aren't we European?' Roberta would say. 'Look at us, using the sidewalk, saving the environment, browsing. What is it they call that?'

In English, Antonio replied. 'Browsing? Oh, window-shopping, ne?'

'Window-shopping. I love that. What are you up to? Me? Oh, I'm window-shopping. I'm shopping for windows. Just a little window-shopping.'

There were a number of reasons not to walk in São Paulo, but Antonio was unconvinced by most of them. The principal reason – that it was dangerous – was simply not an issue, considering where he spent most of his time. In fact, you were far more likely to be threatened sitting in your car in traffic in the nicer parts of the city than you were to have a problem on foot. In Rio, OK, but in São Paulo, street mugging wasn't that common. The villains were far more inventive than that.

Another reason his friends always pulled was the lack of pavement, of *sidewalk*. This was more nonsense, Antonio told them. That, he said, time and again, was about distance, not convenience. No fucker's going to walk along the Marginal; if you need to take the Marginal, it is too fucking far to walk. São Paulo, despite appearances, despite its vastness, its concrete desert, was a city of neighbourhoods like any other; the key to happiness within it, Antonio reckoned, was making sure you spent most of your time in one or two closely linked neighbourhoods.

And now Antonio walked through one of the very nicest, Jardim Paulistano, close by in fact to where he went to school.

Born and bred São Paulo, Antonio was. Proper Paulistano. Proper in that it was his birthright to claim this, and he did so, and proper as a true Paulistano knew his place in the city, respected it, and respected the rules and traditions that governed that place, that position in the city, that *role*. He knew what he was about. The city did that for you rather well –

São Paulo defined you.

The city's motto:

*I lead I will not be led.*

As the song goes: *quem e seu dono? Ninguem, São Paulo.*

Who is your owner? No one, São Paulo:

No one's the boss of you.

Pretty easy to find a bit of purpose, a bit of direction, when you're basically told who you are and what you should be doing with your life.

Antonio walked through the pockets of residential streets between Faria Lima and Avenida Brasil, a rectangular maze of low-rise, expansive housing, curving, narrow roads, dead ends, private lanes and cute cul-de-sacs, genteel-looking shops and restaurants, expensive cars and private security booths on every corner.

Women exercised. Women dressed up. Women nattered. Faces were *wealthy*. There was a lot of money in the faces around here, he thought, remembering chucking-out time at school, with all those expensive faces nattering. They'd ploughed a lot of money into their brows this lot, their unfurrowed brows.

On Gabriel Monteiro da Silva the houses were slightly set back from the road. There were trees. They were placed, these trees, strategically. The road led *somewhere*. It had that possibility, Gabriel Monteiro da Silva. The schools were *loaded*.

Despite the traffic, it always felt an unhurried and civilised place –

Cars queued. Women tottered. Nannies shepherded. Kids ambled. Kids chattered. Teenagers smoked. Teenagers gabbed. Teenagers flirted.

These teenagers sat outside Primo Basilico, a pizza restaurant that doubled up in the afternoons as a clubhouse for rich kids –

Been there, Antonio thought.

He certainly had been there. The sixth form at the British school would all pile down after lessons, sit and drink coffee, the occasional beer, and smoke. They loved to smoke, back then. One after another, passing them round and round, and lighting them up one after another: chain smoking was exactly right.

Most of Antonio's classmates had been going there since they were three years old, their cousins and siblings paving the way. Before that uncles and sometimes even parents.

Jobs for the boys –

They were families of the elite. This meant politicians' children – including the family of one infamous former mayor of São Paulo after whom the phrase *roba mais faz*, steals but get things done, was coined. Acceptable to be a crook if the rubbish is being collected on time and the buses are running. It meant the children of media figures, of lawyers, of the city's rule-makers: the head of the Polícia Civil had sent his two sons there. It meant the children of famous people, most notably, of course, Sir Michael Jagger.

It meant a sort of mafia.

But it didn't only mean this.

Antonio arrived at the school aged fourteen on a scholarship. This was not well known. His parents were white collar, middle class, absolutely: his mother worked as an administrator in a private university; his father was a minor bureaucrat in the lower echelons of city hall.

'I'm a cog in the labyrinthine system of legal admin,' he'd say. 'It's overwhelming to all but those who can afford to use a despachante. I'm needed. I'm performing a vital service.'

That was how he'd speak, like he was a kind of paperwork Batman.

Antonio wasn't convinced. Whatever good his father was doing still left him in shabby suits and driving – driving himself – around in a Volkswagen estate.

His parents worked hard, and he knew it, but their earnestness was suffocating. Antonio was an only child and he bore the slow decline of expectations that his family experienced; when he was twelve years old, he remembered waking up and realising that *this is it,* this is *really* it.

Not long after this, he'd got up in the night and overhead his parents talking in the living room of their tasteful, modest apartment in Pinheiros. An apartment that was fifteen minutes' walk from Gabriel Monteiro da Silva, from where Antonio was now.

'But don't you see,' his mother was saying, 'he can sense it, he can *feel* this stasis, this entropy.'

'Where did you learn words like that?' his father said.

His mother ignored him. 'This is not about you and me, it's not about where *we* are, entendeu? What he can sense, what he can feel is that we know we can't offer him any more than we already have. Like, there is nothing else. We need him to know there can be.'

'And sending him to a posh school run by exactly the sort of people I work against is some sort of answer, porra?'

'Horizons. It'll broaden his horizons. He'll… meet people, sabe?'

'People that can offer more than us, ne?'

Antonio knew, despite the silence, the gesture his mother made at this moment:

*I'm not discussing it. I know this is exactly what we always promised we wouldn't do.*

'And how is this supposed to happen, querida?' his father said. 'We're supposed to just, what, turn up there with him? Demand they let him in?'

'I've spoken to a few people at the university.'

'Same people that taught you about entropy, eh, menina?'

'Actually, you know what? Yeah, porra. People I talk to, sabe?'

'Uh-huh.'

'There's a way. A scholarship. And we can do it without Tônico even knowing, so if it doesn't work out –'

'How?'

'Transcripts from the last couple of years at school. And we plead a case. We tell them why it's important to us and what help we'd need.'

'Important to us?'

'Sim.'

'Help.'

'Porra, you know exactly what it all means.'

'Uh-huh. And I suppose we have to prove why we need this help while we're grovelling about what this means to us?'

Antonio knew the answer to that, even at twelve years old.

Main thing was though –

He was excited. He'd get in. He was as smart as a tack; it'd be a cakewalk. He'd heard that most of the posh lot were thick as fuck. Inflated opinions of themselves, so he'd heard, so he'd seen in his brief experience with them at the odd birthday party.

They *oozed* entitlement.

It was this: they couldn't actually believe that someone worse off than them – socially, financially, opportunity-wise – could possibly be better than them in any way. They couldn't fathom it. It was an alien concept.

Antonio knew this, and yet, even at twelve, he was excited.

Roberta was good on it all. 'You know what we live in? What age?' she said to him once on one of their early walks through the city. 'The age of entitlement.'

'The age of enlightenment?'

'You heard.' She smiled. 'The age of instant enlightenment, perhaps.'

He laughed. 'Oh, very good.'

'I'm serious. All this social media malarkey, all this rampant consumerism, everyone lives in their heads these days. No one gives a monkey's about anyone else, sabe?'

He grinned. 'Oh yeah?'

'Porra, tou falando sério!'

Antonio knew she was being serious.

Roberta continued. 'Everyone's like head down, block out every single sensation other than what they're feeding into their gobs and feeding into their brains off their phones, entendeu?'

'Uh-huh.'

'It's a classless phenomenon too, you know. Look at the queues at the coffee stands at the bus stops, certo? It's the same thing as in fucking Starbucks. Head cowed over phone, thumb flicking, other hand shovelling in coffee and pão de queijo.'

'That's how you distinguish class, querida? Starbucks?'

Roberta made a face. 'Mate, you know it's about the price, not the quality.'

'The great sociologist.'

'No, but think about it: the basic goal of globalisation is that everything is the same, everywhere. So, it follows: everyone, sabe?'

'So the mobile phone and readily available coffee is what's dissolving class boundaries, then?' He laughed. 'Try telling that to all your friends on the march on Sunday.'

Roberta grinned. She took his arm. 'I guess I just mean that doing something like this – you know, *walking* – is pretty valuable to me.' She kissed him. 'It means a lot. It's not something many people appreciate. You know?'

He did know.

He decided to wander up to the school, have a little look, at least from a distance.

He stopped just past the Pão de Açucar supermarket where the road cut Gabriel in two. The school was on the other side of the road; he could see its great green doors, its security measures softened by the neutral colour. Where he stood was a small, old-school padaria. They'd occasionally eat lunch there in the sixth form. Cheap burgers. Mixto quente. Bottled beer. Labourers and manual workers and dustmen sat at the counter. Dirty and sweaty, lined faces, they drank shots. Antonio never understood why no one complained about him and his friends being there. The labourers and manual workers and dustmen seemed unbothered by the flash, lairy rich boys wearing loafers and no socks. This always surprised Antonio; he assumed a default antagonism. His mates didn't care, either. There was some truth, he thought now, in the idea that the rich and poor get on fine; it's the middle classes that have all the hang-ups.

He went in.

He ordered a Serra Malte beer – a middle-class signifier, Roberta joked on their second date – and sat outside at a table that had a view of the school. It was a little after five o'clock, so there weren't many kids or parents milling about. He could hear cheers, chanting; the gymnasium stretched out almost to the road. Basketball. Or volleyball. He didn't especially care for either, gave up sport when he could. School sport. He still played tennis at Clube Harmonia, the most exclusive and pleasant of all the extremely expensive São Paulo sporting establishments. His parents could never afford the fees, but one of his closest school pal's granddad's membership number was 002, which meant some serious privilege. They swung it for him, on the house.

Cheers.

His beer arrived and he poured a dose into the tiny glass, made sure the bottle was secure in its little – fuck, what's the word? He chuckled. Roberta called it a camisinha, a little condom. Well, it was a form of protection, keeping it cold.

The beer was cold and delicious.

Serra Malte was, unmistakeably, a quality lager. Your thinking man's lager. A notch up from Original, which was the default choice of lager for your São Paulo thinking man, but Serra Malte had the edge: it was harder to find; it was *rarer*.

He smiled to himself as he ran through this little routine. This was what he and his friends would do, routines. He smiled as he thought of them, of evenings and lunchtimes passed in this way, riffing.

They were funny, his friends.

Friends. You're stuck with them, really. That old Paulistano shrug, apologetic raise of the eyebrows and the simple admission:

*What are you going to do? He's a mate.*

Take Rafael, he thought. They went *waaay* back. Rafael was a few years above in school, but his cousin was a mate of Antonio's, so once they started going out, started drinking, they all mobbed up and those few years stopped mattering. And they became friends, and that meant you had your mate's interests at heart: you had their back. It was childish, perhaps, but it was true. His father told him, when he was around seventeen, that women could never really *be* friends, there was always something getting in the way. And by that, Antonio supposed, he meant men, competing for men, that there was always that danger, that your friend might nick your man, so women could never really be friends, and, of course, lads would never do that to each other was the implication.

'Que isso?' Roberta said, when he told her. 'That is a quite disgusting view of the world.'

'I know, that's why I told you.'

'I mean, que porra essa?' What the fuck?

'I did say I realised that it was, that it's curious to me that he could even believe it. That's why I told you.'

'The man's a monster.'

'Look –'

'I mean. It's not. I can't. I – entendeu?'

He did understand.

He also knew that it was total nonsense. He poured himself more beer. God, it wasn't half crisp, this thinking man's lager.

The traffic on Gabriel thickened. The heat seemed to balloon above the road. Clouds were gathering. Angry-looking clouds mobbed up, gathered above. Cars were itchy. Cars revved and nudged. There was impatience in the air. You did not want to get stuck on the Marginal in a storm. And these cars looked Marginal-bound. Their disposition was prickly. Their body language was entirely unwelcoming.

Antonio reckoned he didn't have long before the storm. It was that time of year. Clockwork. He could shelter the twenty minutes or so in the bar, then walk up to Roberta's in the fresh air, in the new air, in the gift of cleared air.

He had a little time yet. He drained his glass and ordered another bottle of lager. He knew he'd be a touch buzzed after his second lager, but he was relaxed and it was part of a bigger buzz, the excitement, the anticipation, of the evening ahead with Roberta.

She was funny about his friends. She liked them, he thought, some of them, but she also thought they were pretty trivial. She tended to value those that brought something, who added something to society, who did something *worthwhile*. Of course, this was based entirely on her own definition of what that was. Antonio and his school friends had, almost to a man, left school and attended an expensive, private and not especially well-respected academic institution: TAAP. This institution was, in Roberta's words, a sort of finishing school for rich kids who would go on to work in their family's companies, or in finance, or not at all.

'I mean,' she'd said more than once, 'what is the point of these people? It's a bubble they live in, a fucking echo chamber, entendeu?'

Antonio would shrug. He'd say that there is nothing wrong with living within certain parameters, certain boundaries. 'It only looks narrow if you ignore the fact of their families, their desires to be a part of a very specific, and loving, community.'

He was keenly aware of the uncharacteristic earnestness of this statement. And it was deliberate. It didn't work though.

'Ah, vai, meu,' she said. 'You're using family to justify their weekends at the club drinking beer, sabe? The fact that their parents and nephews and uncles are all there too does not make it some noble exercise, entendeu?'

In some ways, it was difficult to argue with. Well, perhaps it was difficult to argue with *her*. There was certainly no chance of any softening in her position. This was frustrating. Antonio didn't think she'd ever really understood how important these friends were to him. He was a scholarship boy; he was both insider and outsider.

When his mother and father had let him down, in his eyes, it was his friends who were there: they were the ones providing him with a life and with opportunities to live it. For him, there was never any question that he would follow them to the same university and the same kind of job. If nothing else, money, and having some of it for a change, was extremely welcome. He had always relied on the generosity of his friends' parents for invitations to restaurants, private clubs, holidays – he had got used to a particular lifestyle, and working for a hedge fund was a conscious decision made to allow him to pursue it.

His second lager was, it felt, even colder, even crisper than his first. He sank back into the plastic chair and watched the school gates, though no one came in or out. For a moment, the clouds broke and the sun beat down. The sun throbbed. The sun ached. It didn't last. The clouds closed up shop. The clouds darkened.

Antonio poured himself another glass and prepared to find a table inside.

The lager, for a second, seemed to rear up in him, together with a welling of resentment –

She needed to be a little more open, a little more understanding, ta ligado? I mean, apart from anything else, the brazen hypocrisy of attacking their wealth, he thought: textbook champagne lefty, text-book rich hippie sórt. Very nice, it is, to study for a worthy PhD at USP, intern at an NGO, and live alone in a cushy gaff in town, ne? Very *activist*, know what I mean? Very fucking Robin Hood.

He laughed at himself. She'd like the Robin Hood bit.

The lager, the cold, crisp, middle-class lager that he drank down, settled him once again and he moved inside as the first spots of rain arrived. On Gabriel, cars sighed. Cars settled in. They would not be moving when the rain really hit. Around the corner from the school, these flash floods could leave the cars floating. After one such storm, he and his friend Fabio went to collect Fabio's car. It was not where Fabio had left it. They found it, a few minutes later, on the other side of the square, nestled perfectly in a fairly tight parking spot.

The thing is, he thought, there was no contradiction, no problem in working his job and sharing the same interests as Roberta *outside* of this job.

And he thought that nas fim das contas, at the end of the day, she agreed.

There were, she said, two ways to address their backgrounds –

Do what she did; do what he did.

That was exactly what they were doing; what they did was absolutely fine.

He found a corner table. He studied the bar. It had changed very little: the same yellowing walls, the same red plastic tables, the same napkin dispensers on these tables, the same tiny TV up in the corner, the same grumpy owner behind the counter, surrounded by the glass of the cigarette display. The clientele was basically the same. The same wearied but good-humoured men stoically working their way through their drinks, working on plates of cheap meat and cheap cheese, working on bowls of tart, bitter olives. There were, Antonio realised, three teachers from the school drinking lager and eating sandwiches and talking loudly in English about the weather. He turned slightly away from them. He laughed. Today, he reflected, an English person talking about the weather was totally reasonable.

The rain battered the street outside, gave the street a real hammering. It came down in missiles. The street was being beaten into submission by this rain, this São Paulo rain. The street, Antonio saw, was giving up. The water level, in only five minutes, had risen above the pavement. Rubbish was collecting in pockets, like branches snagged in the eddies and rapids of a river. Soon, the mud and the dirt, the spent cans of drink, the empty packets of crisps, the garbage, would all flow down the road. On this street, that was fine; it cleared quickly. This was not the case elsewhere. Elsewhere there would be mudslides and lost cars; cars may, in extreme cases, float off and into the river from the Marginal –

'Oi, cara, oi, playboy –'

A ratty little fucker was in front of Antonio's table, his hand out –

'Posso falar alguma coisa? Pode?'

Can I say something? he was saying. Can I talk to you?

Antonio shook his head. Antonio raised a palm. 'Não tem cara, desculpe, viu?'

Antonio wagged his finger. I've nothing, sorry, he was saying, shaking his head and wagging his finger, grimacing as if he were really keen to help, but sorry, mate, I've got nothing –

The lad was not, however, perturbed. He was scrawny, weaselly, with bad hair and few teeth. His clothes shone. He glistened. His wet head dripped.

'No, you don't understand,' he was saying now, 'Rafael, ne? No, Rafael?'

'Do I know Rafael?' Antonio's face creased in confusion and annoyance. 'Que isso, cara?' What are you going on about?

The clientele began to notice. The owner began to notice. There were one or two whistles. One or two shouts of *vai embora, seu caralho*, get out, you little fuck, go and ply your rent-boy trade else-where, bicho, that lad's too good-looking for you, son, little bitch looks like the devil sucking on a mango, and then laughter –

The guy was panicking now. 'Rafael, ne? Here. Take this.'

Antonio shrugged. 'Meu, me deixe em paz, eh, cara?'

Come on, mate, leave it out.

'Here,' the guy placed a piece of paper on the table. 'Rafael,' he said again. 'For you. Take it.'

'Que isso? Você ta viagando, cara.' You're having a laugh, mate.

'Pra você,' he said. It's for you. He made a face.

What the fuck is this? Antonio thought. 'Que porra essa?' he said.

The guy nodded. He looked down at the paper. Nodded again. He scuttled away, into the rain, to bar-wide whistles and jeers, some applause.

Antonio raised his eyebrows, shook his head: what the fuck was that all about?

He smiled at the bar. He swooned. He played it for laughs. He gave a mock bow. The gallery laughed, whistled. He feigned camp delight. Who me? Why, thank you. He fluttered eyelids. The bar roared. The English table faked interest.

In a moment, everyone was back to their drinks.

Antonio looked at the piece of paper, folded, with **Rafael** written across it.

He unfolded it. There was a time: **4pm**.

There was a place: **South side of the park, Praça Alexandre de Gusmão**.

There was a date: **20 March**.

What the fuck *is* this? Antonio mulled it over. The lads at the bar were joking, weren't they, about the rent-boy business? If that rodent was trade, God help us all, Antonio thought. But the park in Praça Alexandre de Gusmão was a hotspot for cottaging and discreet fuck jobs: the place was crawling with underage strange offering services in the shrubbery after dark. So he'd been told.

But Rafael? It must be something else. The lad was as hetero as a bull. Though, you know, could be bluster, overcompensation. Nah, it couldn't be. I mean, I'm very much a whatever-floats-your-boat kind of a fella, Antonio thought, but this would be very surprising indeed.

It had to be something else. Muito odd this, he thought.

He finished his beer. He pulled his phone to check the time. It had been on silent. He had two missed calls: Rafael. And two text messages: Rafael.

Muito odd.

The text messages:

**Where the fuck did you get to? I've spoken to Matheus and arranged for us both to take a few days off next week. Holiday, certo? You know what I mean.**

**Keep to yourself – sério. Abraço**

Muito odd, all this. Coincidence? Of course, but still –

He needed a pow-wow with old Rafael. He'd get in early doors and have a word. Deliver this love letter, perhaps.

He smiled. Whatever. It was time to go.

The rain had eased. The roads shone. The roads *glistened*. The smell hung –

Petrichor. Roberta had taught him that word. Of course she had – Roberta.

He *grinned*.

The train from London Waterloo to Bournemouth had not changed. Neither had the fact that Ellie generally sat on it hungover.

She was humming. Really hum-*dinging*, she was. She was necking water and sipping coffee and picking at a particularly unpleasant ham and egg brioche drenched in a sort of Benedict sauce that was exactly the wrong temperature and was kind of congealing, but the egg was doing something right, at least, she thought.

She sat in First Class. Style Queen.

She was disappointed, however, that South West trains no longer offered any complimentary food and drink. She was quite ready to get stuck into a gin and tonic by the time they reached Southampton Parkway. The British Airways snacking tray this was not. She made do with a dehydrated coffee buzz, rode it hard; it put her in mind of teenage experiments with dodgy bags of speed, where you had to will yourself into a wired state. This was better, but what with the obscene pricing of branded coffee these days, not a great deal cheaper.

Southampton Water was always a shock. The train drifted through the industrial outskirts of the city before suddenly finding itself crossing a fairly significant drop of estuary, as if by accident. If you slumped low enough in your seat it was impossible to see anything *but* water, and there was an odd sense, as the train slowed down, that the tracks had simply run out, that the train had ploughed on into the water under its own momentum and would, at any moment, sink.

Ellie's phone rang.

'Hi, Mum.'

'Where are you, darling?'

'Just about to come into the New Forest.'

'OK, perfect. I'll pick you up as planned, OK?'

Ellie shook her head, gave a rueful smile. 'That's the plan.'

'Thank you, darling,' her mum said, pointedly, but not without humour.

'Thank *you*, Mum.'

Ellie hung up. She looked out at the New Forest. She relaxed, as she always had. It was a soothing experience. There was a wildness to the place, but also a calm, an order. The heather, the bracken, the yellow-green hue stretched out, becoming, in parts, a marshy, boggy playground for the ponies that wandered wild. She'd never seen one actually run, she thought. The way they seemed to gather, move in groups of four and five, picking their way through clusters of trees, feeding on patches of grass: there was something reassuring about it. She felt, as she often did at this point in the journey, while watching them interact, as if she were narrating an animated children's film with talking ponies. It was a pretty good idea.

The coffee buzz softened; the gentle hum of the train's air conditioning eased, in tune with the environment. She spotted two groups of walkers, flashes of red and yellow waterproof clothing and expensive North Face hiking boots; bare legs and backpacks, maps and aluminium walking sticks: it could be her mum.

It was good to come home. It had been four years, just under. She hadn't seen her mum in four years. This was not as remarkable as it perhaps should have been. Time passed. And while it passed in the same way that it always had, being abroad somehow distorted it: you're learning, you're growing at a different rate when you're living abroad. The simplest admin task requires skills and knowledge you don't even know you have until you try to undertake it. Time speeds by; your ageing feels accelerated.

And, of course, what with technology and blah blah blah, it no longer felt like you were cut off; her relationship with her mother had rarely been better over these last few years, she thought now, smiling.

As the train approached Bournemouth, she remembered the last time that she had seen her mum, sitting on the rocks in Poole harbour, where the wooden groynes used to be, watching two pink, naked toddlers splashing about below them, their mother reading hungrily, the kids laughing and squealing. Here was another mother and her daughter, the same duty of care, the same desire, the same love –

'You can come back any time you want. I'll always be –'

'Mum, *please*.'

Ellie remembered her mother turning to her and cradling her head in her hands. 'I'll miss you is all.'

'You don't have to do this, Mum.'

'I'll never stop being your mum, Ellie.'

Ellie remembered now her steadfastness, her need for independence.

'I'm doing this on my own, Mum.'

She remembered how her mum smiled and wrapped her arms around her. She remembered how she had squirmed a little, then had let her. She remembered the children eating ice-cream cones on the sand, smearing it over their faces and bodies. She remembered their mother hopping from one to the other with a tissue that was quickly disintegrating, the paperback abandoned.

And now, as she stepped off the train, she remembered the overwhelming feeling of family, of having a mother, of being loved and looked after by *your* mother, of knowing that however awful you can be, she will love you, that however irritating she can be, you will know why, the feeling of safety, of comfort, this overwhelming feeling of *home* –

And at the end of the platform she was waiting for Ellie, her purse clutched to her, her hair recently cut, her make up fresh and understated, her body tense with anticipation, yet aiming, clearly, for some sort of nonchalance, for some sense of distance, and Ellie too, but it dissolved immediately, it melted, it dripped out of them, and they held each other and sobbed.

And that's when Ellie realised –

She'd go back to São Paulo as planned, she'd finish this story on the Lava Jato, she'd attend the march on Sunday, she'd tie things up, complete everything she'd worked so hard for, everything she had *risked* –

Then she'd come home.

Home, where she belonged.

She would come home –

In a few days, she'd have done everything she'd set out to do.

*Home.*

On the night before Ellie was due to fly back, she looked over the notes she'd made, the transcripts of interviews she'd conducted, both in São Paulo and over the last two days with Paulistanos in London, the quotes about the city she'd gathered. She was preparing a longer piece, a piece based on real people, on real Paulistanos, and she felt that when she returned to England, when she returned home, she'd get the distance she needed to really write about the city. *Paulistano.* It was a punchy title.

Ellie began to see how best to understand the city. It's about voices, words and living as a Brazilian – experiencing *saudades, alegría, jeitinho.*

One thing that struck her about the interviews: preoccupations change, but despite years passing between them, they all reference exactly the same problems that Brazil faced now, in 2016, problems of division, problems that many of her friends felt would only get worse as the Lava Jato got deeper; there was a belief that this investigation, this Lava Jato would bring down core democratic parties, figures, structures –

And the next logical step was a populist, neo-dictatorship.

Was this possible? Ellie didn't know, but many of these quotes spoke for themselves.

*I've been involved with USP for many years, as a law student in the 1990s to doing research at post-doctoral level and teaching film studies at the Film, Radio and Television Department since 2008. Both the city of São Paulo and USP have been gradually changing in the past two decades, and it would be fair to say that the city is now much kinder to its students and recent graduates than it was twenty years ago. I feel a much greater, tangible enthusiasm in the younger generation for all things Brazilian, from politics to culture and arts. USP has contributed to this renewed enthusiasm by continuing to develop indigenous and original research. We're a more international institution, each year attracting more students and visiting researchers from abroad and setting up international cooperation agreements all over the world. And as with other public universities in Brazil it does not charge tuition fees, remaining at least in principle true to its modern democratic origins in the 1930s, when it played a significant role in turning São Paulo into Brazil's most important city.*

This was Ciça, a university professor of nearly forty. They had spoken four years before. Four years! Look at the optimism! She really should contact her again, Ellie thought.

Finance was, of course, never far from anyone's agenda.

*That fucking credit card system! Man, that is the worst thing that exists in Brazil, and in São Paulo it's worse than anywhere else because of this material culture. It's a way of devaluing money. No one knows the true value anymore, what they should get in their lives for what they have. They say that you can stagger payment over twelve months without paying interest, but of course the interest is already included. Of course it fucking is! Look at the size of the discount you get when you pay in cash. Look: you buy a pair of shoes and divide payment over a year, but by the time you actually own the shoes, you need another pair! And then you do the same thing again. For a nation with so many uneducated people, this financial system is not an opportunity. It's irresponsible. They're lying to us.*

She looked at her own notes, from 2013:

*Today São Paulo is one of the most expensive cities in the world. In 2025 it will be the sixth richest city on the planet. It is currently*

*home to twenty-one dollar billionaires, ranking it in sixth place
behind Moscow, New York, London, Hong Kong and Istanbul.
Seven of these billionaires became so only in 2011. A Big Mac in São
Paulo is the fourth most expensive in the world. The most profitable
Louis Vuitton store in the world is in São Paulo. The GDP of São
Paulo in 2011 was larger than the combined GDPs of Argentina,
Chile, Uruguay, Bolivia and Paraguay. São Paulo has the highest
Ferrari sales in the world. It is little wonder then that Paulistanos
are obsessed with status and wealth. How did this happen and why?*

Two colleagues, Marcos and Tulio, business partners in London
in a Brazilian restaurant in Hackney Ellie had visited only last
night. They talked about football, of course. Look at the contradiction: unity and disunity. And look at the analogy: tragedy, family,
philosophy.

*In 1994 there was a big moment in my life when I watched
Palmeiras against São Paulo in the semi-final of the Paulista
championship. It was the day of Senna's funeral. He was a
Corinthians fan, but in the moments before this huge match, the
two sets of supporters of Corinthians' fiercest rivals started chanting
his name. 'Senna, Senna, Senna!' It showed me how we could all
come together. It was a tragedy, but it meant something to the city to
express our unity, our love. That is São Paulo.*

*Supporting Palmeiras is a lifestyle. We're passionate, educated, there's
an Italian fan base too, so it feels close to home. Point is, we've got
a different philosophy to the fans of Corinthians and São Paulo.
They're more interested in conflict. We're about unity, manners,
family, friends. That's something you don't see in London. Not as
much, anyway.*

She'd spoken to Ruth, another restaurateur now based in London,
but one who had worked the airlines.

*As a flight attendant you can see the difference between Paulistanos and other Brazilians. Leaving São Paulo for another state is like going to another country – there's less freedom, less tolerance, fewer chances for a woman to be independent and live a life separate from marriage and raising children. In some places, the women would get on the plane as if they'd just left the beauty parlour! Hair straightened, nails long and painted, heels high; for them it was an event to travel. Paulistanos are more sophisticated. They know what they're doing. You look at them and you can't tell if they're high-flying executives or lowly employees. Both types are at home. I'd work the thirty-eight minute flight from São Paulo to Rio, and the hicks from smaller states would order everything they possibly could to get their money's worth. Beer, Campari, coffee, vodka, wine! Paulistanos don't do that. I prefer the Brazilians in São Paulo. I go home wearing Converse and my mother's like, 'Uh-huh?' sucking her teeth and raising her eyebrows. A thirty-two year old isn't supposed to wear trainers. I'm supposed to be dressed in pearls and sensible pencil skirts.*

Ellie was fascinated to hear from those Paulistanos who had left. There was something about their pride in the city that had altered, yet its core remained. They were quick to judge, and quick to defend; quick to point out frescura, if someone is being a little combative, or unnecessarily rude, snobbish even: *frescura*, or being *fresca* or *frescinha*. Like everything in São Paulo, there was a class element to it as well: the perception being that someone who is *fresca* thinks they are better than you.

And there was bitterness too. Adriana, an educational administrator now living in London, had worked at one of those swank, wealthy international schools in São Paulo, one of those schools that churned out playboys and patrocínias. Ellie had met a fair few of them, dated one or two.

*Working at an international school was tough. The school was full of rich kids, and, though they were charming, they represented the city's prejudice. They lived in a bubble. There was a hierarchy at the school, and the Brazilian administrative staff were firmly at the bottom. What upset me was that I was treated as inferior, in my own country. My own city. It was a shock, you know? I felt more of a foreigner than ever before. And the teachers that did come from abroad would never have the same quality of life at home that they have in São Paulo! The free rent, high salary and all the administrative help they need. I'd look at them and think: 'I know where you're coming from and I know where you're going. You're the same as me.'*

This was a starting point, perhaps, these interviews, these feelings, these ideas.

It was all about the discourses of power, the structures of power, and that's what Ellie wanted to interrogate.

When she returned to São Paulo, she was about to see it in all its ugly glory – power. Who had it, who deserved it, where it went when it disappeared.

She opened a new document, tapped out PAULISTANO at the top and started to write:

*Order and Progress, it states on the Brazilian flag.*

> *'Love as a principle and order as the basis; progress as the goal.'*
>
> *Arguably, for modern-day São Paulo, the followers of Antonio Comte who deposed the monarchy and secured independence for Brazil in the nineteenth century focused on the wrong words. Undoubtedly there is a principle of love in Brazil, and São Paulo represents nothing if not progress as an ultimate goal; but order?*
>
> *'I lead, I will not be led.' Economically, the city is the beating heart of Brazil. If it stops, the country dies. More and more, this is true in all areas of society and the rallying cry is deeply Brazilian with its double-consciousness, its affection and passion, and sense of longing, nostalgia, of saudades, captured in a banner I saw more than once at recent political protests:*

*'São Paulo, I'm not proud of you, but I love you.'*

When this was all done, when she had the story she was looking for, it would be time to come home.

Sunday, 20 March. The March in March –

This weekend they were picking sides. Attendance meant you were parking your flag. Today, they were coming down firmly on the left, with Dilma, and therefore making a statement to the conservative elite that the Workers' Party was not finished.

Happy, peaceful thoughts.

Antonio was wide awake. It was six in the morning, and he'd been fairly awake, his sleep patchy at best, he now thought, since about half four. He was, it was safe to say, on edge.

Roberta slept on soundly, oblivious, next to him. *The sleep of those without secrets.* She gurgled occasionally, every now and then gave a surprisingly loud snort, or honk, not quite the full snore, not *quite*, that might have made him nudge her or adjust her position, but enough to remind him that he was keeping something from her, *what* it was, in fact, that he was keeping from her. *The sleep of those without shame.*

It had, so far, been a wonderful weekend, had been a pretty fucking wonderful few days ever since their dinner, the evening after the morning after the morning after. The evening of the day he'd been given that strange note addressed to Rafael. *The sleep of those without doubts.* The evening *before* Rafael had fronted up about what this holiday malarkey actually meant.

'Mate, just allow it,' he said. 'It's a precaution, that's all.'

'Precaution for what?'

'We might need some time away from the office, that's all, for this off-the-books job, entendeu? Here. In São Paulo. We ain't going anywhere.'

'So it's just daytime then? Working hours, like?'

Rafael grinned – mean. 'If you're worried about your bird, don't. You'll be back home in time for your tea.'

'Don't be a cunt.'

Rafael smiled – genuine. 'Settle down, I'm just fucking about, mate, relaxa, sabe?' He breathed out. 'We might not even need to take the time off. But we *might* need a day or two. It's important. And it's well worth it, dollar-wise. It's easier this way, trust, cara. Simpler to pre-empt it than fuck off from our desks without telling anyone exactly why. And if we *don't* use it, it'll be there for you down the line, you know, pending, and Bob's your mother's brother and you and Miss Prissy can fuck off shopping to Miami for a few days. Or Guatemala, you know, dig a fucking well.' He winked. 'Whatever takes her fancy, entendeu?'

*Bob's your mother's brother.* He said that in English. Antonio couldn't help but laugh. The lad's been watching some dodgy films, he thought.

Fact is, he was reassured; he *was* thinking about Roberta. If he had to take a day or two off in São Paulo, it was doable. It was work, after all, even if it was off the record. And while that worried him a touch, while he wasn't entirely sure what he was getting himself into, Rafael's superior, Senhor Matheus, had green-lit it, and off the record was how the system often worked.

None of this, of course, helped much with the nagging guilt he felt for not sharing any of it with Roberta. He looked at her now. *The sleep of those without suspicion.* And as the date on Rafael's misplaced invitation arrived, and the hours and minutes crept towards the time printed on this invitation, Antonio felt overwhelmed by what it all might mean, felt numb, paralysed, and this paralysis extended out towards Roberta. The knowledge that he would be difficult with her today, reticent, irritable, thanks to this paralysis, *compounded* the anxiety he felt as it brought that nagging guilt crashingly into focus.

Roberta sighed, muttered something in her sleep. He eased his arm out from under her neck. She hugged her softest pillow to her and sighed again. Antonio lay back and placed his hands beneath his head, watching as the light gathered pace outside and the wood in her tasteful, elegant, but ineffective slatted blinds brightened.

Why hadn't he said anything to Rafael about the note?

It was, essentially, the same basic reason he hadn't said anything to Roberta –

Fear.

Fear of embarrassing Rafael.

Fear of embarrassing himself.

Fear that he would discover – from either or both of them, intentionally or not – that he was doing something really quite stupid indeed.

Fear, he realised, that was rooted in uncertainty, in the notknowing, and talking about any of this would reveal this lack of knowledge quite sharply, reveal this lack of certainty, which, in turn, would trigger another kind of knowledge: that at best he was being an ingénue, at worst, really quite stupid indeed.

Roberta stirred and he looked at her.

She was, he had to admit, outrageously sexy. Objectively speaking, to *objectify* her, as she would say, she was seriously fucking hot. Mischievous eyes, a tangle of brown hair, loads of legs –

And the sex. Well quite, the *sex*. Antonio smiled to himself. Let me put it this way, he thought, before Roberta, he'd only ever used the phrase *make love* ironically.

It is easy to say to someone that you have never felt this way before, Antonio thought. And, to an extent, that's the case in every relationship, you haven't ever felt this way before as you've never felt this way about this particular person before –

But it was true. He had never felt this way before.

He understood, now, what those words meant.

Roberta stretched. Her eyes closed, she smiled, turned to him, wriggled into him, buried her head in his chest, her hands found his neck, she said, simply –

'Amor.'

He kissed her. 'I'll make you some tea.'

'Wait, just two minutes.' She held him. 'Please.'

He kissed her again –

The tea *could* wait.

Eight hours later and Antonio was all alone in a fuck-off big crowd, spinning out from a good slap of strong weed and cursing the fact that he couldn't hide his agitation and simply enjoy the day with Roberta, that he couldn't help being a snide little fucker and that *she* couldn't give him a fucking break considering what he was going through.

Which was stupid, he knew. But still. Silly cow, she should have known that *something* wasn't right. Fucking Rafael. What a fucking joke, eh? he thought. The lad's having a laugh, stitching me up like this. Because that's what this is, Antonio thought, a stitch-up. He didn't know how, he didn't even know what he'd done even, but he did know that what Rafael was doing was very likely connected to the very thing they were protesting about, in theory, that day:

The greased-hand and lined-pocket chain-of-corruption agenda that Dilma was hammering, that Dilma was claiming did not take place on her watch, or even in her party before her watch, the funnelling-off of funds out of the country.

Yeah, right.

There were fucking millions of people on Avenida Paulista, and Roberta had skedaddled with some purpose, some real urgency. There was no way, at this point in the rally, that he was going to find her. And, to make it considerably worse, he had her mobile phone in his pocket. It had seemed like a good idea at the time. Left-wing get-together or not, there'd still be some cruel little prick lifting purses, rifling through bags. It's hard to pickpocket a pair of good, fashionable, slim-cut jeans: a benefit of this narrow-legged new world we all now lived in.

Yeah, right.

His head *swam*.

The pre-march joint also seemed like a good idea at the time. Get into the whole hippie vibe. Say things like vibe. Christ, you didn't need to even have your own: there was a great cloud of it bursting and sagging just above.

He tried to focus. Colours everywhere. Shouting. Smiles.

This was defiance.

Defiance of the people that ran the city.

For a moment, a righteous energy surged through him –

It didn't last.

God he was a prick. Why couldn't he have just agreed with her rant?

All she'd said was that there was no debate, that impeachment *claimed* to be a debate, but that it was, in fact, the opposite. Almost those exact words, he thought.

'It is *closing down* the debate,' she said. 'Polarising the country, dividing families, friends, colleagues. Dividing *us*, sometimes. It is us and them now, entendeu? That simple, that basic. Two sides, us and them and no grey, no nuance, just black and white and it is terribly sad and that is not democracy, not what politics is, should be, we no longer deserve the democracy we'd earned.'

He could see the drugs drive this rant on.

'Dilma had been a part of achieving it, right, I know that, but now, who knows, ne? And she's either a snake in the grass or a terribly wronged woman in a society that is more misogynistic, conservative, backward-looking than ever. Who the fuck knows, sabe? I do not. That's all I can tell you.'

And she looked angry. Not hurt, not sad, not confused, not even bitter. Angry.

And this, for some reason, pissed him off.

'Settle down,' was all he could bring himself to say.

What a cunt.

No wonder she bolted. She was absolutely furious. Fair enough, really.

But now what?

Christ he was stoned. How did these hippies do it? It's exhausting, terrifying. This weed was *killer*. Imagine LSD or DMT! It's a fucking full-time job, being a hippie. He was definitely a 'bit of a sharpener and let's dance to some fucking Motown' kind of a man. Stoners were, in the end, fucking useless. Lazy. Everyone knew that. They never actually *did* anything.

The crowd heaved. The crowd swayed. The crowd throbbed.

He could make no sense of any of it.

Slogans. Banners. Music. Groups. Workers. Maids. Students. Activists. Anarchists. Face paint. Klaxons. Flags. Megaphones. Balaclavas. Pipes. Whistles. Handclaps. Cheers. Singing. Placards. Jokes. Cartoons. Thumbs-up. V-signs. Masks. Balloons. Red. Red. Red. Red. Red. Rainbows. Faces. Arms. Legs. Backsides. Shoulders. People. People. People.

He had to get off Avenida Paulista. There were too many people. It was suffocating.

And Lula was expected on stage in not too long and the hypocrisy of cheering that backward, gyppo hick was making Antonio angry, especially after it was now pretty fucking clear that Dilma had made him her chief of staff so he couldn't be prosecuted and sent to jail, as being left wing doesn't mean you can't also be a thieving gyppo cunt after all, and why didn't I think of that when Roberta was getting all arsy, and if the fucker's going down then I don't see why I need to be here any longer –

But not being there any longer was a tall order.

People fucking everywhere. There was a considerable body of them, a growing, slithering body, between Antonio and the other side of Avenida Paulista.

And he was stoned, he reminded himself.

Logistics, at this point, were not his friend.

He saw the pokey little shopping centre across the road from the museum, Conjunto Nacional. He should use that as a beacon, a lighthouse. He could then duck off the strip, pass the park, and hotfoot it up Alameda Santos towards Roberta's place and hope to fuck she'd decided to do the same.

Roberta. What a wally, he was. Is it so hard to simply love the one you love? To bury all the inconsequential shit of the last week or so – and it *was* inconsequential – and simply *put her first*?

Well, he thought in a fug, spaced out, his brain literally taking up more space, we live and learn. And she says I'm good at that: learning.

Yeah, he thought, his brain, his dispersed brain, his new, hippie brain catching up with his movements, his *plans*, I'll go to Roberta's and wait for her there. I'm off. Ciao, fuckers.

Crowd-surfing was out, he thought. He plotted a line from where he was at the end of Rua Augusta to the shopping mall. It would, under normal circumstances, even factoring in traffic light changes, take fewer than five minutes. He got his elbows ready, he got his regretful face on, he put his head down and he bustled –

It took longer than five minutes. There was dancing in the way. He bought a beer from a vendor to try and rid himself of some of his edge. Then another, from another vendor, as it had worked.

At Conjunto Nacional, he stopped for a moment, drank it in. He looked up and down Paulista. He smiled, despite himself. He could turn this story into something funny. Roberta would get it. They would laugh. There was one thing he knew about them: they were quick to get over themselves, quick to realise when they'd been ridiculous, quick to laugh at their ridiculousness, each other's and their own. He remembered the first time they'd travelled together and she'd forgotten to put her toiletries in a plastic bag and was pulled by security. He went over to check everything was alright and she snapped at him, and he took offence and flounced off saying, 'I was *just* trying to be supportive.'

They laughed very quickly about that.

It would be OK. It simply would. *They* would.

The road either side of the shopping mall was jammed. Ram-jammed. The shop fronts that opened out onto Avenida Paulista had been quickly shut up, their grills pulled down. The main entrance was still just about accessible. He took a deep breath and heaved, hefted his way through the crowd, into the mall, where it was clear and cool, really cool, and he didn't think, in fact, he'd ever been this thankful to be on the inside of a shopping mall before, let alone one that was as low-rent as Conjunto Nacional, and he could get through to the other side, and the lager had really *softened up* his head, really *eased* him into a much better mood, so he'd cross the mall, he resolved, then nip down the side of the park and take Alameda Santos up to Paraíso, where –

The park. Fuck. Praça Alexandre de Gusmão.

He looked at his watch. Not long until four. In his dope-fudged brain, with the dope-edged roundabout mood swings of anger and regret, frustration and excitement, he'd forgotten all about one of the key reasons he was anxious in the first place.

Well, this might be interesting, he thought. He smiled. He was a touch unmoored by the beer-weed combo. Yet, he thought, he had nailed the ratio, got it just right, you know, bang on, even if he did say so himself.

Jesus, imagine old Rafael having his cock sucked behind a tree! Now *that* would be a valuable bit of information. He laughed at his own insincerity. Not my style, he thought, knowing that was true. But it wouldn't hurt to know, would it? And, after all, it was on his way to Roberta's, wasn't it?

He left the shopping centre and snaked across the road. The backstreets were quiet. The backstreets were blowing political rally debris. The backstreets were empty, cleaned out by some cataclysmic event.

Antonio drank it in.

South side, the note had said. He should hang about, hang back a tad, scope the square, all corners like. Which side was fucking south anyway?

He stumbled over a loose paving stone. He chuckled.

He thought: Rafael, homo –

Nah. The lad's got something going. Some of the birds he's been with are scandalous. Not that that means anything though. Yeah, he's got something going.

Let's go and have a gander.

At the top end of the square was an underground car park. There was always someone manning the entrance, but only once you'd gone down a level from the street. Antonio figured he'd walk in to the park by this entrance, hang back there. If he saw Rafael he could tell him something like Roberta was in there fetching her vehicle, something like that.

The park was dead. Not a soul about the place. The rally noise filled it. It echoed – eerie. Antonio wasn't sure what he was doing there exactly. But he'd come this far; might as well put one little mystery to bed.

On the far side of the square, right down on Alameda Santos, he could make out a few lads horsing around.

He decided to head that way.

He got half a dozen or so yards into the park.

In front of him –

A figure, scurrying.

This figure scurried straight at him.

This scurrying figure: the snide rent-boy postman.

Antonio, frozen, eyes wide:

Fuck.

'You,' he said, as the scurrying figure hurried past. 'You –'

The figure turned. The figure scurried on. The figure spoke. 'You!' he said. 'You need to go. You need to go. I've seen you now, I've seen you.'

Antonio, frozen, watched the man rushing away. Antonio turned back.

Beyond –

Two men dressed in black, arms extended.

Beyond them –

A young man in a pink shirt, sharp trousers, shiny –

Rafael.

Antonio, frozen, watched as the two men dressed in black extended their arms and, noiselessly, shot Rafael in the chest.

*I've seen you.*

Antonio, frozen, watched Rafael crumple.

Antonio, frozen, watched the two men dressed in black drag the body into the bushes and disappear. He heard a shout. He heard the roar of a motorcycle.

*I've seen you.*

Antonio, frozen, dumbstruck –

He heard the scurrying figure call out: 'Go, caralho, go, you need to go, to disappear, bicho. Vai embora!'

Antonio headed back out of the park and did a left.

*I've seen you.*

As he did, he found first his phone then Roberta's, turned them off, pulled the Sim cards, destroyed these under his feet and chucked the phones back into the bushes in the park, at the opposite corner to, at the opposite corner to –

At the opposite corner to where Rafael had crumpled.

*I've seen you.*

To where Rafael had been shot in the chest, and lay –

*I've seen you.*

To where Rafael lay crumpled, dead.

*I've seen you.*

Antonio kept moving. He pulled his wallet. He found an ATM. He boosted all the cash he could. He bent and snapped his bankcard. He pocketed the cash. He emptied his wallet. It did not take long. It was fashionable among the playboys and fuckheads to keep a money clip and a single bankcard in a slim wallet.

Antonio noted the convenience of this fashion.

Antonio noted this note.

*I've seen you.*

Antonio: brain scrambled.

He hotfooted.

He moved *fast*.

*I've seen you.*

He kept moving –

*I've seen you.*

Where to?

*I've seen you.*

Where to? Where to?

# PART THREE: **FORTUNE'S ALWAYS HIDING**

**Interrogation room, Polícia Civil HQ**
**São Paulo, 22 March, lark-time**

'I don't suppose you've ever sat on that side of the table, have you, son?'

Leme shook his head. Leme smiled. He rolled his neck. He stretched his arms. He went eye to eye with his questioner. He *glared* him down.

'I'm choosing to sit here, don't forget,' Leme said. 'I'm doing your job for you, mate. If it weren't for me, you wouldn't even know there'd been a crime. That poor cunt's body would be on the slow rot, a worm-frenzy. So leave it out, entendeu?'

Leme's questioner raised an eyebrow. He angled his head left, then right.

'Fair point well made,' he said. 'Still, you *are* on that side of the table, aren't you? So be nice, certo?'

Leme nodded. Fact is he liked old Lutfalla. They'd never quite crossed paths professionally, but he was alright. Decent rep, known to be a worker, nothing too shady in his locker, family man, sense of humour, put his hand in his pocket when the need arose. Leme could have had a lot worse sitting across from him –

Luck of the morning-shift draw.

Well, late-night shift really. Leme was likely the last task old Lut had to get done before home and bed and a day or two off, play with the kids, shout at the wife, wank in the shower, that sort of thing.

Lutfalla yawned.

'You tired?' Leme asked.

'Exhausted, mate. Last thing I fucking need, *this*,' he said.

'It wasn't exactly top of my list of things to do either, mate.'

'Let's start there then.'

'You what?'

'Some people are saying that this is you turning yourself in, right? That's what some people are saying.'

'I guess it's not a million miles off, is it?'

Lutfalla smiled. 'You confessing to something?'

'Don't be a cunt.'

'I said be nice.'

Leme shrugged. 'Protective custody, you know, for now.'

'What does that mean?'

'It means that someone's stitching me up.'

'Oh yeah?'

'Two days, two bodies. And I'm at both scenes, corpses good as new.'

'*Two* bodies?'

Leme said nothing.

'You said two bodies.'

'I figure we work out the first one, it's easy to work out the second.'

'We know who the second one is, mate.'

Leme nodded. Leme grimaced. 'I mean work out *why*, entendeu?'

'Right.'

'You didn't know there was another stiff?'

'No. I did not. Enlighten me.'

'Sunday. By the rally. A youngish, playboy type. In the park off Paulista.'

'Alexandre de Gusmão, you mean? The square? OK, that's likely a botched homo whack-job.'

'I don't think so.'

'No?'

'The Militar boys showed up just when I discovered the poor lad.'

'Right.'

'And the tip-off came from our second corpse, our good friend – our *former* good friend – Senhor Fat João.'

Lutfalla said nothing. He rubbed his eyes. He rubbed his hair. With both hands, he rubbed his cheeks, his stubble.

Leme sat tight.

'What do you expect me to do here, Mario?' Lutfalla said. 'You call in the stiff, but you refuse to say what you're doing there at the end of the fucking world finding the little rat fuck. That's why you're here, certo? You know that. Então? You best not be messing me about, sabe?'

'Like I said, the little rat fuck led me to the first body. So I went to see what he might know that might shed a little luz on the matter.'

'As far as anyone here is concerned, there is no other body.'

'Donkeys in the fucking shade, ne?'

Lutfalla smiled. 'And that's your problem. Your reason for being at our dead friend's gaff is a reason that's news to us.'

'Thanks, Sherlock.'

Lutfalla made a face. 'Tell you what,' he said. 'I'm going to log this as all good, give you the all-clear, the whole slap-bang investigative-work trip that paid out a tasty dividend. But I'll also log that it's on hold, decent-result-at-half-time situation. I don't know what's going on, but I ain't going to stop you trying to find out. This is done, for now. You've got a day, maybe a couple, tops. OK?'

Leme grinned. 'Nice one. You're a good lad.'

It wasn't rocket science what Leme had to do next –

And double-quick. Set up a meet with Fat Silva to find out why the slovenly fuck had sent him to Fat João's palatial pad on the day that life, and all its opportunities, were cruelly taken from him. Actually, there was no need to set up a meet and old Silva never liked a surprise. Leme knew where he would be: home or breakfast. Leme knew that Lutfalla would give him a bit of breathing space. Leme knew that Superintendent Lagnado would be enough hours behind play to give him a chance. The fact is he needed the same information he needed twenty-four hours ago.

The name of dead guy numero uno –

Leme jumped the stairs two at a time. Less chance of running into anyone on the stairs. The elevator *heaved*. He arrowed across the open-plan space. He pushed into the tin-can office he shared with Lisboa.

'Well, well,' Lisboa said. 'If it isn't Harrison Ford in the fucking *Fugitive*.'

Lisboa gunned the engine. The engine sputtered. The engine growled. He aimed his rust bucket up and through Jardins. They bounced through the slick-swank shopping pocket of Oscar Freire. Leme noted Diesel, Louis Vuitton, Levi's, Gucci. They hopped the grid system, diagonally, rode traffic-light luck. They said nothing. They angled across by going *around*. Crow flies and whatnot it was no more than two clicks to Silva's. They skipped the school bus jams – *just*. Fifteen minutes of honking and cranking, crunching and kerb-bothering, they parked. Silva's building looked *tired*.

Leme watched as Lisboa shambled over to the condo entrance. Lisboa spoke into the intercom. A moment later, the porteiro, a youthful pup of a doorman, came out. Lisboa spoke to the young pup. Lisboa's message was communicated, Leme thought. Lisboa stomped back across the road: *pissed*. He ducked his head into Leme's window.

'Out, you, I know where he is.'

Silva looked *tired*. He was taking on a full Brazilian: eggs, bread, cold cuts, yoghurt, sweet breads, fruit, sausage, flask of coffee, vase of orange juice, cigarette burning in an ashtray just east of his bursting plate, his plate spilling food, *glutting* food –

'I wondered when you two would show up,' he said.

'Here.' Leme passed him a napkin. 'You've got egg on your face, son.'

Silva knew the expression. 'It appears that way, doesn't it?'

Crime pops up all over the shop. About six months after Leme and Renata first got together they were invited to spend the weekend at the country house of friends of Renata's. They were looking forward to it. The condominium where the house had been built was not far out of São Paulo, an hour, hour and a half, but the air was always fresher, the space greener. There was a swimming pool. There would be barbecued meals. There would be plenty of booze. A handful of

Renata's close friends were going. Leme was most excited by this last aspect. He was going to get involved, going to become a part of her life. They'd reached that point; they spent their weekends together, regardless. In fact, that point was the point: it'd happened naturally, seamlessly.

Leme had three days off and eased into the Friday. Renata was working in her legal aid office in Paraisópolis. She had to work late, in the end. She always had to work late. Working late cost her her life, to a point, in the end. But not this weekend. She was late getting home, she was late getting packed, she was late getting showered, she was late getting dressed, she was late having a quick – just a quick – supper, a bite really, just to be sure, you know, she was doing the driving after all –

So they were late on the road. And a Friday, a Friday evening at that. Traffic was *heavy*. An hour, hour and a half, was more like three, three and a quarter. The condominium was quiet, on the outside, dark, when they arrived not long before midnight, hopeful that the evening would be in full flow, and they'd catch the end of dinner and something of the weekend spirit, late-night booze-fuelled Friday fun, and all that ruckus. Leme was *psyched*. He was well up for it. He was about to establish to everyone else what he and Renata already knew: that this was the real deal.

They arrived at the security gates, showed ID, bit of back and forth with the security detail, and ghosted through.

It was one of those condos where the architecture made no sense. Each house a testament to its owner's folly. Like a sort of Disneyland for flash, garish gaffs. Flash, garish, *second* gaffs of course. Most of these flash gaffs were lit up, obviously full for the weekend, kids playing, adults playing, driveways rammed with flash cars, sounds of food cooking outside and splish-splashing in pools. Renata crept along the grid of roads, looking for the turn to her friends' place, windows down, air cool, air expectant. They found the turn. This road was quiet, dark. The houses were empty. This was common, certainly possible, not everyone fled the city every weekend. They crept further, slowed right down. When Renata recognised the house, she stopped the car. 'We're here,' she said. 'I'm sure this is it.' Leme scanned the street. No one around, lights off, house, it seemed, deserted. 'Stay here,' he said. Leme skirted the grounds. A sprinkler in the back garden sprayed water left right left right left right. This was triggering the security light. It flashed on off on off on off. The windows, most of them, were ajar. There was a buzz of electricity. There was silence. There were, he thought, whimpers, sobs.

Leme nudged the front door and it swung open. He called out. Shouts, swearing, who the fuck are you, you said you weren't coming back, we haven't moved, take what you want, don't touch the women. Leme turned on the lights. He identified himself. He told them to stay calm. He asked what was going on, what had happened. He said: one of you, just one of you, tell me. And stay down, stay down on the floor, stay down with your hands behind your head until I say so, just for now, just in case, don't panic, I'm one of you. A man told him what had happened. He told him in a tone of disbelief. He couldn't fathom what had happened. He couldn't fathom that it was over, almost over, and yet far from over. He couldn't fathom it, it made no sense to him, he couldn't *process* any of it. Leme nodded. Wait here, he told them. He went upstairs. He checked from room to room. Women, in each room, whimpered and sobbed, their hands behind their heads, whimpered and sobbed face down on the floor. They were all OK. Leme brought them downstairs. He instructed the guy whose house it was to call security. To call security, now. He instructed the man to tell security there had been a breach. He went to the fridge and handed out beers. He found a bottle of whiskey on the kitchen counter, some glasses. He poured shots. There was some hysteria, but then there was a calm, a relief. Then euphoria, a softening. What doesn't kill you, etc. We made it, we fucking made it. Fuck them! We made it. I love you. He went to fetch Renata. She was confused, scared. When he told her what had happened, she broke down sobbing.

They'd been making dinner when three men in balaclavas carrying guns walked through the front door, and two more men also in balaclavas, also carrying guns, came in through the back door. With guns to their heads, the men were forced to lie face down on the floor, downstairs. The women were taken upstairs. Renata sobbed. The women were taken upstairs and two of the men stayed with them while the other three men stripped the house, and all the people in it, of valuables. They told the men to stay where they were, that any move to help their women would be punished, that the throats of their women would be cut, after they'd been raped. The men sobbed. The men yelled. The men could do nothing. There were guns trained on their heads. The women were OK. It was a threat. The threat was enough. The robbery went off without incident.

Leme went next door. The same scene. He went to the house next to that. The same scene. Five houses had been turned over. Five sets of occupants terrified and stripped.

They never caught the gang that did it.

Silva said, 'I know about Fat João. I'm sorry. I *didn't* know. Why would I? And even if I did, why would I do that, eh? To you? We're mates.' Leme nodded. Leme was fairly certain all along that Silva hadn't grassed. 'Anyway, you're in luck,' Silva said. 'My young protégée is coming along in a minute and might have something for you.' Lisboa shot Leme a look. The look said: don't be too quick to forgive, this might not add up.

Leme never told Renata what that night had done for him, long-term, not really. It had made it clearer than ever that she would be his wife, that he would be her husband. The idea of it, the two of them split like that, appalled him.

The *idea* of it.

Later, it made him think about how crime, about how the ordinary horror of crime, crime in São Paulo, was democratic. You could, like Renata, in her legal aid office in the favela, work in a place where criminals lived and operated with impunity, work with people directly touched by these criminals, touched in their daily lives by the rules and routines of these criminals, and you could live happily alongside them, work alongside them, *for* them, and you could live by these rules and routines. Or you could get deeply unlucky, like Renata had, and you could die by these rules and routines, die at the hand of a stray bullet.

Or you could just go away for the weekend and stay with your friends, your rich middle-class friends, and something terrible could happen. Or not. It was democratic.

Of course, Leme found out later that Renata's death, killed by this stray bullet in a firefight between police and thieves, while an accident, wasn't simply an accident.

Even that felt democratic, in its way, to him now.

Ellie jumped from the back seat of a cab. 'Ah,' she said, 'the three amigos. The three wise men.' She paused. She pointed at Silva's plate, raised her eyebrows, laughed. 'The three little pigs.' Lisboa glared at Silva. 'We're not the three anything, sweetheart,' he said. Silva raised his palms. 'I know how it looks.' Lisboa nodded. Silva said, 'Ellie here has something. Can we just suspend the hostilities until she's told us what it is? Favor?' Leme nodded.

'Right,' Ellie said. 'So this is what I *have*, as Francisco puts it.' The three wise men kept their counsel, kept schtum. Ellie went on. 'I got back Sunday morning. I headed to the rally. Yesterday, that's Monday, I get a call from my friend, Lis, we used to work together, she went travelling, she's back, whatever. Anyway, so her friend Roberta's in a right two and eight, you know, a state? Her boyfriend's missing. Well, they had a row at the rally, she stormed off and she hasn't seen him since. It hadn't even been twenty-four hours, sure, but he had her phone and he's not answering and not replying to emails and Lis had been calling round, subtle, you know, and no one had heard or seen hide nor hair and whatnot. So the poor girl's on the hysterical edge of concerned, entendeu? Lis called me as she knows about my, you know, my *connections*, the three little pigs, as it were –' She made a face at Lisboa. 'So here I am. I thought you could help. That's why I got in touch, *Leme*. Nice of you to follow up properly.' Leme ignored this. 'And Francisco, when I told him last night, seemed to think I might be able to help *you*, which, I'll be honest, was something of a surprise.'

'What's the lad's name?' Lisboa asked.

'Antonio. Antonio Neves.'

'Where does he work?'

'He's a finance guy. Sleek little hedge-fund operation called Capital SP.'

'We better pay them a visit,' Lisboa said.

'Not sure how much point there is in that,' Ellie said.

Lisboa raised a hard eyebrow – oh, yeah, fucking educate me, gringa, it said.

'Roberta was there yesterday. They told her this Antonio had taken a few days of holiday. All legit. Cleared with the fucking line manager and blah blah blah. First she'd heard of it. Didn't help with her strop, that bit of info.'

'No, I don't suppose it would,' said Leme.

Silva gestured at Ellie. 'Now tell them the other thing.'

Ellie grinned. 'So later on yesterday, Lis *and* Roberta both get emails calls texts whatever, totally separate, no obvious connection, about some rumours of someone who's missing. Some lad in that posh playboy circuit had been asking around, apparently.'

'Asking about what exactly?' Lisboa said.

'This is the odd bit: asking if anyone knew of anyone missing, entendeu? Like he was just sort of curious.'

'And please tell me neither of your friends mentioned this Antonio?'

'They're not stupid.'

Lisboa coughed. Ellie glared. Leme gestured: go on, please.

A bala perdida, a stray bullet, is not as random, not as unlucky, not as *rare* as you might think. Adilson, a friend from Leme's condo, one of a group of middle-aged tennis players who liked to drink courtside after their bad-tempered doubles, was shot in the chest. When he got out of hospital Leme saw him sitting by the pool in customary fashion, Speedos and lager. A little quieter, a little recalcitrant even, but basically the same. There was a group of friends and well-wishers surrounding him and he knocked them aside to embrace Leme.

'Feel this,' he said. 'It's still there. Can you feel it? The bullet.'

It was hard and lumpy like a growth. If you pushed firmly, you could trace the edges, Leme thought. It was like someone had forced a bottle cap under his skin.

'They weren't able to take it out,' he said, 'without causing further problems.'

He laughed. He raised his can of lager.

'What doesn't kill you, eh?'

He was hit by a bala perdida. Nine a.m., and Adilson had been walking to work in Itaim, a respectable and desirable area of offices and residences, quiet streets and fashionable restaurants. Shots were fired; a robbery. He felt his legs give way and warmth in his chest. His head spun and there was a sharp and nagging pain in his back. When he looked up, he saw his dead father talking to God. That's the last thing he remembered before coming round in hospital. He was fine now, the bullet worn like a badge of honour, a greying lump of skin that didn't tan like the rest of him. Thing was, there were rumours that it wasn't a stray bullet at all. Story was that the woman he was fucking, her son didn't like it. This lad was a coke fiend, Leme had heard. The delusional sort. The scratching-around-in-the-dark and cooking-up-plans sort of fiend. He didn't like old Adilson. And he had the sort of wedge that could arrange a stray-bullet whack-job. That's the story going round now. Democratic.

'You know what's next, right?'

'Gabriel Carvalho. Here's his address and his work details.' Ellie pushed a piece of paper across the table. 'It doesn't sound to me that this lad's got a great deal up here.' She tapped her forehead.

'Definitely one of your mob then,' Lisboa muttered.

Leme sat tight. He gave Lisboa a pointed look: we're fucking off out of it.

'What can I do now then?' Ellie asked.

'She's got a great story, which might –'

'She does nothing, Francisco,' Leme said. 'Fuck all, zip, certo? This is very useful and we're grateful, but you tell your friends to sit tight, hold tight and do nothing. Give me their contact details.' He handed her his notebook and pen. 'And tell them I'll be in touch. Apart from that, nada. Ta ligado?'

Ellie nodded. Her eyes darted.

The normalisation of crime was something else that made it democratic in its reach. If democracy is about creating opportunities, then crime in São Paulo did that in unexpected ways. Opportunities in how you respond to it. Crime creates scenarios, Leme thought, the idea of which is appalling, unimaginable –

And yet. A democracy of opportunity. Leme was put on a kidnapping case a year or so ago. The daughter of a media magnate. A serious name. *Serious* cash behind this serious name. Key point: Leme wasn't put on the case until *after* it had been resolved. Opportunities, democracy.

The media magnate, the media *baron*, got the call on a Monday. The call was detailed on three fronts: 1) that the location of where the kidnappers held his daughter was known by no one outside the core senior leadership group of the kidnapping gang 2) that this senior leadership group would accept not a cent less than the total amount of money they believed to be a fair trade for the baron's lovely daughter 3) that any contact with the police would result in the baron's dutiful daughter being relieved, bit by bit, of a series of fairly significant parts of her body. So far: standard. Leme rolls in with a firm jaw and a swagger expecting to marshal the rich ingénue legacy-makers into a dignified submission, and what does he find when he knocks on their door? The lovely, dutiful daughter, safe and sound, bubble gum popping away and clearly quite enjoying a week or two off school.

The magnate had balls, Leme later decided, of pure titanium. After the call, the magnate hung up, saying nothing, agreeing to nothing, asking for nothing. He then set in motion a number of instructions for his accountant. First, he sold his primary residence. Second, he sold his secondary residence. Third, he sold his other place. Fourth, he sold his boat. Fifth, he emptied his bank accounts of any cash. Sixth, he moved any residual savings in his Brazilian accounts into a number of his offshore interests. Seventh, he signed over all the stock and shares he owned in the conglomerate of media companies in which he had controlling stakes. This last one was the most complicated of the transactions, which was why he left it until last. He really didn't want to have to go through all that. It was a titanium ball-ache. But he did have to do it. The senior leadership group of the kidnapping gang demanded it. Indirectly. Imagine: you hold the daughter of an extremely rich man, you are blackmailing him for a fortune; what is the one, foolproof way this blackmail, this threat, cannot possibly work? If the incredibly rich man is not, in fact, incredibly rich, if, it turns out, he has nothing. Word got to the senior leadership team that the magnate was ridding himself of property, cash and assets, and the proceeds of any sales distributed among business contacts, family. They panicked. It was the untangling of the knot of media company interests, the symbol of it, really, that pushed them too far. The magnate showed that he was not prepared to pay a ransom to such an extent that he was, genuinely, leaving himself destitute and with no possibility of a future. The magnate at no point communicated with the senior leadership team; they could see it happening with their own eyes. They knew his portfolio; they watched his wealth plummet. They were left, after seven days, with a young woman who couldn't be, and wouldn't be, paid for. Fair play, they thought, and let her go. Execute her, and things get sticky. Word is, Leme heard, they were in awe of the size of the magnate's titanium balls.

And the punchline: all the assets, all the property, all the controlling stakes were his again after another week. It was all paperwork; nothing actually changed hands. Leme had asked how he did this. 'I've got a lot of cousins. Sales generate wealth. If anything, I *made* money.' Which gave Leme another idea, of course. Democracy. Normalisation creates democratic opportunities. Leme was one hundred per cent that the magnate didn't set the whole thing up, that was clear.

But what was also clear: his example meant someone else certainly would.

As Silva sloped off looking forlorn, Lisboa boosted the car, kicked the engine into gear. Leme hung back. 'I'll call you later,' he said to Ellie. 'We need to have a word.' She nodded. He smiled. 'Stay lucky,' he said.

It was still early. Second breakfast-time. They swerved out of Paraíso and headed to this Gabriel lad's home address in Jardins. The address *reeked* cash. The address said: old school, old money. Gabriel, Leme would not be surprised, lived with his parents. This would help swing the right kind of conversation. In Leme's experience, rich kids liked to keep their parents out of any police enquiries. And then later they called their parents' lawyers.

'You're quiet,' Leme said.

Lisboa grunted. Leme left it. He knew Lisboa was going out on something of a limb. It wasn't the first time. Lisboa was family. Better than family. Leme *knew* he could rely on him. At this point, he reasoned, he wasn't actually in the frame for either murder. At this point, he was just out of shot. It wouldn't take too much though to line up the photo and snap. At this point, Lisboa was assisting with an investigation sanctioned by Lutfalla's interview. That was the only way to put it, at this point.

'I don't trust Silva,' Lisboa said. 'He always seems to know a bit too much.'

'Prides himself on it.'

'Pride comes before one, as we well know. Let's hope it's him and not you that comes a cropper, copper.'

'It's not like that.'

Lisboa sighed. 'The man's only ever going to put himself first, entendeu? I don't like his style.'

Leme left it at that.

Not long after the kidnapping incident, Leme was pulled into another one-way-or-another type of dilemma. One lunchtime at the swank British school in Jardins, the security guards told the employees no one is allowed out, no trips to the supermarket or whatnot, everything cancelled. You're all staying in, protective custody, yeah?

Turned out the local bank had been robbed about half an hour earlier and the two villains were hiding out somewhere in the neighbourhood. This was a posh neighbourhood, spacious houses, foreign cars and private security booths on most corners. In the immediate, emergency-call aftermath, the ground-force police only managed to catch one of the thieves. Not long later, the other was shot dead by a student's bodyguard. This bodyguard was waiting around outside the school and noticed someone suspicious, pursued him, realised who it was and killed him. Shot him in the chest and head. A very professional job.

No one cared.

Most Paulistanos shrugged it off, clicked their teeth and said:

'Ah, menos um, ne?' Oh well, that's one less, right?

Normalisation. Democracy. The security guard was, Leme had heard, fighting off multiple offers of work. The democracy of opportunity.

Leme left it at that as there wasn't much else to do, at this point. The case, Fat João's murder, if it could even be considered a case, would only unfold if they unfolded it. The case reeked. The case had 'police beak offed by the criminal fraternity' written all over it. Or, 'police beak offed by his own runner'. Leme didn't run snitches, but if that's how the big boys wanted the cookie to crush, then it didn't take Einstein to join the dots. The key was to ID the dead playboy. But they knew that already. The new information was this lad Antonio. Leme hoped, for Ellie's sake, for the sake of her mate, that it wasn't him. But if it wasn't him, then where the fuck was he? That was question number two on this morning's agenda. Question number three was precisely what old Carlos was up to. Fat João was wrapped up in a rug. This was an old-style PCC gang calling card. The idea was cute: swallowed up by a part of your own home, meaning you've sold out the cunts who protect you. The rug, literally, pulled out from under your feet. It also made the cremation that bit easier. In Rio, they piled tyres over your head until you were coiled up to your chin and then they burnt you alive. This was a tad more civilised. The PCC fancied themselves as a classier outfit than their coastal competition. Of course, it wasn't unknown for our friendly Militars to mock up a PCC execution if it suited. What Big Carlos was currently up to was therefore very interesting indeed. Wherever this Antonio lad was hiding, and whoever dealt the cards on poor old Fat João – young Antonio was looking like hot property. Everyone, Leme figured, would be extremely keen to find him. And if he *was* the dead playboy, then the fact he's now known missing by his missus and her best mate *and* Ellie, who was not exactly famous for keeping things to herself, meant that there would be some heavier questions coming Leme's way about why he was found at the scene. Leme did not have long. And if Lutfalla had reported with any truth their conversation earlier that morning, then Leme did not have long at all. How long before Carlos let slip Leme's place in the dead playboy scenario? Carlos was keeping that card close to his chest, or up his fucking sleeve. This was, Leme thought, a thin-ice, heavy-skate situation. They needed to crack on. Time was very fucking far from being on his side. Time was three nothing up against Leme and playing keep ball. Time was *toying* with Leme. They had to, as the saying went, keep riding the bike; if you stop pedalling, the bike stops.

And if the bike stops, you're fucked.

Lisboa jammed the brakes and jammed the car into a messy double-park. He jerked his chin right. 'Here.'

The point about the two investigations – the kidnapping, the sanctioned security guard whack-job – was that by the time Leme was put on them, by the time the Polícia Civil had begun any kind of official investigation at all, there was nothing left to investigate, já era, the city had already made up its mind, had already passed judgement, had already acted as judge, jury, and, in the second case, executioner. Leme didn't have to *do* anything. São Paulo sat in the saddle and the wheels turned.

Leme popped the glove box. He fished. He found his moody security company executive ID badge. He pulled a metallic case of fake business cards. He pulled a fake company letterhead. He would go easy on the lad; give him a chance. 'Stay here,' he told Lisboa. 'But get out, show your teeth, as it were.'

'Yes, sir.' Lisboa saluted ironically.

Leme marched. The garden path was *looong*. Leme buzzed maid-quarters. The maid trotted down. The maid kept good house.

'Pois não?' the maid asked. Can I help you?

Leme played charm school. His eyes dazzled. He flashed teeth. He flashed all of his moody credentials. 'I need to speak to the young man of the household,' he said.

The maid smiled, made nice, nothing more. 'He's asleep.'

Leme grinned. 'Wake him up.'

The maid crossed her arms. She raised her eyebrows. She grinned back. 'May I ask to what the young man of the household owes the pleasure of this visit?'

'You can ask.'

'So?'

Leme smiled – thin, this time. He didn't have time to fuck about. If charm school wasn't going to work, he'd have to play old school. He glanced left then right.

He leaned in.

'Look, love, fact is I'm a detective in the Polícia Civil and I need a word with young Gabriel, and I will have one, at least one word. Two choices: you go and wake him up and tell him the neighbourhood security firm have a few questions that might help with a public nuisance order, that *he* might be able to *help*, and you show him this card, or I go round the front door and tell Mr and Mrs upstairs you weren't prepared to let an officer of the law into the house for a friendly chat. Alright?'

The maid nodded. The maid took the card Leme held in the air.

'Wait here,' she said.

Leme wondered what it is he even *did* do, sometimes. The whole city had a code, a system, an understanding. It wasn't so much the Wild West, as a lot of people made out, more a sort of self-policing social contract: São Paulo was like one big favela –

Run by the bad-apple one per cent.

Leme's own building had a clever little routine. When you drove into the garage, you identified yourself at the bulletproof-glass booth in which three or four of the seguranças sat. But car-jacking in Morumbi happened.

A pair of thieves stops you at a traffic light, one hops in the back with a gun trained on your head. When you approach your building, they crouch down low and tell you they'll kill you if you do anything suspicious. So you wave nonchalantly at the glass booth and ghost inside. Then, the thieves go from flat to flat stripping them of valuables, load up and leave in the car in which they arrived.

It's a clever scam, Leme thought, if a little high-risk. In his building they had a system. If you do happen to drive in with a couple of malandros tucked away in the back, you park in a special bay which the security guys have designated as a signal to them you're in trouble. Once parked there, all hell breaks loose. Leme didn't think it had ever happened.

Point is, it might. And if it did, and Leme was put on the case, he wouldn't have to do anything. Everything that needed doing had already been done.

Leme looked this Gabriel lad up and down. Slick pair of pyjamas he was wearing. Really Hugh Hefnering up the place. 'I'll keep this simple,' Leme said. 'You cooperate, all good, as they say. You don't, you see that big fella down there?' He pointed at Lisboa. 'Well, he'll give you a slap until you do, entendeu?'

Gabriel nodded.

'Right then,' Leme said. 'So I've heard from a decent source, decent sources, in fact, that you've been asking around your friends, and their friends, and *their* friends if anyone knows of anyone missing in action, sabe? You follow? That sound familiar, lad?'

Gabriel looked shifty. 'What do you mean?'

'I mean you've been making some enquiries, is the phrase. I want to know why. And who for.'

Gabriel looked muito shifty. The pyjamas *shone*. 'I really don't know what you're talking about. I'd love to help but –'

Leme raised a finger. He then pointed with this finger at Lisboa.

'I'm telling the truth. Listen, I swear –'

Leme nodded at Lisboa. Made a face: don't mug me off, pal.

'Really, I promise.' Gabriel raised his palms.

'You're telling me you *haven't* been asking around.'

'I haven't been making any enquiries, Senhor, I swear.'

'Easy. Not quite the same thing.'

Gabriel shook. Gabriel breathed. He made a 'calm down' gesture with his hands. He said, 'Why don't you give me your card, and I'll get in touch if I hear anything at all that might relate to whatever it is you're talking about.' He paused. Gathered himself. 'I could make some enquiries for you, entendeu? That work?'

Leme looked this Gabriel up and down, looked this rich prick Gabriel up and down again. Leme smiled. Leme crackled.

'Nice jammies, son,' he said.

Leme slammed the door. Lisboa pulled away. Minor tyre squeal. Rubber and exhaust.

'Well?' he said.

Leme said, 'Kid's terrified. Playing the big man, doing us a favour, that kind of chat. Whatever he's up to though, he's going to tell his line manager, sharpish, know what I mean?'

Lisboa nodded. 'As the saying goes,' he said, 'if you're going to sup with the devil, you better make sure you use a long old spoon.'

Leme snorted. 'That a saying, is it? We best get after young Antonio.' He tapped Antonio's work address into his phone. 'The chances of him being at the office are slim to none,' he said, 'as the saying goes, of course, and none's just fucked off out of it.'

Lisboa grunted. Lisboa drove. 'We have to start somewhere, mate,' Lisboa said.

What Leme *did* do was live with Antonia. He grieved, still, of course he did, grieved for Renata. Living with someone new was in no way a comment on his grief. Grief doesn't leave; absence remains. His life with Antonia was a treat. Living with someone, it turned out, is a lot of fun when you like that person, when you get on, when you love that person. Antonia was *funny*. And Leme was funny! He hadn't ever thought he was funny. But they seemed to spend a fair bit of time in stitches, hooting with laughter. Laughing at each other, making each other laugh. They talked, regularly, about themselves, about their relationship. 'It's not tiresome talking about our relationship with you, sabe?' Antonia said. 'I must say, it's something of a surprise. The words alone make me shudder, and not in a good way.' They talked about the future and what that future might look like. For Leme, love, this time, was different: it felt like nothing he'd ever experienced, infinite possibilities unfolding in front of him. This love, he realised, was awe-inspiring. Renata would always be a part of his life. It was she who encouraged Leme to be happy, showed him that he could be. This, Leme now understood, is what love is. We let each other go and we understand. Love, like São Paulo, has no past. Only *now*. And *now* being now, now brought with it certain other conversations, other feelings, feelings that Leme hadn't known existed, feelings that Antonia shared, which was something else of a surprise to her, feelings to express. Quite a surprise, it was, when she said, yes, yes I do want to have a baby with you. I do want that very much, yes, yes I do. They had stopped worrying about contraception long ago; Leme realised that the main reason for this was that he didn't mind if she got pregnant. Obviously, that didn't feel like the most enthusiastic starting point, but the fact was it didn't panic him, and that grew quickly into something much more. Their Catholic approach to contraception then took an even further back seat. It felt very good indeed when he came hard inside her.

Leme's phone yapped. Text from Ellie:

**Capital SP: dodgy lava jato doleiro work. More in an email soon... Ex**

Good girl.

Leme and Lisboa crowded the reception desk at Capital SP. They *squeezed*. They felt bad for the receptionist, crowded behind her desk, squeezed and jostled by these strange men. Needs must. They made big.

The receptionist did not hang around with these big men and their Polícia Civil badges. She said, 'There are two men on holiday according to my calendar. Antonio Neves and Rafael Marquez.'

*Rafael Marquez*. A new name. Leme and Lisboa shared a look. Right then.

Lisboa nodded. 'And you don't know when they're back?'

'Thursday, it says here, but I remember that when Senhor Matheus authorised the holiday request, he said they might be back Wednesday, or even today.'

'But they're not?'

'They're not. Not yet, at least.'

'And they booked this time off together?'

'Rafael submitted the request for both of them, yes. His boss, Senhor Matheus authorised it, like I said.'

Lisboa looked at Leme. *Rafael submitted the request for both of them.* Lisboa looked at the receptionist. She shrank. Her desk dwarfed her. *Time off together.* He said, 'I think we need a word with this Senhor Matheus.'

The receptionist nodded. She picked up her phone. She spoke in hushed tones. She spoke fast. She replaced the phone.

'You can go up,' she said. 'Third floor. He'll meet you out of the elevator.'

Leme hadn't told Antonia anything. Not this time. He did not want to know what she would think of it all. He knew, of course, what she would think of it all. She had previous with Carlos. He wondered how far this Lava Jato beef really stretched. How many respectable companies, firms, businesses were implicated, perhaps even without knowing they were. Antonia was a lawyer. She had a certain amount of form herself, of course. Her company had been involved in some fairly questionable dealings. Leme knew this. It was how it was. That intersection of private-owned and state-run, or state-owned and private-run was murky. Bureaucracy and administration, legal nit-picking was a clusterfuck. But not understanding what was strictly legal and what was strictly not, was no defence. Or, more pertinently, understanding that other people didn't understand what was strictly legal and what was all-out dodgy, was not a defence. What was tolerated was not the same as what was right. And as much as Leme didn't want Antonia to know about what he was up to, about the pickle he was well and truly in, he didn't want to know if she had some role to play in this unfolding head-scratcher of a corruption situation. Leme loved Antonia. He had not spoken to her since telling her he would not make it home on the evening after discovering Fat João. This was not usual, but it was also not unusual. Leme missed Antonia.

Leme and Lisboa stood shoulder to shoulder in the glass lift. They had a three-sixty view of the really quite impressive facilities. Lisboa tapped the glass. 'There's two goldfish in a bowl,' he said. 'One says to the other, "You wanna hang out later?" The other one thinks about it and says, "Yeah, probably."'

Leme smiled. 'You know what they say about people and glass houses.'

Lisboa elbowed Leme, quite hard, in the ribs. 'Don't be soppy, eh.'

Leme was born in Paraíso and grew up first there and then in Morumbi near Paraisópolis. That old joke: France has Paris, we have Paraisópolis. His first school was the only school in the area for kids that age. Morumbi had once been a farm. Construction happened at quite a lick. Leme grew with it. The school was public. It was just your basic school. Morumbi, then, was not so sharply divided. Paraisópolis was a fraction of the size. There were none of the swank condos that now lined the roads. The first, Portal do Morumbi, was founded by residents the same year Leme was born. The second one that rose up and spread itself out in a fat, proprietary, *imperialist* gesture was Portal da Cidade, where Leme now lived. When he was eight years old, his best friends were Rodrigo, Zé Duda, and Pão de Queijo, cheese-bread, his nickname earned by his hatred for cheese-bread, his disgust for it, the smell especially. Whenever anyone had any cheese-bread, they threw it at Pão de Queijo.

Rodrigo was mixed race, Zé Duda and Pão de Queijo were both black. Leme was neither, in first generation terms. But Leme's mother was from the favela and she made sure he saw the world in the same terms as she did. It meant being understanding; it also meant being uncompromising, tough in how you move through the world. Leme's dad had never allowed Leme to forget how close he had come to a favela half-life. 'I rescued your mother,' he'd always told Leme, 'gave her a life she wouldn't have had, you wouldn't have had.' It was never exactly clear to Leme what his mother had been rescued *from*. Leme's memories of his mother were abstract now: a figure at home, tending home, tending to Leme and his father. Leme never got to ask her about *her*. It never occurred to him. And then when it did, when he was old enough, it was too late. When Leme was very young, she'd take him at weekends to the public swimming pool on the outskirts of the favela Paraisópolis. He'd splash around half-naked with dozens of other children, baking in the midday sun, throwing footballs at each other, laughing and shrieking with delight. She'd watch as they'd form small groups with friends, race each other underwater, chase each other through the shallows, diving into the deep end. She'd sit under an umbrella in a swimsuit that would never get wet, chatting with other mums about school and work, anxiously checking every few moments that Leme was within his depth, that his head still bobbed in the clear, blue water. At first, Leme remembered that he'd struggle to make friends and he'd spend more time sitting with his mum and the other women, basking in the sun and half-listening to their adult jokes and concerns. Then, as he got a little older, he spent more time with his friends; he spent his weekends without her. He remembered her saying: 'Watching you grow up, young man, fills me with both pride and fear. And the great fear, Mario: not making the most of what God gives you. Do that, keep faith, work hard, put your family first and you'll be alright, be rewarded in the next life, the one our *Padre* guarantees every Sunday.' Leme remembered that. He wasn't sure his father rescued her from anything.

They were funny, Leme's little friends. Aged nine, Leme changed schools. A better school. It was where, later, he met Lisboa. It was not a posh school, not British, American, *international*. But it was a better school. Leme lost touch with his friends. But he didn't move, he still lived in the same neighbourhood, still lived his life in the same places like any other kid, and then like any other teenager. When he was thirteen years old he was walking home, not too late, dark, but not too dark, still plenty of people kicking about. Morumbi had turned by then into the cheek-by-jowl, poverty-wealth scenario that dominated it today. But that didn't stop Leme walking home, walking the streets he had always walked, walking his neighbourhood. As he reached the corner of his street, his street, in his neighbourhood, his street, where he lived, where he had always lived, four boys surrounded him. They were boys, his age, but they were bigger, they looked tougher, they had edge. They wanted what Leme had in his pockets. It wasn't much, but that wasn't the point. Leme felt the threat of weapons without the visible threat of weapons. This edge these kids had was sharp. Leme swallowed. He felt lightheaded, faint. Some energy seemed to leach from him. He breathed. He swallowed. He felt hands rifle pockets. And then: 'Mario? Não! Mario!' And Leme, even in the faint panic of being boxed in, of being worked over, of being scared, recognised the ringleader. 'Pão de Queijo! Seu caralho.' Leme played it very cool. He faked nonchalance. The mugging was off. They swapped a few old jokes. They asked after one or two of the old gang. It was nice, Leme reflected, when he did get home. Pão de Queijo, he thought, laughing, shaking his head. When he got older he told the story a few times. He told it with humour, a sort of 'you'll never fucking guess what Morumbi used to be like' kind of humour. Older still, he thought about how depressing a story it was. He never saw Pão de Queijo again.

The office was *long*.

It oozed dark wood and leather. It *sang* privilege. The office was a butler with white gloves *bowing*. It welcomed you, this office, made you feel perfectly at home.

'Let's have a drink, shall we?'

Leme and Lisboa looked at each other. Their expressions said: why the fuck not?

There was a globe in the middle of this long, oozing office. One of those old ones, wooden-topped, elegant, absolutely not for children, not a toy, no Senhor, nem fodendo, no fucking way –

Senhor Matheus popped the lid. He took out a crystal decanter and three fat glasses. He poured three fat measures. He hesitated. 'Chorinho?' he said. A teardrop, a drop more? That same expression: why the fuck not? Senhor Matheus poured all of them a chorinho. He handed them their drinks. The fat glasses sat nicely in the palms of their hands.

'Single malt,' Matheus said. 'Lagavulin, sixteen years.'

'Thought so,' Lisboa said, fairly seriously.

Leme said nothing.

They sat for a moment enjoying their sixteen-year-old Lagavulins. Good time to drink whisky this, Leme thought, a sort of early elevenses. Better than a second breakfast. Then Matheus suggested that they talk freely and off the record. And again, Leme and Lisboa, that expression: why the fuck not? They weren't, after all, expecting that.

'It appears,' Matheus continued, 'that you want to know something about two of my employees. I also want to know something about them.'

'We'd like to know where they are,' Lisboa said.

'I'd also like to know where they are.'

'Holiday, no?'

Matheus leaned back in his extremely leather chair. 'They are supposed to be on something like a holiday, yes.'

'But they're not.'

'I don't know *where* they are.'

This, to Lisboa, did not seem a hugely helpful statement. Leme lifted a palm. 'Why don't you tell us about this not-quite holiday they may or may not be on.'

Matheus nodded. 'They're both doing some off-the-books work for us here. For me. Rafael has been doing this work for me, for us, for, I don't know, around two months. He told me last week that he needed some help, and he suggested Antonio.'

'Off-the-books work.'

'I know,' Matheus said, 'that you won't have any interest in the nature of this work. And if you did have any interest in the nature of this work, which I know you don't, you wouldn't be here talking to me. Off the books,' he put down his fat glass, his fat, empty glass, 'does not mean off limits, does not mean illegal, entendeu?'

Lisboa nodded. He offered his glass. Matheus filled it.

Leme checked his phone. Email from Ellie. Subject: **Capital SP**. He read fast. Leme nudged Lisboa. Lisboa took Leme's phone. He scanned lines.

'Is there something I can help you with there?' Matheus said.

Lisboa looked at Leme. Lisboa raised an eyebrow. Leme nodded.

Lisboa said, 'You done much business this last two months or so for your Petrobras or Odebrecht clients?'

'There's such a thing as client confidentiality, you know.'

Lisboa looked at Leme. Lisboa looked back at Matheus. 'I thought that was an oath your doctor had to take. I'm pretty sure we could get a warrant, or whatever it is we'd need.'

'As I said before, I know you're not really interested in the work we're doing here.'

'Perhaps not, but I suspect some of these clients of yours might be interested in where some of their money is going.'

Matheus smiled, shifted in his seat. He grimaced, played cuckold, the wronged man. 'Which is why I want to find my employees as much as you do.'

'So what's the point of this conversation?' Lisboa said.

'I haven't heard from them. Well, I haven't heard from Rafael, he's my contact, since Sunday morning.'

'Right.'

'And I should have done. They're supposed to be doing this work for me, for *us*, and checking in as they're doing it. They've been doing neither of these things, as far as I – as far as we – can see, certo?'

'And you want to report them missing then?'

Matheus smiled. 'They're on holiday.'

Leme nodded. He glanced at Lisboa. He flicked his fingers to say, right, embora, let's fuck off. Two of this Matheus's employees –

*Two*. Leme had what he needed.

It was something, one of your former best mates trying to mug you. Yep, it was definitely something. Talk about your mugging off! Bit snide, even if, at the end of the day, it was accidental. It was Leme's first direct experience of crime. And the thing was, he didn't feel anything but an understanding. Not an understanding in the sense of some liberal, enlightened position that blamed all crime on the poor, desperate circumstances in which the poor, desperate criminal grew up, he didn't have a *sociological* understanding, no, nem fodendo, not at all. He simply understood that it had happened and why. And the key to why was that it *had* happened. That was what Leme learnt in his first direct experience with crime.

Ellie's email went like this: I had word from a contact in UK. He confirmed money coming into London from Capital SP, but indirectly. And business has been much more brisk the last few months. Money goes from public work contracts to Petrobras, to the cartel of construction companies that Petrobras has an exclusive deal with to carry out these public works (incl. Odebrecht, Camargo Correa, Andrade Gutierrez, Mendes Jr, UTC), then to the public officials and politicians who make them happen. The kickback percentage, at each stage, plus commission, is then funnelled off into Panama, which has the laundering structure to set up thousands of shell companies and legitimate but essentially fake firms all over places like the British Virgin Islands. Key figure is a law firm called Fonseca, apparently. All the legal work goes through them. Money then trickles off in increments to all these offshore launderettes (very English word there for you) and then after this into financial hubs in multiple forms – accounts, funds, businesses – like London for pick-up or further travel. Capital SP is doing some straightforward laundering of client money hidden in existing legit trades. But paying well over the odds for stock, investments, etc., other stuff I don't understand. And helping themselves to a fair bit, so my contact reckons. That's what I have. I won't say a word to this chick Roberta, don't fret, querido.

Leme thought: rich people are savages the world over. And they're the ones that want protecting. Barbarians. What they want: dirty cash, clean hands.

Part of understanding crime was understanding how you react to it, Leme learned. Two years after the not-mugging, Leme was with some friends, messing about near their homes. One of his friend's older brothers pitched up. A favela kid, a young black kid with a shank, had just jumped their youngest brother, and this tooled-up little cunt had jacked the youngest brother's watch, a watch that had been given to him by their grandmother, a watch that had once belonged to their late grandfather. Well out of order. Leme's friend's older brother told Leme and his friends that he knew where the fucker was and that he needed them to come with. 'And bring that bat, porra,' he instructed another of the group, pointing at the baseball bat they were using to smack old cans into the wasteland that bordered the favela. Leme remembered how they'd begun by smacking cans of fizzy pop into this wasteland, and then moved on to empty beer bottles, and then rotting fruit. All three had made a very different, very satisfying sound when hit cleanly off the bat. It was a solid bat. It was a bat for a job. And so, it was a gang of scrawny, spotty, teenage no-marks that stood in front of the pathetic, terrified, little favela kid, the black kid carrying the blade, this favela kid who'd swiped the watch. Leme remembered being nervous about the solidity of this bat, the tangible existence of it, and nervous about how it might be employed to satisfy the solid rage that Leme's friend and his brother were feeling. What Leme hadn't reckoned with was his friend's brother's imagination. The bat was a very tangible, very *real* threat. And only that: a threat. What Leme's friend's brother did to the poor, pathetic little black kid cowering from the threat of this bat, was make him eat the watch. This kid, this thief, this *mugger* ate their watch. He put the watch, piece by piece, into his mouth, and he chewed, he crunched and he swallowed down the small bits of metal and wire and spring. He coughed and he retched, but he swallowed, he *ate*.

The desire for a revenge that might match the rage of the two brothers, might come close to illustrating how unhappy they were, how out of order it all was: that was what won out. The watch, the family heirloom that they were so upset to lose, was put, in the end, to good use.

This was Leme's second direct experience of crime, and the first of its consequences.

Next stop: a meeting with Ellie and this friend of hers, Roberta –

They had to start somewhere. Antonio had to be somewhere.

Lisboa silent, stoic, steaming: left arm tanning out the window. Sunglasses mirrored. Necking coffee and digging into a bag of Pão de Queijo –

Lisboa offered. Leme didn't eat it, wagged a finger, clicked his tongue. I'm alright, mate, thanks. Suit yourself.

The heat was tremendous. They turned right off Brigadeiro, the main drag on their route. The whole Avenida seemed to chunt and shunt, ripple and shimmer, cough and belch. They arrowed in on Brasil and did a left onto Veneza, one of the side streets in the grid of Jardim Europa, not far from the slightly swankier Jardim Paulistano.

Lisboa grunted. He tapped the rear-view mirror. 'Been about ten minutes. Two of them, I think. Look like couriers.'

Leme angled the mirror. There was a motorcycle two cars behind. Black leather get-up. For a courier, he was dawdling. Those fuckers died, one a day in São Paulo on average, so keen were they to rip it up to their destinations. A mug's game. But this lad was not in a huge rush, it seemed.

'Sure there's another?'

Lisboa nodded. 'Yep. Hang about.'

Lisboa, out of the blue, floored it. They raced to the end of Veneza, did a left, then an immediate right, cornering tight, rubber *burned*. He slowed. This was a short, quiet road with a roundabout, fed from four sides, halfway down it, which came out onto Oliveira Días, just off São Gabriel. The roundabout was at the centre of a square grid of streets. In other words, if they were being followed, and the tail was a good one, they shouldn't have lost the tail.

Lisboa trod water.

Two motorcycles came at them as they crossed the roundabout, one from either side.

They growled. They ripped like chainsaws.

They skidded to a stop either side of the car. They pulled weapons.

The riders yelled hands out, out where I can see them.

Leme and Lisboa did as they were told.

The riders kept their visors down.

Leme and Lisboa looked dead ahead. Their hands were on the dash. Full sun. Their hands *roasted*.

The road was empty. Leme saw a third motorbike at the end of it, square on, blocking any potential traffic.

There was a faint blue-red flash, sharp and sudden, but brief in the late-morning sunlight, like the flash of the optician's torch in your light-flooded eyes, hard to see. But if you did see it, it registered. Leme saw it. Rider all in black. Not kosher.

Huh.

Not a coincidence.

The riders pulled guns.

The riders extended their arms.

The riders pointed with their guns.

The windows were open. The heat was still. The air was still –

The silence bristled.

The guns snuck, a touch, through the open windows and into the car.

The guns were suspended there, just inside the car, inches from Leme's head, inches from Lisboa's head, suspended there, just for a moment.

Leme and Lisboa held tight. Their palms sweated. Their palms slipped.

Hold tight.

The riders held tight. The riders held their poses.

Then:

The poses broke.

The riders tapped with the guns on the roof of the car. They holstered the guns. The rider on Leme's side leaned slightly in.

He said: 'Entendeu?'

He wheeled away. He made a gun shape with his hand. He pulled the trigger.

All three bikes skedaddled.

Leme and Lisboa breathed. Lisboa said, 'I think we know what that means.'

Leme nodded. It was a traditional warning, the tap on the roof, a sign of things to come if other things weren't squared, straightened.

Leme tapped the dash, twice. Let's go.

It's how you react to it, crime.

The city took care of itself. The neighbourhood took care of itself. One day, when Leme was fifteen, he went round to Lisboa's house after school. Lisboa's dad was a cop, a detective in the Polícia Civil, and was why, in the end, the two of them ended up on the force. He was a good lad, a fair man, and he understood the good in *doing*, in effecting change, in being a *force for good*. Lisboa had a younger cousin, a girl of twelve. That day, she was expected at the house too, her parents were busy and she needed minding for a few hours. She was late. Not too late, but late enough. Lisboa's dad came home quick, nonetheless. Moments later the cousin came through the door crying and shaking. A young lad had followed her there. He had followed her before, but he was just a kid, he'd never done anything, but this time he had tried to touch her.

He tried to what?

What did he do?

He tried –

When?

Now.

Where?

Lisboa's dad grabbed the cousin and was out the door in seconds.

Leme and Lisboa trailed him. Lisboa's dad found the kid round the corner. The cousin said yes, that's him. Leme and Lisboa watched.

Lisboa's dad picked the kid up, picked the small, terrified, confused kid up, picked him up by his neck, a hand tight round his neck –

And put him up against the wall.

Lisboa's dad put this scrawny weasel, this sex-pest, pervert kid, put him hard, put him hard up against the wall.

He said something to the kid.

Whatever he said, the cousin never had any problems again.

That threat, Leme thought, *solid*.

Ellie's eyes twinkled. Ellie's eyes danced. It might, Leme thought, be a touch indelicate, given the circs. Her mate Roberta was *grey*. It does that to you, worry. It gets at you, keeps at you. It leaves you greyed out, deathly pallor, all that. It's a cunt, worry, a relentless cunt.

Ellie, meanwhile, was enjoying being back in the game, it appeared, thrilled to be in the mix. She was conducting the whole show.

'Tell them,' she said to Roberta, 'tell them about Gabriel.'

Roberta told them what they already knew.

She spoke quietly, with a sniffle, a sort of shock. It had still only been a day and a half since she'd seen him, she said, since she'd heard from him, she knew that, knew it wasn't very long, knew couples had fought and blanked each other for far longer, but it worried her, and no one knew where he was, she'd had her friend Lis asking, carefully, for her, and now this business with Gabriel, some lad everyone knew, you know, on the scene, not exactly friends, but not exactly *not* friends, she said, just wondering, he was, if anyone wasn't about, it didn't feel good, let alone this business with the holiday –

Lisboa interrupted. 'Have you spoken to Antonio's parents?' He looked bored, restless, not digging the investigative thrill like young Ellie. Itching, it looked to Leme, to get on, to get about it.

'No.'

'Why not?'

'I didn't want to worry them.'

'OK, but *you're* worried.'

She nodded. 'My friend Lis knows they haven't heard from him. But it's totally normal. It's the time-off thing that I can't handle. Why would he do that? He wouldn't do that.'

'She hasn't slept,' Ellie said. 'Look at her.'

'You're sure he wouldn't?'

'I don't –'

'Oh come on, give her a break.'

'You're absolutely sure he's not been keeping something from you?'

'Mario, tell him –'

'I –' She shook her head. 'I can't believe –'

'Do you know Rafael Marquez?'

'Yes. Not very well.'

'Can you be nice? Mario, please.'

Lisboa ignored Ellie. 'And you know him through Antonio, I guess?'

Roberta nodded. She gripped her coffee cup tight. 'They were at school together, he's older, I think college too, they work together.'

'So they're mates?'

'Isn't that pretty fucking obvious? Porra, meu.'

'Antonio's got a lot of mates.'

'You say that like it's not a good thing.'

Roberta smiled – rueful. 'I don't think it *is* a good thing.'

'Is this relevant?'

Leme looked at Ellie. She mouthed sorry with exaggerated, ironic deference. Same as ever with this one. Older, but cheekier with it. Bit of experience, and it's pride before one and all that. Leme, with a look, pleaded patience.

'Why is it not a good thing?'

Roberta steeled herself a touch. She straightened her back. She drew deep. 'Antonio has always felt in debt to his friends.'

'Literally?'

'No, not literally, I mean his background is a little different, he's not a playboy by birth, entendeu? He's a scholarship boy. He's a clever fucker, but he chooses a life that isn't challenging.'

'You mean working where he does?'

Roberta nodded. 'Not my place to judge.'

'And yet.'

'Yeah.'

'So you don't like his friends.'

'It's not just that. It's his loyalty to them.'

'Mates come first.'

'That's a bit fucking sexist!'

'Ellie, be quiet,' Leme said.

'It's simplistic,' Roberta said. 'It's more than that. Point is, he'd do anything for them. If he made a promise, whatever it is, he'd honour it.'

Leme shot Lisboa a look: let's wrap this up. Leme glared at Ellie: keep schtum.

Lisboa nodded. 'I understand. Here's what we know: Rafael Marquez is also off the grid. He booked the two of them the holiday from work. They were supposed to do some off-the-books job for their boss.'

Leme's phone flashed, ringing. Antonia. He silenced it. He turned it over, face down. He hadn't spoken to her today. He should.

Roberta reddened. Her anger surged. 'The fucker! I –'

Lisboa raised a palm. 'Wait, just a moment. Is there anywhere that you know of that Antonio may have gone? Somewhere, I don't know, secret, somewhere he went, I don't know, to go fishing or meditate or whatever.'

Leme smiled – quiet. Lisboa nailed the tone.

Roberta shook her head.

'And this Rafael, do you have any –'

'None at all.' She pursed her lips. Her brain whirred. Her brain sang.

Lisboa, nodding: 'Right, this is what we need you to do.' He looked at Ellie. 'You too. Listen very carefully, love.' He focused again on Roberta. 'I want you to go and see one of Antonio's closest friends, preferably one who is also close to Rafael. I want you to tell them that two Polícia Civil detectives came to see you.'

'Wait, hang on. What the fuck?'

Lisboa glared at Ellie. He touched Roberta's hand. 'We want to find him too, and not because he's done anything wrong. You tell this friend that we're looking for him and Rafael. You tell the friend that it was confusing, but you hadn't seen Antonio since Sunday, you'd had a row, tell him, basically, the truth. Don't focus on how worried you are. And don't mention our names.' Lisboa looked pointedly at Ellie. 'Point is, in moments it'll get back to this Gabriel. We just don't want you to be the one feeding the information, certo?'

Roberta nodded. Leme stood. 'Stay stylish,' he said. 'Everything's going to be alright.' He looked at Ellie. 'And you, behave, entendeu? We'll talk about that email.'

Ellie waved them off, blew them both an ironic kiss, swooned.

Leme eyes *rolled*.

Those were the stories they told themselves, about how the city worked, about justice. About what was just and was unjust. About what exactly justice was. About how exactly justice *worked*. If it ever really did. These were the questions they asked themselves. And there were many answers. When they asked each other what those answers were, that was when there were problems. It was easier not to ask.

Leme looked at his phone. A message from Antonia: **It's happened. I love you.** Leme shook. Leme surged inside. It's happened. I love you. Leme knew what that meant. It meant everything.

Leme held tight. Leme rode track. 'What now then?' he asked Lisboa.

Lisboa weighed this question. 'Lunch, fuck it.'

That look again, they both had it: why the fuck not?

They were, it turned out, ravenous. Worry was a persistent fucker. If worry didn't let up on poor Roberta, if worry hadn't left her alone *for a moment,* it was funny how Leme's appetite had gone largely unscathed. Worry had been a little slack with Leme, bit workshy, to be fair. Leme smiled.

He was feeling pretty fucking euphoric. He had to compartmentalise. Stick it in a happy place. He had to take each game as it comes. You can only beat what's put in front of you. And what was in front of him at this point? That was the task at hand. Figure that out. Meantime, late-lunch chow-down. Stick it in a happy place.

'You're quiet,' Lisboa said.

Lisboa drooled juice from his hefty steak. Lisboa sucked salt from his fries. Lisboa heaved lager. He seemed to be both mopping up and refilling at the same time. A perfect storm. Appetites in sync, appetites *feeding* off each other.

It was quite special.

'I am.'

'Focus on getting some food down you, lad.'

'I'm not struggling.'

Lisboa jabbed the air with his knife. 'Eat now or forever rest in peace, entendeu?'

Leme smiled. 'I do know what you mean.'

'That's what we do, us funny people, we riff, sabe?'

Leme forked fries.

'It's the back and forth, we thrive on it.'

Leme raised his eyebrows.

'It's the camaraderie, the team spirit. Call and response, ta ligado?'

Leme gulped lager.

'It's the joy of working with someone you know, the simple pleasures involved in the art of conversation. Solving problems *together*. And it is an art.'

Leme wiped his chin. 'Leave it out, Ricardo.'

Lisboa snorted. Lisboa guffawed. Lisboa wolfed chow. 'You're let off until I'm done with this steak.'

Leme ate circumspectly. They were at an outdoor table at a neigh-bourhood restaurant in Itaim. Leme needed to talk to Antonia. Compartmentalisation only worked so much. *It's happened. I love you.* Leme needed to get on the blower.

He dabbed at his mouth with a napkin. He shook a toothpick from the plastic dispenser. He killed the end of his beer. He stood up.

'Just got to make a call,' he told Lisboa. 'Antonia, entendeu?'

Lisboa nodded. He swallowed. He grunted. 'On you go, mate,' he said.

Leme pulled his phone as he left the table. He stepped onto the street and turned right. He wandered twenty or so paces down the road, where it was quieter, and stopped outside a residential build-ing. Light breeze, shade. Trees swayed. Leaves breathed in the wind. No restaurant chat and clatter. Nice spot to share in some beauti-ful news. He flicked to calls made and hit her name. He turned a circle as he waited for the connection. Come on. Nothing. He examined his phone: 'calling Mobile.' No dial tone, no ring tone. Calling Mobile. Come the fuck on. He hit hang up. He redialled. He turned another circle. The buzz from nearby bars was low. The odd clank of a condo gate opening and closing. The odd honk of a car horn, the shout of an angry driver – distant. His phone: nothing. Fucking phones. Fucking phone reception. Either way. Again: no sound, just stamped across the screen: calling Mobile. He smiled. It'll work, there's no rush, be patient. The exact words she would speak, her patience with his impatience. Then: voicemail. Odd, phone off. Could be in a meeting. Or it could be reception his end. Try again. Same delay. He examined the screen. Again: calling Mobile. He put the phone back to his ear –

'Hang up.'

A voice behind him. Leme felt something in his back.

'Hang up. Turn around slowly. Hands where I can see them. Easy, there are people about. Phone wallet cash and anything else, certo?'

Leme did what he was told. He was fairly sure he was not being mugged.

He faced his assailant. He was dressed in motorcycle leather, trousers and boots. He wore a black cotton long-sleeve T-shirt. He sweated, lightly. He had that lazy, post-exercise economy and confidence in his movements. He did not look like he was going to be messed about. He knew what he was doing.

'I know you,' Leme said.

The man nodded. 'You do.'

'What do you want? My partner's just over there.' Leme nodded back towards the restaurant. 'And you're not going to use that here, after all.' Leme nodded at the gun half-concealed in the man's sleeve. 'What's your name again, young man?'

'Junior.'

'One of Carlos's boys. Paraisópolis driver, four years or so ago, ne? And we met again on Sunday, I believe.'

'Isso mesmo.' Exactly that.

'Old Carlos want to see me, does he?'

Junior shook his head.

'Come on, son, spit it out.'

'You're looking for a playboy lad called Antonio. I know where he is. I know the name of the body we found you poking around at. I know why Fat João was put out of his misery. And I want to help.'

'And I'm going to trust you, am I?'

Junior gestured with the half-concealed weapon.

Leme nodded towards the restaurant again. 'And my partner?'

'Best you come alone.'

'So you don't fancy a Militar promotion after all, then.'

'Something like that. Get in the car. Driver's side.'

Junior pointed a few yards down the road. Leme did what he was told.

'Key's in the ignition.'

'Where we going? Not fucking Lapa again, I hope.'

Junior shook his head. 'Just drive for now,' he said. 'I'll tell you my story and then I'll tell you where we're going.'

Leme gunned the engine. It growled. It roared. It settled, *purred*.
Leme raised an eyebrow, appreciatively. 'Nice wheels,' he said.

Junior nodded.

'Então,' Leme said. 'Let's have it then.'

Junior gave it to him, his story. Leme had to admit –

It was a good one.

Crime: it was how you react to it. Leme listened to Junior's story.

Junior left the apartment in Lapa. Fat João was well dead, pronto
corpse-stiffness. Must have been something to do with his bad diet,
the body freezing up that rapid. Big Carlos was downstairs in the
condo garage. Junior took the elevator. They sat high in the back seat.
Militar SUV, like a tank. Driver popped the engine then popped the
siren. They blue-red-flashed it, a high-tailed wail out of there. Driver
swerved left right left right, pavement-riding, traffic-bullying, horn-
honking: the works. They roared down the Marginal, in and out
of the safety lane, up and over the central reservation. Emergency
service. Junior told Leme the emergency was getting old Carlos to a
steak dinner.

They piled off the Marginal and into Morumbi. Headed for a
high-end joint on Giovanni Gronchi. Leme knew it. Leme made a
face: it's all *right*. Driver waited in the SUV. Junior and Carlos settled
into a booth. Muito romantic, Leme said. Junior glared. Carlos said,
food first then we'll talk. Carlos ordered for both of them. A fat por-
terhouse, a baked potato, a portion of fries, a salad, you know, pay
lip service to the old greens, the old cholesterol levels, corn drenched
in butter, a bottle of red –

Two beers each as a warm-up.

Junior was *hungry*. It happens, Leme said. Believe me. Carlos was
methodical in his approach, scientific. He first ate his steak, all of it,
without touching anything else, then his baked potato, same format,
then his fries, then his salad, and then his corn, with his hands,
butter all over his fat chin. He drank a full glass of red wine between
each component. Leme shook his head. The man's a monster. No

argument, Junior said. Carlos mopped up, ordered a second bottle and got to it. Why do you think our rat cunt friend there had to go? Carlos asked. Junior didn't know. Well, he knew, Fat João was a rat cunt, but he didn't *know*. He made a mistake, Carlos said. One that might cause us problems. Junior waited. Junior's belly heaved. It throbbed. It was very present, Junior's belly. That lad on Sunday, Carlos said. The dead playboy. It's connected. Junior told him that he thought it might be. Yeah, Carlos said. Fat João helped set that up. Junior nodded. But not before he fucked up. Junior waited. He had a message to pass on to this playboy, Carlos said, only he followed the wrong fucker out of the office. He delivered it to the wrong playboy. Junior nodded. We only found that out after the event, entendeu? How? Junior asked. The lad was a rat cunt, how do you think? Fair enough. Now then, Carlos said, your little stunt earlier might have worked out for the best. What little stunt? Leme asked. Junior told Leme about Gabriel. Leme didn't let on that he knew about this Gabriel. You're lottery-level lucky, my son, Leme said. I'm surprised Carlos didn't do you straight off the bat. Carlos poured them more wine. So, you've let the side down, in principle, but your show of allegiance to the flag and your bit of quick thinking means I'm going to give you something. Junior waited. Carlos smiled. The toothy gash of his grin was purple and dark. The name of the dead playboy. It might be a poisoned chalice, so to speak. Junior nodded. He knew. This was a see-no-evil hear-no-evil sort of a deal. Rafael Marquez, Carlos told him. That piece of gold is your way into our team, young man. Junior nodded. Poisoned chalice, Leme said. Right.

'I've got two questions,' Leme said. Junior nodded. 'One: why did this Rafael have to go? Two: did you do Fat João yourself?' Junior nodded. 'First answer: money and lies. Part of a clean-up. The kid was skimming – heavy. This doleiro business is classless now. It's money, money, money – everyone is in on it. That's enough, as you know.' 'This what Carlos told you?' Junior nodded. 'Second answer,' he said. 'I was there, that's all that matters.' Leme nodded. 'Church.'

It's how you react to crime. On a normal day in November in 2011, Leme's wife Renata went to her office as she did every day. She was a lawyer who worked in the favela Paraisópolis, legal aid, not quite pro bono but not far off. Like every other day, Renata worked hard. This day, she was helping a man with a land dispute. His wife was heavily pregnant. He wanted to build an extension to his rough, brick-and-wood favela house. This man lived next to a bar and a tyre shop and the owners of these businesses were not happy with these plans. In fact, they were blocking them, not legally, but literally blocking this poor man's plans, filling the space with their own crap where he intended to extend. Instead of a single extra room to house his growing family, there was a pile of tyres four deep and ten tall, surrounded by crates of empty beer bottles. Renata had spent all day talking to these owners. Back and forth, negotiating a compromise, showing them how they would be helping her client, and how they would be helping each other, and finally how they would be helping themselves. By mid-afternoon the two business owners had their lackeys shifting tyres and crates. By the end of the afternoon, Renata's client arrived home from work to see the cleared space and then he was buying drinks for the two men, and all three of them toasting the right decision for each other, for themselves, for the community. And then, in the early evening, just as Renata was preparing to head home, before it got dark, her client arrived at her office to pay his respects, to thank her and to bless her. He stayed for a long time. Too long. She left in a hurry. She fumbled her keys. Fireworks crackled and spat at the top end of the favela, meaning: danger. There had been more frequent invasions of the favela by the Military Police. They were warming up for Operação Saturação, an all-out assault to end the war on drugs. It would claim lives. Renata dropped her keys. Men in flip-flops carrying automatic weapons snaked around the backstreets. Renata's office was located on a corner where five dirt roads met. It was a community hub. A por kilo restaurant, another bar, another tyre shop, a greengrocer, a butcher, her legal aid office. It was the closest thing in the favela to a high street. The men drinking in the makeshift, hole-in-the-wall bar moved slowly inside, pushed tables in front. The grill came down quickly at the restaurant. The shops slammed doors, locked windows. They all knew what was coming. Renata scrabbled for her keys. She needed to get back into her office. The flash and single siren wail. Motorcycles skidded. SUV doors flung open. Renata was paralysed, unsure what to do, dithered right then left. She aimed back for the office; it was closer than her car. Then: machine-gun fire from all sides. Policemen and thieves. A kid with dreadlocks and gold teeth spraying lead.

It's called a bala perdida, a stray bullet.

It's how you react to crime.

Junior continued his story.

Driver dropped Carlos home then delivered Junior to his. The car ride was relaxed. Junior asked the one question: what about this Rafael's body? Carlos just shook his head. Who? He smiled – mean. Junior got it. Knowing the kid's name meant he was involved. They were after full deniability. Fuck knows where the kid's going to turn up. I can think of a few places, Leme said. Junior shook his head. Carlos told Junior that it was done, they had insurance, there were whispers that a Polícia Civil lemon was in place for the stitch-up. Rumours, Leme said. Junior smiled. Yeah, well. At home, Junior got on the phone, sharpish. He called Gabriel. He got the name Rafael Marquez. He told Gabriel nothing. He got another name: Antonio Neves. Colleagues. Friends. Finance guy at Capital SP. Junior instructed Gabriel not to tell Carlos this second name. Gabriel pleaded no can do. Junior was persuasive. You can be per-suasive, son, Leme said. You've really come on, entendeu? Junior glared. Junior got on his bike over to Gabriel's. The parents let him in. Junior played the race card: the quota-filling intern at Gabriel's office. Gabriel: shit-scared. Junior bled Gabriel for information. It was forthcoming. Junior got on his bike to where young Antonio was hiding out.

'And that's where we're going,' Leme said. 'Good work, detective.'

Junior smiled – snide. 'You're the lemon, right. You need to help me. I'm not senior enough to pull this off.'

'Too junior, mate.'

'Very funny. You can help me resolve this.'

Leme nodded. He could.

Leme wondered about his phone wallet cash. There would be missed calls. Certainly from Lisboa. Antonia may have seen that he'd called. She may not have. She'd certainly know that there was no word exactly. Junior pulled his own phone and tap-tapped into it. He held his gun and kept one eye on Leme. 'You can put that thing away, mate.' Leme nodded at the gun. 'I ain't going anywhere.'

Leme didn't exactly react to that crime. It was hardly one he could comprehend. That it happened. How it had. How it. How. There were no referents, no precedents, no ways that he could contextualise it, no attempts to situate it in the city, in the city's self-governance, in the city's understanding of justice, in the city as judge, in the city as, in the city –

For a year, Leme sat in the favela, in his car, watching, looking at the scene, looking at where it happened, sat in his car, every morning for a year, looking, watching, sitting, where it happened, every day, for one year –

Why?

He didn't know. It was a compulsion, a need, it was, it –

'You remember when we first met then?'

Junior grunted. Junior nodded.

'Quite a night,' Leme said.

'For you maybe.'

'Rookie.'

'Just drive, porra.'

'Just like you that night.'

Junior shrugged. 'It was what it was, porra.'

Yeah, Leme remembered.

Leme used to be friends with old Carlos. Pretty tight, they were. Always had a laugh and old Carlão had his back, you know, a mate, a good lad. And a year or so after Renata, Carlos got some information. About a young drug dealer with dreadlocks and gold teeth. And it felt like something. It felt like an opportunity.

Junior was Driver that night. Heavy Mob, Big Carlos and Leme. They snaked through the favela in unmarked SUVs, lights down. During Operação Saturação there was a heavy presence of Militars. They kept an empty shack high up in the labyrinth. It was pretty much a lookout point. Not many other houses about. Well, relatively. It was still dense as fuck, but some of the buildings were decrepit, some abandoned. This was right in the fucking jungle. From the middle, uppermost point of Paraisópolis, you were three miles from the main road in every direction. This is what many people will never understand: the favela is alive; it *crawls*. It has its own life, cut off. When you're in it, you're *in* it. From high up in the air, during the day, in the blanket of sun, the heat so intense the heat itself seems to sweat, it looks like a great sprawling rubbish dump, or an anthill, seething with ants, *throbbing* with ants. Or a pile of rotting food, slowly devoured by maggots. After dark, lights flickered, electricity buzzed, the air cooled, the laughter from the counter-top bars was fresh, the smell of cheap pork and black beans hung, kids played until late, flip-flops smacking out clear like bells, the whole place eased into night.

They headed in and up. Two vehicles. These were tiny, poorly lit streets, with shop-front bars, mosquitoes buzzing around naked bulbs, crates of empty beer bottles stacked up in the street. Stoic, ageing drinkers, backs bent by unforgiving manual labour, legs cracked with rickets, sat at rusting tables, not talking. Hills dropped up and down; the houses listed at peculiar angles, lines of washing strung between them. Each house unique; each house the same. The same exposed cheap brick and rustled corrugated iron, the same painted-on house number, childlike, daubed as in a school project, the same family noises slipped through the holes in the walls for windows, the same thick smells like clouds. Here, you had to be up in the middle of the night to feel it. The houses that bent over Leme in the tight street, extensions hanging low, seemed to sway with the wind. There was a low, constant crackle in the wires strung criss-crossed above them, straining to carry the current around the Paraisópolis warren.

Leme had never been this far in, this far up.

In the Militar safe house, a young man, a kid, a black kid with dreadlocks and gold teeth, a young black kid sat tied to a chair, dripping blood.

Junior outside in the car; the rest of them got to work.

It didn't take long. The bucket of water and the plastic bag. Suffocate, drown, rinse, repeat. Carlos got the confession. Then it was open season. Boots, chair legs, half-bricks. Leme was there. Leme was involved. It was menos um, one less, no doubt, but it was one less villain who happened to have, who happened to have, who more than likely, who –

It was some sort of justice.

Leme was there. Junior was there.

That's all that matters.

Traffic was tight. They dallied. Junior relaxed, gun holstered. Leme fatalistic.

'I'm impressed with your calm, son.'

Junior smirked. 'Done some growing up.'

'Broke your cherry, did you? Old Fat João, I mean? I imagine that does leave you rather more relaxed.'

Junior, smiling, shook his head.

'What was with the whole PCC-imitation execution then?'

'Who's to say it wasn't the PCC?'

'Don't be a cunt, lad.'

Junior considered this. 'You probably know as much as I do.'

'I doubt that.'

'There's whispers that the PCC truce with Comando Vermelho is coming to an end. Seems there's money to be made from Lava Jato. This business is like fucking sand: it gets everywhere.'

Leme nodded. 'And Fat João has links with Rio.'

'Close enough. It can go either way, entendeu?'

'More insurance.'

'E isso aí.' Right on the money.

'Old Carlos is really stacking the deck, ne?'

Junior smiled. 'Just drive, porra.'

Lights changed. Leme crunched into first gear. They were on Nove de Julho, Paulista-bound. Late-afternoon traffic-level not too shabby. Buses and school vans. Motorbikes in and out of lanes, patience thin. From Avenida Paulista, could be any number of destinations. Leme's dinheiro was on a dirty little room in a half-built condo.

'I reckon Carlos stacking the deck is about saving face or saving his own skin.'

'Você que sabe.' You're the boss.

'He's a dirty bastard. Up to his ears in filth, dodgy schemes and whatnot.'

Junior said nothing.

'Someone's had a word. He's doing a favour.'

Junior tightened. They rode bus rhythm: stop, start, weave left, weave right.

'It's a thought, ne?'

Traffic hum. Traffic song. Traffic lullaby. Leme eased the gas. Leme rode the gas half time. Leme hit the Paulista traffic-light optimal speed right on the nose. Eased the gas and drifted through, no stopping, no pause, clean as a Portuguese whistle. Textbook light timing. Junior looked sleepy. He had the look of a nap-ready milk-drunk toddler, eyes lolling.

Leme drifted. Antonia. *It's happened. I love you.* Leme dreamed. Antonia. *It's happened. I love you.* Leme leaned back, sank – happy. Antonia. *It's happened. I love you.* This was her. This was them. This was theirs. Antonia. *It's happened. I love you.*

Leme remembered. Leme looked back.

It was easy, it turned out, to fall in love again, to love again.

They moved in together around the same time as the Cracolândia land deal beef, and the crisis that entailed. They got over that without any real drama. They understood each other. They knew that neither of them had done anything to threaten the two of them as a couple; that seemed like the most important thing. They worked together, in fact; they became a team. They had overcome adversity. Not long afterwards, they went away for a weekend. Monte Verde. A mock Alpine-style resort. They booked a cabin. There was a hot tub and a bar. They piled the car high with red wine and French cheese. They were going to feast on fondue. Antonia drove. Two and a half hours out of São Paulo and up up up. Windows down. Cool air. Green. No mobile phone service. Dirt tracks leading to rivers and streams. Gates opening to farm roads and crop fields. Hedges. The sun no longer beat down, it no longer burned. It *shone*. It glistened. Antonia smiled. Her face shone. Her hair shone. Her hair glistened. Leme laughed. Leme dozed. They played rock and roll on the stereo. They sang Stones. Their song: Loving Cup.

Their cabin overlooked a valley. Their cabin was on a hillside. There were complimentary bubbles in the mini-bar. Leme popped the cork. They drank from deep wine glasses. Bucket-sized. Pure class, Antonia said. They stripped for the hot tub. They made love. They made a naked dash for it. There were no other guests about, and it was private, after all, their hot tub. They knocked back their bubbles and toasted each other and they drank and they laughed and they made love again, quietly, with a degree of circumspection, in amongst the bubbles, their heads light, their smiles full, their love full, their love ballooning, their love bursting, their love –

Monte Verde had a single road, Leme remembered. They ate raclette in their warm jumpers. They sat at an outside table under heaters. The restaurant was full of couples sitting in their warm jumpers, playing at being in Europe, in Switzerland, eating raclette. The reality was that the temperature, as Antonia joked, was about as cold as a São Paulo shopping mall. There was a lot of expensive gear, waterproofs and scarves, warm jumpers and fur-lined boots, swaddling the city getaway crowd. They went quickly back to their cabin, their red wine and their hot tub. They placed manicured logs in their luxury wood-burning stove. They caught and crackled. Flames licked the glass. They eyed a thick, shag pile rug. They smiled at each other.

It was quite a weekend. They walked wooded trails. They ate melted cheese in their warm jumpers. They wandered chocolate shops. They pottered. They browsed knick-knacks and curios. They drank beer at lunch from huge mugs. They made love on their shag pile rug in front of their wood-burning stove. They made love in their hot tub.

Sunday morning, they headed home, the first time they had returned to their home together. Leme drove. Antonia dozed, her head on his shoulder. She murmured. He stroked her hair when he could. They played no rock and roll; it was peaceful. Leme felt content. Leme felt excited.

It had been easy, it turned out, to fall in love again, to love again. Whatever anyone says, he thought now, his eye on Junior, perhaps it really is simply about the right person. All that business about timing and whatnot, and it's not you it's me, and I'm really focusing on work, and I'm not ready, it's too soon, I'm not over her, when in fact meeting Antonia and loving Antonia were something separate and something singular. Antonia. *It's happened. I love you.* He wondered now, his eye on Junior, what Renata would make of all this. He smiled. Antonia. *It's happened. I love you.* Everything was different now.

Leme was *goood*.

Junior got into a rhythm of his own.

Monosyllabic imperatives. Right. Left here. Left. Next right. Left at the lights. He held his phone in front of him, pointedly, like a weapon. He examined its screen with serious intent. He held his weapon loosely, like a notebook. They'd done a right off Paulista

225

and down Rua Augusta. The neon bristled. The student bars heaved and cackled. The motels did a brisk trade with women who came in and out of neon-fronted strip bars with happy-looking Johns. There were queues of boho types outside the theatres. An angry bouncer relieved a tourist of his cash. Men and women devoured enormous deli sandwiches in padarias. Business as usual.

'We there yet?' Leme asked.

Junior gave him the sidelong fisheye. He was a bit moody. Nervous, Leme thought. Not really a surprise considering the lad was about to screw over his boss, a boss who did not take kindly to being screwed over, who, in fact, was known to ruin the lives, even *end* the lives, of any cunt that dared to even think about screwing him over. Yeah, Leme thought, twitchy, edgy. The man's early poise and quiet swagger had done one; Junior was shitting it.

'Don't worry, porra,' Leme said. 'I've got this. Stroll in the woods, mate.'

Junior grunted. 'Another five minutes, porra. Shape up.'

Leme nodded. Here we go. Here we fucking go.

At the end of Rua Augusta, once you've got past the skin clubs and motel-brothels, past the cheap bars and artsy performance spaces, past the hip nightclubs and twenty-four-hour bakeries, and past Parque Augusta, with its desperate junkies and crack-addicted, toothless whores engaged in their terrible transactions, once you've crossed beneath Viaduto Júlio de Mesquita Filho, you arrive at a quiet square, benches and low-hanging trees, circled by Rua Avan-handava, which is home to a few old-school Italian canteens, most famously, Famiglia Mancini, run by families that don't ask too many questions. These restaurants are frequented by the detectives and more senior members of the Civil Police based at the 4th Distrito Policial Consolação station that flanks Parque Augusta. So when Junior indicated that Leme was to ghost round the back and creep quietly past the Mancini Pizzeria, the Madreperola seafood place, the swank Walter Mancini restaurant, and then the eponymous family canteen, Leme felt pretty secure. Just past the eponymous family canteen was a cheap hotel, not much more than a doss house, and slightly behind it, an auto repair shop. A narrow entrance closed off by a garage door ran between. Junior tapped at his phone and the door opened. They went through, and down to a tiny underground car park, clearly not used by the hotel. There was space for, perhaps at most, if cleverly arranged, two other vehicles. The detritus was oily: rusting parts, rags and half-empty paint buckets. Leme made it for the auto repair storage facility. It was tucked almost under the Museo Judaico de São Paulo. Nove de Julho rumbled overhead. Belly-of-the-beast type of scene, Leme thought: right in the gut of the city.

Leme killed the engine, killed the lights. It was murky down there. Damp. It was not welcoming. It seemed like a strange sort of a safe house.

'Where's the kid?' Leme asked.

Junior gestured with his chin at a doorway in the corner. 'There's an office.'

Leme nodded. 'You thought about what you're going to do next?'

Junior shook his head.

'Best course is probably do nothing.'

Junior grunted.

'No need for anyone to find out how this came to pass, entendeu?'

'Uh-huh.'

'So,' Leme said, 'you going to get the kid or what?'

Junior opened his door. He waved his revolver to show Leme he was to do the same. Leme did as he was told. Junior flicked a wall switch, and a naked bulb buzzed, sputtered, lit. Leme's eyes adjusted. He'd stopped the car in the middle of the concrete space, driven right into it. Behind, the ramp bent sharply to street level. In front of the car: the oily detritus, and to the left, the doorway, no door. No light came from the space on the other side of this doorway. It was, definitively, your basic shithole. To the right there was a broken-looking chair, a filthy blanket. Leaning against the chair: a battered acoustic guitar, strings torn from it, snapped and hanging loose, its neck twisted, its body warped and scratched, the victim of some outrage. A couple of ropes lay coiled like whips. Next to these: a small pile of empty, rusting tins, beans and frankfurter, tops opened up and levered to the side, food forked straight from it, cold. Dirty.

Junior held out a hand. 'Keys.'

Leme tossed them over. Junior caught them, pocketed them – deft.

'Então?' Leme nodded at the doorway.

'Wait here.'

'I'll take a number and have a seat,' Leme said.

They were not far from Cracolândia. There had been further attempts to clean it up a little, but they were largely half-hearted. Leme remembered poor old Leandro, from Antonia's law firm, plucked from the favela on an affirmative action internship and used as a go-between, poor old Leandro who found himself accidentally treading on Militar cash-dope turf down there in the streets of very hell, his throat cut in his own home for the privilege. Leme had last worked the Centro in 2014. There had been a spate of brutal killings, six seemingly random attacks, a couple of homeless men, a prostitute, a working mother travelling to her job, a professional beggar, a man out jogging mistaken for a drug dealer: only the prostitute survived, though she remained in a critical condition for months afterwards. She had no insurance, of course, and no job security. Four were killed with an axe. Three of the bodies had been decapitated. The man out jogging was stabbed and burned. They caught the killer easily enough: a witness noted the number plate of a car apparently fleeing a crime and called it in. They traced the number plate to its owner, Jhonathan Lopes de Santana. Leme was part of the team that arrested him. He was, it appeared to Leme, indifferent to what he had done. He had targeted the homeless, beggars, drug dealers and addicts as it was 'less serious' than killing taxpayers. He told the police he would have continued to kill. He had the number thirty-six tattooed on his leg: his intended victim total. He had etched a drawing of an axe into his arm, using needle and knife. There was nothing in his background to suggest he was a threat to society. His motivation, he told police, he didn't really know, but it was likely because he watched a lot of war videos. He was inspired, he said, by the ISIS beheading films. Leme remembered his eyes. They were blank, but puzzled, like he didn't know why he had done what he had done, but he did know he *had* done what he had done, and that was OK. It had happened before, the homeless and the destitute, the worthless and the scourges of decent society murdered by a single killer or a gang. It was not vigilante justice; more like an experiment. It was how you react to crime. Leme didn't know how to react to this young man, this monster. How to react to such a thing, how to fathom that his lack of contrition was more like a simple acceptance of what he'd done? The story was well-known; it was all over the national media, some international outlets. If friends or acquaintances ever asked Leme about it, he told them he'd had nothing to do with the case.

Leme waited. A light came on in the dark space behind the empty doorway. He heard quiet, scratching noises, as if furniture were being moved around, or the place was being straightened, tidied up a little, a quick geral. The room couldn't be much bigger than a cell, he thought. Then: a much louder noise –

The garage door jerked and crunched open, a low hum as it rose and slid into place. A black car with blacked-out windows pulled in.

Here we go.

The woman, who had been on her way to work, had got up early. She lived with her daughter in Brás in a simple house and was walking up to the Centro to her job as an administrative assistant in the law faculty of the University of São Paulo. She had left early that morning as she wanted to get a head start at work so that she could then leave early to cook a birthday dinner for her daughter, who turned thirty that day. It was five thirty in the morning when she was killed. She was dressed in nondescript clothes; her daughter later told police that she always walked to work in clothes like those so as not to attract attention, and changed into her office outfit when she arrived. Lopes de Santana told police he thought she was a prostitute on her way home. It was the clothes, he said, they were baggy, comfortable, thrown on, casual, but the woman wearing them alert and confident. She was the kindest, most warm-hearted woman you would ever meet, her daughter said to the press. It was a wrong-place wrong-time situation, the police told the daughter. The woman's name was Maria; she was fifty-nine years old. Lopes de Santana shrugged. She was a whore, he thought.

The back and passenger doors opened. Leme felt a surge of fear, a light-headed rush like he might faint. He had felt this before, many times, and he controlled it. Junior appeared in the doorway, his weapon raised. The Heavy Mob climbed out from the back seat, either side. Then, on the near side, closer to where Leme stood, one of them yanked Ellie out by the arm. She looked dazed, said nothing. After this, a pair of sturdy, meaty, leather-booted legs swung out from the front seat, and Carlos heaved himself out after them.

'Oi, oi,' he said.

Leme looked at Junior. Junior shrugged. 'Ah, it is what it is, porra, entendeu?'

Leme shook his head. 'Vagabundo,' he muttered. 'Seu caralho.'

Leme had known Ellie for more than four years. He remembered the way she had spoken, in paragraphs, opinions formed, considered and communicated, a mixture of insight and understanding, self-deprecation about how messy she could be. That joke: thank God, she'd said to a new lover, my last boyfriend's cock was so big I had cystitis pretty much constantly. Leme remembered that. He remembered her voice. He looked at her now, quiet, confused, scared, and he thought of her voice, he thought of her voice to give her strength, to give *himself* strength. The strength she showed when her friend Ana, her best friend, her only friend really, went missing. I met Ana in São

Paulo, the first words she said to him. I wasn't prepared; I know that now. For her or the city. The city leapt up at me the moment I arrived.

Leme looked at her now. Was she prepared for this? Confused, mute, in danger. She was brave, Ellie.

Look where that had got her.

'Carlão,' Leme said. 'This is out of order, mate.'

Leme remembered Ellie, her first impressions of the city she wasn't prepared for. From the air, São Paulo goes on forever, she said, a dense building site, dust and pollution hovering above skyscrapers, flashing lights distant in the cloud, bridges that cross the stinking river. Futuristic and apocalyptic, Leme remembered that idea, had liked it, the image: helicopters dropping off businessmen on the roofs of their workplace, their heads encased in helmets, their brief-cases handcuffed to their hands. That is the fantasy. She'd looked at him then, made a face. The reality arrived as the plane touched down. The heat rose from the gutters. Sticky with sweat, I strug-gled to collect my baggage, she told him, Paulistanos talking loudly to each other and into mobile phones in a perverse-European lan-guage, mellifluous and harsh. Foreigners shouldered away, baking in the artificial light. I noticed the manner, the entitlement of the men. The expectancy of the women. In the well-dressed, at least. And then the shuffling resignation of the darker faces. The oversized vests and shorts. I wondered where I would fit in. Pink-cheeked and pale, creeping patches under my arms. There were a couple of sharp glances, head to thigh. My skirt was too short for an airport.

Leme looked at her now. Look how far you've come, querida.

'Settle down, Mario,' Carlos said. 'This is just a straightener, entendeu? Your little friend here is a curious cat, that's all. And we all know what happens to them.'

Leme shook his head, smiled – rueful. She was, he thought.

Her voice flashed through Leme. Hold tight, he thought. I started off in one of those flat-services, he heard her saying. The magazine had set it up but told me that I probably wouldn't be able to afford it for too long. That wasn't too encouraging. I moved out from top-floor quality to a fifth storey with dodgy plumbing and permanent stains. My balcony attracted smoke from the passing trucks. When I first moved in there, I tried to sit out in the evenings and read, sip at a glass of wine, but I'd be quickly forced inside by the fumes. And the noise. The noise! The noise: a constant low thunder pierced by car horns and angry shouts from the drivers. On my first night, sweating in the heat, I'd opened the bedroom window and lay awake until dawn, writhing around under the sheets. I thought, as I stood under the electric shower, terrified the water would react with the open wires, my head fuzzy from lack of sleep: does no one go to bed in this city?

Look where it has got you, Leme thought. *Look.*

Her voice echoed. On my first day at the office, a group of my colleagues invited me out for a drink. We went to a local bar, Vaca Veia, which they told me translated roughly as old cow. I wasn't sure what to make of that. They drip-fed me Caipirinha until the bar became a carousel of grinning, flushed faces, wild, gesticulating arms and noisy laughter. There was a confident man outside the ladies toilets: he handed me a shot. I staggered back to the flat-service and passed out in my clothes, waking a couple of hours later to throw up in the pristine toilet. My mouth tasted of scorched limes and after-shave, my skin raw from stubble. That first night, with its seductive mix of abandon and professional intent, had offered adventure. The cloying looks of my colleagues the next day, the sweaty paranoia of my hangover, did not.

This voice flashed, echoed, this voice, this girl, this woman, this woman who had done so much for Leme, with him, and he looked at her now, and his eyes said: *Hold fast, querida.* Hold tight.

Leme looked at Carlos. He nodded at Junior. 'Your boy deserves a promotion.'

Carlos smiled. 'He's a stone killer, this lad.'

Leme watched as the Heavy Mob moved either side of him. 'Well, he's a good actor. Played that bad-guy-on-the-turn very well indeed. Bravo, *Junior*.'

Carlos laughed. 'Sometimes it takes making a little mistake to understand which side your bread is buttered, sabe? Young Junior here catches on quick.'

'As the saying goes,' Leme said, 'love or fight, ne?'

'What a wordsmith.'

'Uh-huh.'

Leme and Carlos looked at each other. Carlos had a firm grip on Ellie's arm. She was standing, but she was slumped, head lolling, Carlos's grip helping her to stay upright. Carlos clocked Leme's concern. He smiled.

'You worried about your little gringa cunt, are you?' he said. 'Mate, she's a floozy doozy, primeiro classe. Told me all about the botched illegal scrape job she had to have last year. One night stand with a Big Man down at Love Story, you know what I mean? The fucker wasn't having any of it. Poor slag had to figure it out all alone. Damaged goods, mate. I don't know why you bother.'

'That's not true.'

'Don't shoot the messenger, son.'

Leme saw the Heavy Mob edge round a touch further, their weapons drawn but held in front, pointed at the ground. Junior leaned against the door frame, cool as fuck. Leme faced the two cars, wall behind him, chair and guitar to his left. Carlos levered Ellie round and propped her up on the bonnet of Junior's vehicle.

'What have you done to her?' Leme asked.

'She's fine.'

'She doesn't look it.'

'Trust me.'

'Ha.'

Leme examined Ellie. She looked drunk, a little high, perhaps. Some sort of pill, he thought, a tranquiliser or some shit like that.

'Why is she here anyway?'

Carlos turned to Ellie and spoke into her ear. 'She's been a nosy cow, that's why, haven't you, querida?' He looked back at Leme. 'She was sniffing around Capital SP, I believe you know it. Productive meeting? We had someone keeping an eye on the place. She was causing something of a ruckus in reception. They were very pleased we could help escort her off the premises.'

'Right.'

Ellie coughed, seemed to shake herself awake. Carlos handed her a bottle of water. 'Here you go, love. Drink up.' He made a face at Leme. 'Told you. She'll be right as rain in no time.'

Ellie drank deeply. She seemed to come out of the daze for a moment. She saw Leme. Her eyes widened. Her chest swelled. Leme felt it too. That look again: hold fast.

'So,' Carlos said. 'We find ourselves in something of a pickle, do we not?'

Leme grunted.

Carlos continued. 'Fact is old Fat João fucked it all up by involving this lad Antonio. He's what takes it out of the realm of a fairly simple clean-up of a couple of wide-boy doleiros who got greedy, sabe?'

Leme nodded. 'So you had Fat João point me to the body so I might be put in the frame. Like you told me before, insurance, porra.'

Carlos smiled – nasty. 'They've got me over a fucking barrel and you know full well why.'

Leme nodded. 'The Gold Teeth beef, I suspect.'

Carlos grimaced. 'Let's just say that some of my activities over the years have been remarked upon.'

'And now you have to take care of a few bits and pieces for the big boys.'

'Yeah, you can call it that. It's quite a racket though. This Lava Jato nonsense is scaring a lot of people, and there is a lot of money to be made helping these pussies cover their tracks.'

'So you're performing a public service.'

'For those who can afford it.'

Leme smiled. 'And Fat João?'

'Do you really give a fuck?'

'I found the poor cunt.'

Carlos nodded. 'Handy that. We can play it out however we like. End of the day, no cunt cares, and we can close the book on it.'

'And this lad Antonio? Where's he then?'

'We don't know.'

'You don't know.'

'He'll come home when he's hungry.'

'And when he does?'

'He's implicated, to an extent. That Capital SP mob are well dodgy. And they've got some important clients. We'll come to an agreement.'

Leme's stare hardened. 'What kind of an agreement?'

'I think there's been quite enough unpleasantness. I suspect he'll be happy to keep his trap shut, with what we know.'

Leme weighed it. Capital SP was connected. Leme was in the frame for Rafael and Fat João: if need be. Leme knew all about Gold Teeth. Leme also knew all about Carlos's excursions into the Cracolândia drug-trafficking game and his subsequent real-estate investments. Two options, as Leme saw it: one, Leme takes a fall as there will be fallout from Rafael, if not Fat João, and there will be a fall to take. Two, well, Leme knew the other option, the safer option, for them, and they could make it work.

'It'd be a balancing-out, porra,' Carlos said, watching Leme's mind work.

Ellie though. Ellie was there. Ellie.

Leme had told her a couple of years ago that she should go home. He told her that you couldn't do the work she wanted to do and stay sane. Look at Silva, he said, the man's a mess, lost all sense of what life is about, can't even think about it, can't even think about what might have been as it's long gone, it's only the story, the next story, and it's no life. Ellie waved Leme away. Ah vai, she said, don't be such a drama queen. Leme laughed. But he looked her straight and said, one day, querida, you're going to come up against something that's too big for you. You should go home before that happens. Her bravado was cute, Leme remembered that. Look where it had got her.

Carlos eyed Leme. Carlos nodded at Ellie. 'We've also got an arrangement. She's going home.'

'Yeah?'

'One of you has to. She'll be on a plane in a day or two. I've had a word with our Federal friends. Her visa's compromised, entendeu? Suits everyone. Trust me.'

Leme nodded. 'On that point, OK.'

Carlos gestured at Junior. He lifted his gun and trained it on Leme. Carlos gestured at the Heavy Mob. They went into the back of the vehicle they'd arrived in and pulled out a rolled plastic sheet. They unrolled it. They pulled a fat rug. Carlos raised his eyebrows at that. Made a face: oh the irony.

Leme nodded.

Leme thought of Antonia. Her face. Her arms. Her arms carrying their child. Antonia dancing a lullaby, cradling their child in her arms.

Ellie looked at Leme. She couldn't speak. In her eyes: understanding. In her eyes: tears. She tried to speak. She couldn't speak. He felt her eyes, the meaning in her look. Strength. She gave him strength.

He tightened. He shaped up. He rolled his neck.

Leme closed his eyes. A tear fell, slid down his cheek. Carlos said something to one of his boys, one of the Heavy Mob. Leme opened his eyes. Junior stood still. Junior did not smile. Leme nodded. Junior looked away. Leme looked at Ellie. He urged her to understand. Ellie like a rabbit stuck on a metro track, train bearing down, confused. Leme nodded. He mouthed the words: *Antonia. Tell her to change nothing*. He spoke the words. Carlos shook his head: pipe down, mate.

Carlos gestured at Junior. Junior took Ellie's arm. Junior stiff-armed Ellie into the passenger seat of his vehicle. He buckled her in. Leme watched Ellie frantic. She shook her head. She sobbed fat tears. She tried to scream. She couldn't scream. Junior jumped in. Junior slammed doors. Junior fed her water. The engine growled. The engine purred. A hard reverse screech and Junior did one.

Leme closed his eyes. He saw Antonia's face. Renata's face. Antonia's face. Their words echoed. He was loved, he is loved.
  Leme breathed –
  Lights out.

# Postscript

President Dilma Rousseff was formally impeached on 17 April 2016. She was charged with criminal administrative misconduct and disregard for the Federal budget.

The Lava Jato investigation paralysed government: coalitions cannot be built without bribes. Prosecutors suspended Petrobras contracts with all major suppliers, key construction and shipping firms in Brazil. The country faced a devastating recession.

Faith in the political system was eroded. In 2016 a series of huge protests against corruption were staged in over 200 cities in every state in the country. In São Paulo, the largest demonstration in the history of the city took place, with over 2.5 million in attendance.

The protests, it became clear, were not just about the government, but the whole, rotten political structure of the country.

In October 2018, the far-right, populist Jair Bolsonaro campaigned to be elected president. He promised to unite the country, purge the corrupt leftists and fight crime with a ruthless and brutal no-mercy, no-leniency policy. He is renowned for his misogyny and his racist, homophobic views. Weeks before the election took place, Bolsonaro was attacked and stabbed while speaking at a rally.

He survived and won the election in a landslide.

# Glossary

| | |
|---|---|
| Abraço(s) | Hug(s) |
| Acho que eu vou embora | I think I'll head off |
| Alegría | Joy |
| Amarelou | In this instance, 'Coward' |
| Amigo/Amiga | Friend |
| Amorzinha | Sweetheart |
| Até mais | See you later |
| Bala perdida | Stray bullet |
| Batendo papo | Chatting, banter, literally, 'hitting chins' |
| Beleza | Beautiful |
| Bem | Well, as in 'all well?' Also, as intensifier, 'well hot!' |
| Boca/Boca de fuma | Place in a favela where drugs are sold |
| Cafézinho | Euphemism for bribe, literally, small or quick coffee |
| Caipirinha | Cachaça and lime-based cocktail |
| Cáo de guarda | Guard dog |
| Cara | Dude |
| Caralho | Derogatory term, generally 'motherfucker' or 'dick' |
| Claro | Of course |
| Certo | OK |

| | |
|---|---|
| Chega! | Enough! |
| Chorinho | Idiom, meaning a drop more, or a top-up when drinking, literally, a little tear or teardrop |
| Coitado/Coitada | Poor thing! |
| Comando Vermelho | Red Command, a gang based in Rio de Janeiro |
| Dedo-duro | Grass/snitch |
| Dinheiro | Money |
| Doleiro | A bagman, money launderer |
| E aí | Hey |
| E isso aí | That's exactly right |
| Embora | In this instance, 'let's go' |
| Então… | So… |
| Entendeu? | Know what I mean/understood/you get me? Etc |
| Favela | Slum |
| Faz o que? | What are you going to do? |
| Filho da puta | Son of a bitch |
| Foi legal | It was cool |
| Frescura | Literally, 'to get fresh', in this instance, act superior |
| Garoto/garota | Boy/girl |
| Geral | In this instance, a quick tidy up, clean up |
| Graças a Deus | Thank God |
| Gringa | Foreign woman |
| Hoje | Today |

| | |
|---|---|
| Isso mesmo | Exactly right |
| Já era | Already happened, or, it's over |
| Jeitinho | A shortcut, often used in terms of bribery/cheating |
| Jeito | Style/method/way |
| Luz | Light |
| Mais ou menos | More or less |
| Malandro | A young punk, or petty criminal |
| Mano | Slang, 'brother', similar to 'dude' |
| Mata saudades | To catch up after time apart, literally to kill longing |
| Menina | Girl |
| Menos um | In this instance, when a criminal dies, a shrug, 'one less' |
| Meu | In this instance, 'mate' |
| Militar | A member of the Military Police |
| Muito bem | Very good, or Very well |
| Nada | Nothing |
| Não e/Ne? | Isn't it/Innit? |
| Não tem problema nenhuma | No problem at all |
| Não tem | I don't have it |
| Nas fim das contas | Idiom, At the end of the day |
| Nem fodendo! | No way am I doing that! |
| Noia | Crack addict/paranoid drug user |
| Nossa! | Wow! |
| Obrigado/Obrigada | Thank you |

| | |
|---|---|
| Ótimo | Excellent |
| Padaria | Bakery, simple restaurant/bar |
| Papo furado | Bullshit/nonsense |
| Pão de Queijo | Cheese-bread |
| Pão duro | Stingy, tight-arse, literally, hard bread |
| Pão na chapa | French bread fried in butter |
| Pastel | A deep fried pastry |
| Pegou? | In this instance, '[drugs] kicked in?' |
| Polícia Civil | Civil Police, which undertakes criminal investigation |
| Polícia Militar | Military Police, which polices the city |
| Polícial | Police Officer |
| Pois é | In this instance, 'you're telling me' |
| Pois não? | Can I help you? |
| Porra | Literally, 'semen', but used as a catch-all swear word |
| Porteiro | Doorman |
| Pouquinho | Small amount |
| PCC | First Capital Command, Primeiro Comando da Capital, São Paulo based gang |
| Primeiro classe | First class |
| Puta | Whore |
| Puta que pariu! | Expletive, similar to, 'Fuck me!' |
| Que porra essa? | What the fuck is this? |
| Que coisa! | Amazing! |
| Quem fala? | When answering the phone, 'Who's that?' |

| | |
|---|---|
| Querido/Querida | Term of affection, similar to 'my dear/sweetheart' |
| Relaxa! | Relax! |
| Rodizio | System that allows certain cars in the city at rush hour |
| Roba mais faz | He steals but he gets things done, coined after a corrupt politician, a former mayor of São Paulo |
| Sabe? | You know? |
| Saudades | Longing, when you miss someone/something |
| Segurança | Security guard |
| Sem graça | Literally 'without grace', meaning gauche/clumsy/tacky |
| Sério | Seriously |
| Ta boa? | You OK? |
| Ta ligado? | Know what I mean/understood/you get me? |
| Ta vendo? | Do you see/understand? |
| Ta entendendo? | Know what I mean? |
| Taxista | Taxi driver |
| Tou falando sério | I'm serious |
| Tudo bem? | How are you? |
| Vai com Deus | God be with you |
| Vai se foder! | Go fuck yourself! |
| Vai tomar banho! | Literally, 'go take a shower!', a play on 'up yours!' |
| Vai tomar no cú! | Up yours! |

| | |
|---|---|
| Vagabundo | Derogatory term, similar to 'arsehole' or 'wanker' or 'dick' or 'douchebag', with an emphasis on betrayal, literally, a vagrant |
| Vamos | Let's go |
| Vamos jantar | Let's have dinner |
| Vamos ver | Let's see, We'll see |
| Você | You |
| Você que sabe | Up to you, You're the boss |
| Você ta viagando! | Idiom, that's ridiculous!, literally, you're travelling (in the mayonnaise) |

# Acknowledgments

The K Blundell Trust, Piers Russell-Cobb, Martin Fletcher, Will Francis, Joe Harper, Angeline Rothermundt, Kid Ethic, Nicci Praça, Rosie Stevens, Lucy Caldwell – for her insight, and her time – and Martha Lecauchois, for our time.